John Bainbridge is the author of over thirty books, including several novels and thrillers, as well as non-fiction and topographical books about Britain. He has also written widely for newspapers and magazines. John read literature and history at the University of East Anglia, specialising in the Victorian Underworld. He is the author of the thrillers *Balmoral Kill* and *The Shadow of William Quest.* John has also written the historical novels *Loxley* and *Wolfshead,* and the detective mysteries *The Seafront Corpse, A Seaside Mourning* and *A Christmas Malice.*

By the same author

Fiction

The Shadow of William Quest
A Seaside Mourning
A Christmas Malice
Balmoral Kill
The Seafront Corpse
Loxley
Wolfshead

Non-Fiction

The Compleat Trespasser
Wayfarer's Dole
Footloose with George Borrow
Rambling – The Beginner's Bible
Easy British Bakes and Cakes

Deadly Quest was first published in Great Britain in 2016 by Gaslight Crime.

Copyright © John Bainbridge 2016   Cover image © I-Stock 2016

ISBN: ISBN-13:978-1537615127   ISBN-10:1537615122

DEADLY QUEST

John Bainbridge

Gaslight Crime

William Quest, and many of the characters herein, first appeared in my novel *The Shadow of William Quest.*

Prologue

London 1854

'Penny?'

The beggar had been hanging around the entrance to the low tavern in Whitechapel, every night for a week. A cripple, almost obstructing the doorway with his crutch. A withered old man of past sixty, still wearing the dark jacket of the Rifles, the 95th regiment of foot, with which body of troops, his placard said, he had fought at Talevera and Waterloo.

'Penny?' he asked again, looking up at the scowling thick-set man who was leaving the drinking den.

'Go and earn it, like I has to,' the man growled. 'Yer always in me bloody way. Every time I comes for a daffy of gin, yer gets under me feet. Go to the workhouse if yer has to. Or drown yerself in the Thames. I don't care. But if yer block me way one more night, I'll let the air out of yer.'

He kicked the crutch away from the step, and strode down the alley towards the Commercial-road.

Bluff Todd was in a bad mood and he didn't care who knew it. He dragged his lead-weighted, wooden life-preserver along the ground as he went, muttering and cursing, brushing aside the three-penny whore who was seeking shelter from the cold wind in the curve of the long high wall of London brick.

'No need ter shove!' she shouted after him.

'Shut yer face!' he muttered, waving his life-preserver, 'or yer'll get some of this.'

The beggar, hearing footsteps beside him, glanced up. A rough-looking man, his dark face stubbled with two days' growth of beard, stood beside him. He was dressed in fustian with a belcher-handkerchief tied around his throat, wore a canvas cap, and carried a heavy stick of blackthorn. The gaslight showed the vivid scar that disfigured his left cheek.

'Watch him, Billy,' said the beggar, 'Bluff Todd's in a dangerous mood. And he knows how ter thump people with that there neddy.'

'Are the others in place?'

'They are. D'yer want my company as well?'

The man shook his head.

'You've been out in the cold too long, Jasper.'

'Nothin' to an old warrior.'

'We'll see to Todd,' said William Quest. 'You go and have a daffy yourself.'

~

Bluff Todd crossed the Commercial-road, entering a dark and very narrow alley leading down to the Ratcliffe Highway. A vile passageway that was as dangerous to wander by day as it was by night, the gaslight hardly permeating its gloom. Some way down, two men with knives blocked Todd's journey, but stepped hurriedly against one of the walls when they saw who they were dealing with. They looked down at the filthy cobbles, seemingly terrified of catching his eye.

He emerged from the alley on to the Highway, busy as always with carts going to and fro from the docks. Even at nearly midnight the pavements were packed with people; workers going to and from their labours, sailors wandering up from the river looking for a drink or a poke, a Lascar holding a long-legged folding table and robbing the inebriated in a game of thimblerig.

A few old whores plied their trade and watched as he passed. He looked at their faces as he walked on. None of them were his. He liked them younger. And he thought the Highway was a waste of time. Far better to get his tails working the streets right down by the river, to get the money from the sailors the moment they came ashore. By the time they'd walked up through the narrow streets of Shadwell to the Highway, they might have been robbed or tumbled already.

Ships were tied up at the wharves of the basin, their tall masts towering up as high as the warehouses nearby. Despite the lateness of the hour, many were still being unloaded, a steady procession of stevedores carrying heavy loads into the great gates of the buildings.

The girl was watching them with considerable interest. Her father had worked at the docks before his accident. Now he was buried in a pauper's grave on top of a dozen other bodies, the earth barely covering his bones. Her mother had drunk herself to death within a month of his passing. With the money gone and two little brothers to support, Phoebe had been forced on to the streets.

She was sixteen.

A ripe age for a whore on the streets of Shadwell.

'Why aren't yer working?'

Her heart leapt and her stomach turned. Bluff Todd's face was almost against her own. She could smell drink on his breath and the stench of his body. They were odours she knew only too well. As familiar in her nightmares as the red and bulbous nose and staring brown eyes.

'I've done four already,' she protested, 'all off the ships that moored tonight.'

Bluff Todd put his face up against hers.

'Four ain't enough, yer lazy little bitch. It's midnight! Yer could've done a dozen by now.'

'They just got paid,' she protested. 'They can afford to go to one of the houses in Whitechapel. They don't need me up against a wall.'

He took her hand, forcing the fingers back until she whimpered in pain.

'None of yer lip, yer little drab, or I'll put a mark on that pretty face that'll stop yer ever working again.'

He twisted the fingers even more until he could see the tears forming in her eyes. 'Yer gives me more trouble than any of the other sluts that works for me.'

'It's difficult, Mister Todd.'

'Not difficult at all. These docks is-a thronging with sailors an' all after one thing. How difficult can it be to give it to 'em?'

'Some of them are too far gone in drink...'

'Don't yer give me that one,' he growled. 'It's cos yer picky. Think yerself above all of this, don't yer milady?' He waved a hand at the wharfs and alleys of the dockyard. 'Imagine yerself working in one of the houses, d'yer?'

'No, Mr Todd.'

'Been approached, have yer?'

She shook her head but couldn't look him in the face.

'Yer thinks I don't know, don't yer?'

'Know?'

'I saw yer this afternoon...'

She would have collapsed with fear if he hadn't pushed her hard against the dripping wall of brown London brick. He twisted her fingers back a little bit more.

'Oh, yes, I knows all right,' he went on. 'Up in Stepney I was. Hard by where they bury the Jews. And there yer was. Sitting on a wall. Talking to a woman. I saw yer and there's no point in denying it.'

She tried to look defiant.

'And what if I was? Just some woman asking the way.'

'Yer thinks I was born stupid? I knows who that fat old bitch is. Mrs Bendig. Her what runs the night house in Leicester Square. Want yer for one of her virgins did she? She does that, yer know? Passes girls such as yerself off as virgins – time and time again.'

'She was just asking the way, Mr Todd.'

'Liar!'

'Don't hurt me, Mr Todd...'

'Hurt yer? I'm not a-going to hurt yer. Not in any way that'll show, anyhow. But yer see, Phoebe, I got to teach yer a lesson. Yer sees that, don't yer? It's all on account of the other girls. Yer'll be setting 'em a bad example.'

'Please...'

He pulled her towards him and steered her into the long alley leading back towards the Highway. Into a little cove of brick where the gaslight flickered. He pushed her hard up against the wall. And then took a step backwards so that he might enjoy her fear.

'But what ter do, eh? What ter do?'

'I think you should let her go, Mr Todd. She's in the way. It's you I want...'

Bluff Todd turned.

At first he could see nobody. And then the figure stepped forward. A slim man dressed all in black, with a crape mask and a hood obscuring most of his face.

'Who the hell...'

'I'm your nightmare, Mr Todd. Your own very worst nightmare. You should have listened when you had the chance. We gave you plenty of opportunity.'

A strange growling voice.

Todd watched as the man reached inside his cloak. Saw the pistol being raised. Hardly able to believe what was happening. His mouth dropped open.

'Now listen...' he began.

The flash of the pistol lit up the alley and dazzled his eyes. It was the last sensation he experienced. Bluff Todd's body fell back against the wall, his arms waving outwards in some instinctive and crazy gesture. A small flow of blood from the red hole in the centre of his forehead dripped into his rolling eyes. His legs folded under him and he collapsed forwards on to the filthy cobbles of the dark alley.

The girl screamed.

~

William Quest had followed Todd along the alley to the Ratcliffe Highway, then down to the banks of the Thames and the great basin where the ships were moored. For a moment he lost his quarry amongst the stevedores and the last of the sailors coming ashore to spend their wages.

'Over there. Down where the other alley goes back to the Highway. Our Mr Todd likes to see to his girls in quiet corners. I fear he's giving young Phoebe a hard time.'

Quest glanced at the large man who had been keeping watch on the dock. Albert Sticks was, for the benefit of the world, his manservant. In reality they were partners in crime, neither of them even recognising the concept of master and man.

'You fought him once?' asked Quest. 'How good was he?'

'Just a side-match in a cellar,' Sticks replied. 'Not a prize-fight as such. He's not really a pug. Not a proper fighter. All bluster and no wind. Didn't take much to knock him down.'

'You have a fancy to knock him down again?'

'I don't like what he does to them girls,' Sticks said. 'He's a bully, pure and simple. A disgrace to the Noble Art...'

'Come on then.'

They left the crowds behind and walked across to the warehouses, following the high walls round to the beginnings of an alley which was hardly illuminated by the two gas-lamps nearby.

And there was Bluff Todd, dragging the girl into the dark recess of the ancient passageway.

'I did bring my neddy along,' said Sticks, waving a wooden cosh, 'but I thinks as how I'll just use my fists. For the honour of the Fancy.'

'I'll leave him to you, then,' said Quest.

They heard the girl whimper and then the sound of voices. Two men there, though they couldn't make out the words. A gentleman talking in strange tones and the more familiar speech of Bluff Todd.

The pistol fired just as they turned into the alley.

Quest grabbed Sticks and pulled him back around the corner into safety.

'He's armed!' said Quest.

'Todd don't use no pistol,' said Sticks. 'He wouldn't know how. He's a bludgeon man, carries a life-preserver. That and a knife.'

The scream of the girl sent them hurrying into the alley.

She was standing against the wall, her eyes wide with horror. Bluff Todd lay dead at her feet. The smoke from the pistol was already forming a cloud around the yellow glow of the gaslight.

'Did you top him?' Sticks asked Phoebe. 'Where's the pistol?'

'It wasn't me... it wasn't me...' she shrieked.

And then they heard the sounds of someone running back up the alley towards the Highway. Quest glared into the darkness but could see nobody. Shouts and cries of alarm were coming from the dock basin. The noise of many footsteps hurrying in their direction. The sound of the pistol shot had reverberated from wall to wall, along the wharves, even into the busy interiors of the dockside warehouses.

The mob was coming.

'Get her out of here, Sticks,' said Quest. 'They all know Todd's her ponce. She'll swing if the crushers catch her near his body, whether they find a pistol or not.'

Sticks swung the girl over his shoulder and sped away into the darkness.

Quest took a last look at the body of Bluff Todd before running up the alley, on the trail of the killer. There was nobody in sight. He paused briefly. There was the sound of running footsteps up ahead. And the delighted cry of something like laughter. But wild, careless, somehow not even human.

One

'I know what you're thinking, sergeant,' said Inspector Abraham Anders of Scotland Yard, as the two men looked down at the corpse of Bluff Todd.

Dawn had come to the dockside wharves and warehouses and with the new light, the old luminosity had faded from Todd's eyes. The body had remained in position since the shot had brought the man down, though the hands and ears had been nibbled by rats from the nearby Thames.

'William Quest.' Sergeant Berry declared. 'Back in business after recovering from his wound. So he wasn't scared off after our run-in last year. Not that Bluff Todd didn't ask for it. The East End'll be all the better for his going.'

'It's still murder, Berry,' said Anders. 'And if Quest's responsible I'll have him in Newgate before the day's out. Quest might think he's got some God-given right to mete out justice on his own behalf, but I'll not have it. Not on my patch!'

He brushed his wild and overlong white hair away from his eyes and glared at the sergeant.

'I will not have vigilantes operating in London,' he added, 'however well-intentioned they are.'

'But will Commissioner Mayne let you arrest Quest?' Berry asked. 'I know he thinks we should have put the knot round the man's neck last time, but he was over-ruled. And the Home Secretary...'

'Lord Palmerston can't be allowed to rewrite the laws of England.'

'Not just him though, is it?' Berry replied. 'Quest has a hold on Queen Victoria's spymaster, that fat bloke Wissilcraft.'

'I swore an oath to uphold the law, Berry, and that's just what I intend to do. I know William Quest's in London. I saw him walking in the Mall only yesterday morning. We'll get a warrant drawn up and pay him a visit this very day.'

'On your head, sir.' Sergeant Berry grimaced. 'It's not like Quest's an ordinary criminal...'

'He's exactly that,' said Anders. 'Abandoning the law to the likes of Quest, letting people do what they like, well, it's the road to chaos and anarchy.'

A cool breeze blew up from the river.

'Thing is, sir, we don't know Quest did for Bluff Todd. He usually uses a sword-stick, not a pistol, and drops a hempen noose by his victims. We haven't found one yet. Nor any clue that Quest was even in the neighbourhood.'

Anders nodded.

'I know,' he said, 'I know, but I just have a feeling. And the worst of it is we may never be able to prove it. But I'll look Master Quest in the eye and see what feeling I get then. And if I see his eyelids as much as flicker, I'll have him in a cell.' He looked down at the body. 'Slaughtering men like Todd's just a sideline for Quest. We know he has political motives. Wants to overthrow our lords and masters. That's his real aim.'

'The sooner the better in my book!' the sergeant grinned.

'I don't dispute the sentiment – only the method.' He summoned one of the constables who was standing some little distance away. 'Constable, get this body to the mortuary at the London Hospital. The police surgeon's expecting it.'

~

The poet smiled at her, brushing a lock of dark hair away from his eyes.

'Quite the most wonderful experience,' he said. 'It just gets better and better...'

'However did you manage until I came along?' she replied.

'It is better with you,' he conceded. 'The others are just so much... I don't know. You can drive them like cattle, but you can't make them think.'

'So I'm your muse then?'

'You... and London. One day I'm going to write a great poem about London at night. As many cantos as *Don Juan*. Loosely based on our experiences...'

'How loosely?'

'Not loose enough to be dangerous,' he assured her, turning over in the bed to take her again.

~

William Quest stood at the window of his study looking down at the pedestrians in Tavistock Place, in the heart of Bloomsbury. He had picked up a book to read but his thoughts were too far away to concentrate on its pages. He held it loosely in one hand while his mind drifted to the events of the night before.

He hadn't been able to catch the killer of Bluff Todd. He'd raced along the alley after the echoing footsteps. At one point he thought he had seen the assassin in the far distance, but had never been able to gain ground.

Quest had emerged at last on to the Ratcliffe Highway, still crowded despite the late hour, with sailors and stevedores and black-faced coal-whippers. The killer had become absorbed by the multitude of passers-by. A hopeless task.

He had wandered back down towards the basin and, in a quiet corner where a warehouse overshadowed the Thames, found Sticks and the girl. She told him what had happened and described the killer. Slim, dressed in black, his face hidden beneath a crape mask and a hood.

'Did you know him?' Quest had asked. 'Was it a friend of yours come to account for Bluff Todd?'

She had shaken her head, her face distorted with fear.

'They'll top me for this, won't they?' She looked desperate. 'Everyone knows how that bastard treated me and the others. They'll think I settled him? Or got someone to do it?'

Quest had held her head between his hands and looked into her eyes.

'What they think and what they can prove are two different things,' he had said. 'Listen to me...'

Phoebe had gazed up at him, questions and confusion on her face. Quest realised he had said the words in his own refined voice, not the broad cockney of Bill the footpad, the disguise he was wearing.

Well, there was no point in going on with the deceit. He kept his real voice as he issued instructions.

'Listen to me,' he had said.

'You're a flash cove... a gent,' she had muttered.

'That doesn't matter now,' he had continued. 'I want you to listen carefully to what I say...'

She had nodded, her hand tightening its grip on his arm.

'If anyone asks where you were tonight, you're to tell them that you were getting drunk in *The Three Cripples* off Field Lane, in the company of a big man called Isaac Critzman.'

'A pull?'

Quest had smiled.

'Not a pull. A charitable gent, trying to help you with money. If anyone asks he is the patron of the Metropolitan Society for the Alleviation of Pauperism.'

'The pauper society. I've heard of them.'

'Good, that's makes it so much the easier. Mr Critzman invited you to visit their office in Albemarle Street. He said his society would provide you with decent clothes and some money. And that he offered you a reference so that you might get a job to take you off the streets. You can remember all of this?'

She nodded.

'Could they really do that for me?'

'If you wanted,' said Quest. 'If you wanted, you could really go there and ask for help. That's up to you. But what's really important is that you tell anyone who asks that he was talking to you at the Cripples until the early hours. You never met Bluff Todd tonight. You were never here. Do you understand?'

'But the Cripples is a low place, full of dips and thieves. Anyone of them'd say I was never there.'

'I'll make sure that a good dozen people noticed you. Trust me in that.' He had nodded his head in the direction of Sticks. 'But for now, this gent'll take you somewhere safe for the night. A roof over your head and food to eat. It'll give you time to think...'

Quest's mind wandered away from the scene as his eyes focussed again on the street outside the window. A hackney-coach had drawn up outside and two men were getting out.

'Company's come calling', I see,' said Sticks.

For a big man, the old prize-fighter moved very quietly. Quest had been so lost in his thoughts that he hadn't even heard him approach.

'Company from Scotland Yard,' he replied. 'Two very familiar faces. Is the girl all right?'

'She spent the night in the lurk in Stepney, fed and watered. But by the time I woke she'd moved on.'

'Do you know where?'

Sticks waved a fist in the direction of the streets.

'Somewhere out there,' he said.

~

'So, did you kill Bluff Todd?'

Inspector Anders stood by the window of the little drawing room, looking across at William Quest who sat back in an armchair near the fireplace, thumbing through the pages of *Lavengro*. Sergeant Berry hovered by the door, quite well aware that the old boxer Albert Sticks had positioned himself outside in the hallway. Berry reached inside his coat and gently touched the hard wood of his billy-stick.

'You think I did?' Quest asked.

'Let me ask another question first, then. Did you know Bluff Todd?'

Quest smiled as he looked up at the policeman. Anders' face seemed more lined than it had been when they had last met in Norfolk the winter before. His hair and whiskers were even greyer. The detective seemed tired.

'I should think anyone who's spent any time at all in Whitechapel would know Bluff Todd. A very unpleasant individual, I always thought. Hard on the girls who work for him. I'm sure you're aware of his reputation?'

Anders gave a slight nod.

'Even unpleasant individuals have a right to life under the law,' he said, 'and to go back to my original question. Did you kill him?'

Quest brushed a lock of dark hair away from his eyes and let out a deep sigh before looking up at the detective. For a moment a picture of Todd lying dead on the cobbles of the alley flicked through his mind. He heard again the bark of the pistol and the smell of the powder.

'I didn't kill him, Inspector.'

'Do you know who did?'

'It's a mystery to me,' said Quest. 'But I'm not surprised that *someone* did. Men like Bluff Todd live on borrowed time. They make a lot of enemies.'

'Do you think it possible that one of his girls shot him?'

'He was shot then?'

Anders didn't like that innocent look on Quest's face. There was a disingenuousness about the man's expression. A look of feigned virtue, as though Quest was playing a parlour game with the two policemen.

'I'm sure you know very well he was shot. It's the talk of the East End. And the death was reported in that newspaper on the table there,' Anders said, pointing at the card table under the window.

'I haven't read any account of this slaying just yet,' said Quest. 'I always save the newspaper until the evening. I've so many more interesting things to read.'

He waved a hand at the many bookshelves lining the wall.

'Please do sit down, Inspector,' he added, indicating a chair. 'Having a policeman standing over me makes me nervous. Sergeant Berry too. I'm not going anywhere so there's no need to guard the door, sergeant.'

Anders sat in the chair facing Quest. Sergeant Berry took a wooden stool close by the door, a leg stretched out across the exit from the room.

Quest smiled.

'I'm sure the sergeant believes I'm planning to flee.'

'Ah, well, he's very aware of your reputation,' said Anders. 'I ask you again. Do you think it likely that Bluff Todd was shot dead by one of his girls?'

'On the money he gave them? I doubt they could afford the powder, let alone the weapon. Surely it's more probable that Todd was shot by some rival? The East End is full of men like Todd.'

Anders regarded Quest for a moment before answering. He always thought of his encounters with the man to be rather like a particularly hard-fought game of chess. However hard he tried to anticipate the moves, Quest always seemed to outmatch him.

'I'll tell you what I think, Quest...' he said at last.

'Please do. I've always thought you a shrewd judge of character.'

'I'm inclined to believe that you didn't kill Bluff Todd...'

'That's a generous assessment, Inspector.'

'I haven't finished yet...'

'I see...'

Anders leant forward.

'You may not have killed him, Quest, but I firmly believe that you know more of this matter than you're telling.'

'I have that reputation,' said Quest, raising his eyes to the ceiling. 'Heaven knows why?'

'We all know why,' Anders replied. 'The events of last year are very fresh in my mind. You may believe that you can operate outside the law with impunity, but take my word you can't. Without the rule of law there can be only anarchy.'

'Some people believe there's worse than that within the rule of the law,' said Quest. 'We live in a very unfair and unpleasant land, Inspector. Millions slave and live in poverty so that a few might prosper. The law to me seems designed to keep the many down. Are you not a foot-soldier of the rich?'

'If I'm a foot-soldier then I'm a trooper of the law itself!' Anders thundered. 'I uphold the law regardless of class. The very fact that I'm investigating the slaying of a low creature like Todd proves that. He was not a member of the Class.'

'He exploited others in just the way the Class do. It's all a matter of degree, surely? Bluff Todd or Palmerston, it makes no difference to me.'

Anders looked around the room.

'You have a brass neck to spout such things, Quest. Here you sit in a fine room in a pleasant house in Bloomsbury. You're well fed, you have a good coal fire and a roof over your head. Are you not a member of the Class yourself?'

'You know my background, Anders. You know where I came from and what I've suffered to get here. I want every last country peasant and rookery drudge to live as I do. You want my creed? There it is. I'm fighting to make a difference.'

Anders had never seen Quest so agitated before. The calmness that always seemed to be on the surface had gone. The chess master had thrown away the game by letting himself be riled. There was genuine anger on his opponent's face.

For a second Anders thought of a frightened and tortured boy being hunted across lonely countryside. Of the shadow of the gallows.

He looked at the terrible scars on Quest's hand. And Quest, seeing him looking, pushed the hand behind the cushion on the chair.

'I had hoped that you might have dropped these pursuits,' Anders said at last. 'If you want to change society then stand for Parliament. A man like you could do a lot of good there.'

'I haven't the...'

'Patience?'

Quest smiled.

'Perhaps,' he acknowledged. 'To be brutal, it's a talking shop. The majority of the people in these islands aren't represented there. And only a minority have the vote. Reform may come but it'll be devilish slow.'

Anders could think of nothing to say. In his heart he knew that Quest was right. Few things ever changed, and he'd had more than a bellyful of his political masters himself. And there was something more. He *liked* William Quest. He'd probably have to bring him to be hanged outside Newgate Gaol at some point, but it wouldn't be a happy day.

'I believe that you didn't kill Bluff Todd,' he said. 'But I would ask you once more. Please abandon your quest for vengeance. There has to be a better way.'

'If way to the better there be, it enacts a full look at the worst,' Quest replied. 'This house is one of my sanctuaries, Inspector. Out there...' He nodded towards the window. 'Out there, people live and die like the beasts of the field.'

And only a little while later, some of the beasts tried to kill William Quest.

Two

There was to be a hanging next day outside the old prison of Newgate.

A few bystanders watched as the gallows were erected, some strangers to the town looking up at the old walls of the gaol, trying to picture the composure of the victim as he sweated away his last moments in the condemned cell.

There would be a crowd of thousands on the hanging day itself, all come along to witness the entertaining spectacle of seeing Colley Rogers 'turned off'.

William Quest knew that doomed gentleman rather well. He had been Quest's fence when he had first come to London and adopted the occupation of pickpocket. A weaselly little man of indeterminate age who kept a shop in Field Lane, adorned with wipes, the more expensive pocket handkerchiefs. All with the owners' initials carefully pricked away. Colley was also not averse to buying stolen silver from burglars and pocket books of good quality leather.

He had been kind to the young Quest, but the boy had soon moved on. The old fence was a little too garrulous in his drink to be safe. Quest was only surprised that Colley Rogers had lasted so long.

It was a fine evening and William Quest had chosen to walk from his home in Tavistock Place to Josef Critzman's walking stick and umbrella emporium in Cheapside. As he strolled along Newgate Street, he looked up at the prison walls and gave a slight bow of the head in acknowledgement to his former partner in crime.

Always sad to see a kindly man topped.

He reached down to give a penny to the crippled beggar sitting with his back against the high wall. The tatterdemalion figure gave a little salute and muttered a thanks.

'Watching my back, Jasper?'

'Yer being followed,' the old soldier replied under his breath. 'They picked up yer trail soon after yer left yer house. Closed carriage with a pair of grey horses. It's gone up and down the street twice in the time yer've bin oglin' the gaol.'

'You saw it all the way?'

Despite his disability, Jasper Feedle could move at a phenomenal rate through the streets of London, helped by his vast knowledge of every short cut in the city.

'They follows yer, I follows them.'

'Just the carriage?'

Jasper shook his head.

'It pulled up in Giltspur Street,' he said. 'Whoever's inside talked to three roughs, who went off through the grounds of the 'ospital. They'll be ahead of yer now. If yer heads down the alley towards St. Paul's Churchyard yer might flush 'em out. Linger awhile looking at the shops and give me time to get down there.'

'Could they be police?' asked Quest.

'No, not crushers,' said Jasper. 'Somethin' I don't like about this...'

'Are you armed, Jasper?'

'Only me crutch. Good enough for them. I see yer've got yer blackthorn?'

Quest acknowledged the beggar with the lead-weighted walking stick before moving on and crossing the road. He walked slowly along Newgate Street, pausing for several minutes to look in the window of a bookseller and printer. He saw the carriage reflected in the glass as it went very slowly by in the direction of Cheapside. An old growler with the blinds drawn down.

He strolled on and saw it move towards the junction with St Martin's Le Grand, where he watched it turn very slowly and head back towards Newgate. Before it could draw level he crossed the road in front of it, to the corner of the narrow Queen's Head Passage. Here he waited and looked full on towards the carriage. The driver looked ordinary enough, though he had a hat pulled hard down over his face.

The carriage slowed....

Quest thought at first that the passenger had ordered it to halt, as though to make conversation. But the vehicle didn't entirely stop. He saw the drawn-down blind ease slightly sideways. Watched as the barrel of the percussion-pistol poked out through the crape. Saw the gun discharge.

The ball buried itself in the wall four inches to one side of his head. And then the growler sped away back down the street in the direction of the gaol. There was a hubbub of conversation as passers-by queried what the noise might have been. But none of them looked in his direction.

Quest turned into the dark passageway and headed down towards Paternoster Row and the great cathedral of St Paul's beyond. He was halfway down the alley when the three roughs confronted him. One carried a weighted life preserver, the others were armed with daggers. They walked side by side towards him. Two of the men had the build of prize-fighters, the third a thin figure with a pock-marked face. Quest looked past them down the alley. It was deserted. Quest almost chuckled, speculating that a wiser man might step back into the busy mainstream of the crowded streets.

A lesser mortal might have done so.

But Quest was filled with curiosity.

The three men rushed forward, one of the burlier roughs head on, the other two along the walls of the passage as though they intended to come at him from both sides at once, both waving daggers. Then for a second they halted. Quest stood still, his own weighted stick down at his side.

He had been in a hundred fights in alleys just like this. There were only so many patterns of attack in such a confined space.

Either one of them would make the first move, or they'd all rush in at once. There were really no other options. It was the way these scraps were done.

They chose to all come at once.

But in their determination to make a rapid attack they ignored their backs. The first indication that the two men at Quest's side had that they were in trouble, was when the rough in the middle of the passage grunted and fell to the ground. His comrades glanced round at the noise to see a one-legged man with a crutch coming towards them, nimbly stepping over the fallen man.

This distraction proved their undoing. The largest of the roughs turned his head back towards Quest just in time to see the lead-weighted blackthorn walking stick coming towards his brow. The force of the blow knocked the man hard against the wall. His head bloodied as he tumbled sideways to the ground.

He was hardly down before Quest and Jasper turned on the weedier rough with the pock-marked face. There was terror on his face as they closed on him. He held his dagger out in front of him for a moment, waving it from side to side. And then he threw it down on the ground, holding his arms out in surrender as he backed against the stonework of the wall.

Jasper leant on his crutch, swinging his arm down in a great sweep to pick up the dagger. Quest stepped forward and held his blackthorn hard against the man's throat, pinioning him to the wall. He could feel his victim shivering with fear through its dark wood.

'Who are you?'

The man remained silent.

Jasper held out the rough's dagger. Putting the tip of the blade against the white flesh of a scraggy neck.

'I hates people wot won't tell us things,' he said.

'Who sent you?' Quest asked. 'Better that you tell us. My friend here isn't renowned for his patience. He's cut many a throat. And I just know he'd like to slice through yours.'

The rough gave a slight shake of the head.

Quest eased back with the blackthorn.

'It's like this, you see,' he said. 'I don't take prisoners. Your friends there are as good as dead. And you are too. Unless you speak. There are only two options for you. In a few moments' time you could be walking out of this alley with a sovereign in your pocket. A chance to get out of London. Or in the same few moments, you could be bleeding like a stuck pig down on the cobbles.'

Quest saw the terror in the man's eyes. He perceived that the fear was not entirely generated by his present situation. He looked down. The man was pissing himself.

'Don't be scared of anyone else,' Quest whispered into the man's ear. 'Just be very scared of us. Unless you tell me what I want to know, you won't live to fear any other party.'

The rough was breathing heavily, his lips trembling.

'You don't know who you're dealing with,' he said. 'He'll slaughter me if he finds out I've peached. We wasn't to kill you. Bring you alive, he said.'

'Who said? Come on... I'll give you five guineas and you can leave London today. And I'll see you safe away. If you don't tell me, I'll kill you here and now.'

The man glanced from side to side, as though hoping that someone might come along. But the passage was deserted. The noise from passers-by in Newgate Street seemed far away.

'You might kill me anyway,' the rough gasped.

'A chance you'll have to take,' said Quest.

'You promise you'll leave me alone?'

Quest nodded.

'I don't know who's getting him to do it, I really don't. He met us in an alehouse in Bermondsey. *The Bold Dragoon.* He always meets us there when he wants something doing,' the words came tumbling out very fast. 'If he finds I've peached, I'm done. If he's blown, everyone'll suffer. I got a family, mister. Over in Southwark. He'll have them. He'll have them all.'

'Ten guineas,' said Quest.

The man looked up at him.

'You have that much on you?'

Quest nodded. He gave the man time to consider his situation. Saw the look of hope and greed come on to the frightened face.

'He fixes things for people, you see. Both sides of the river. He's not a man to be crossed. Oh Jesus!...'

'Tell me his name and where I can find him?'

'I don't know his name. Only what they calls him.'

'So what do they call him?'

'You'll have heard of him,' the man was almost whimpering. 'Everyone's heard of him, though some thinks he don't exist. But he does... he does...'

'Who is he? Where is he?'

'The safest place in London for him. The place what gives him the only name he has. Baptised by the lowest in that foul place. The worst rookery in London. He's the King of Jacob's Island...'

~

'How old are you, sweetheart?'

Mrs Bendig leant forward over the table, patting Phoebe's arm with a very fat and beringed hand.

'Sixteen, ma'am,' the girl replied.

'A nice age,' Molly Bendig replied. 'And you're a beautiful looking girl, too. Fortune favours you, my dear. But when we talked the other day, when I met you in Stepney, you told me you wasn't available to come and work for me?'

'I wasn't at the time, ma'am. But I suddenly finds myself available. And you did say if ever I was to find myself available, I was to come to you.'

A crease of a smile appeared among the great rolls of fat on Mrs Bendig's face. She reached forward and turned up two glasses and opened the gin bottle. She poured out much of its contents.

'Have a glass of daffy, my dear. It'll help you to relax. Does wonders for me when I'm a bit agitated. So, now you're available?'

'I am, ma'am.'

'No need to call me ma'am. Mrs Bendig'll do. I like my young ladies to think of me more as a friend than an employer. And you're available as from right now?'

'I am, Mrs Bendig.'

'And you're available all because some clever bludger's topped that old bastard Bluff Todd?'

Phoebe looked pale and nodded.

Mrs Bendig leaned forward and drew a large finger down the girl's cheek.

'Wasn't you, was it, my lovely?'

'No, Mrs Bendig. No indeed!'

The brothel keeper let out a raucous laugh which echoed into every corner of the vast greeting room of the night house. She tapped the side of her nose.

'Just thought as how I'd ask. If you had, your secret would have been safe. There's many a young lady come to work for me what only got here by topping her ponce. A drip of poison in his gin or a pillow over his head when he's been drunk. Deserved it most of them. I never know why you pretty girls ever bother working the streets.' She leant forward once more. 'Always a room here for a pretty girl in my night house.'

'I didn't kill him, Mrs Bendig. Honest, I didn't...'

Phoebe looked across into Mrs Bendig's great face. Noticed how her many chins seemed to envelop the top of her generous and very exposed bosom.

Mrs Bendig sighed.

'I'll tell you something I don't tell many,' she said. 'I was young and pretty like you once. And I knows about working the streets 'cos I done it myself. Not here in London, but up in Manchester.' She looked thoughtfully up at the ceiling. 'Wild times, my child. Wild times. A foul place to sell yourself, Manchester. And not much money about. Labourers, mostly, that's the class I used to do when I was young. I thought I'd spend all my best years being poked in alleys and ginnels. Well, you knows what it's like, don't you? But then I says to myself, "Molly, you deserve better'n this." And I was determined to have it too.'

She took up the glass of gin and poured it down her throat. She played with the empty glass on the table.

'And that was how I met Mr Bendig. Horace ran a grand house right in the heart of the town. A big place too. Twenty girls, available day and night. I worked there for him a whole year before I captured his heart. And then he says to me, "Molly", he says, "I can't abide the thought of you with all those other men, and you just giving me a go once a week."

Mrs Bendig poured out some more gin. A tear ran down her vast cheek.

'Now wasn't that the loveliest and most romantic words as you've ever heard, my sweetheart?'

'Yes, indeed, Mrs Bendig.'

'So we was married within the month. Well, not in church exactly, but as good as... And by the next month I was running the place for him. And the second house as we took on. We was famous all over Manchester. And then... and then...'

She brought a silk handkerchief up to her eyes.

'My poor Horace was took!'

'Oh, Mrs Bendig!'

'Took he was, my lovely. Just as we was doing so well, and he was talking of packing it all up and moving to the country. Just as he was getting religion from the Methodists and thinking of abandoning the trade forthwith...'

'I'm so sorry, Mrs Bendig,' said Phoebe, reaching forward and taking the older lady's hand.

'Oh, you're a kind girl, a sweet child. I can see as how you understands...'

'It's a cruel world,' said Phoebe.

'Cruel ain't the half of it. I comes home to find the crushers all over the room. Someone had slit poor Horace's throat. There he was a-lying in our own bed. And they accused me! I had to get a dozen of my girls to swear as how I was at our other house at the time. Poor Horace! So I sold up and come to London. And within a year I had this grand place.'

She looked around the big room with pride. Her night house off Leicester Square was now the first port of call for gentlemen seeking good company in London. Here they would dine and drink at the long table. Molly Bendig at the head as hostess. And then those still capable would make their way upstairs to the many bedrooms, where they could seek the expensive company of one of Mrs Bendig's beautiful and refined young ladies. Molly Bendig was the talk of a certain class in London.

And the importance of some of her customers ensured that her business thrived without interference from legal and moral organisations.

The hostess beamed a smile at Phoebe.

'I can see as how we're going to get on just champion,' she said. 'And I know that a great many of my gentlemen are going to fall under the spell of such a pretty face as yours. You can move in forthwith. I'll house you and dress you and present you at the table this very next Saturday night. But there's just one thing, my dear...'

The smile had vanished and there was a steely look on Mrs Bendig's face.

'Just one thing. I do expect loyalty from my young ladies. You work in the house and here in the house only. No assignations on the side. No private meetings with gentlemen. Is that clear?'

Phoebe nodded.

'Just so long as we understands each other, my sweetheart,' said Mrs Bendig, holding the girl's hand just a tad too tight.

Three

'You are surely not thinking of mounting an expedition to Jacob's Island, Will?'

Josef Critzman looked thinner and older than ever, every month of his sixty years. His hand trembled as he poured the tea. Despite being absent from Poland for thirty years, he had never lost his accent.

Quest thought that the old man seemed very ill. They were sitting by the fireside in the back room of his walking stick and umbrella shop in Cheapside. The muffins had been eaten long since and the shop's proprietor had just made the hot drink.

'Of course he's not,' said Isaac Critzman, his brother, a man as fat as Josef was thin. 'Will might as well throw himself in the Thames right now as to go to that foul place. It's the one rookery in London that even we daren't enter. The last member of Monkshood who tried was never seen again...'

'Poor Stripey, I told him not to,' said Jasper Feedle. 'He was so sure as how he'd be safe in his disguise. Had his tale all ready. As how he was on the run from the jacks of Scotland Yard. He thought his brother might be a-hidin' there.'

'And I advised against it,' said Josef. 'Why should his brother have even been there? It was just a rumour.' He turned to Quest. 'I beg of you, Will, please do not do this thing.'

Quest sipped his tea and looked around the room. The two Critzman brothers sat at the table, Jasper in a rocking chair, warming his hands by the fire. Albert Sticks stood in the doorway keeping one eye on the empty shop.

'They did try to top you, lad,' the latter said. 'You should never have let any of the three go. We should have shoved 'em in a cellar and worked away until they told us more.'

Quest said, 'But they didn't try and kill me. They wanted me alive. The ringleader told me as much.'

'Whoever was in that carriage fired a pistol at you...' said Sticks. 'Jasper says as how the ball only just missed your head.'

'Yes, missed,' said Quest. 'And at such a short range! The worst shot in London could have hit me from six feet if he'd wanted.

That bullet was designed to send me into the alley. So that his associates could bludgeon me and take me off.'

'But why?' asked Isaac. 'Why you, Will? And is this an attack on you alone or on the whole of Monkshood? Are others to be threatened?'

'I don't believe so,' Quest replied. 'From what our friend in the alley said, I was to be the target. The King of Jacob's Island wants my company. We don't know that he's even aware of Monkshood. Let's not assume the worst until we can find out more.'

'And you seriously expect to find out more by going into his lair?' asked Josef. 'It is folly, Will!'

'My brother's right,' said Isaac. 'You know what that place is like. Near surrounded by foul water, the Folly Ditch itself convenient for the disposal of a body. Every last house in the rookery linked to its neighbour by tunnels and secret passages. And it's the haunt of the most violent of creatures. Men, aye, and women, who've long experience of killing interlopers. You'll be dead long before you get anywhere near their King. It would take an army to root him out.'

'They say as how Mr Dickens got death threats just for writin' about the place,' said Sticks. 'And that was years before they'd crowned their King. It's not like the other rookeries, lad. Not like the Acre or Rat's Castle. There might be villains in both those places but there's poor folk as well, with good hearts to give 'em a balance. But the Island? Well, you might as well throw yourself into a bear pit.'

'It is a place beyond redemption,' said Josef. 'If ever the devil has an outpost on this earth it is there...'

He looked across at his brother.

'Isaac, given these new circumstances, I really do believe that we must postpone our tour of the abbeys and cathedrals of England. Until these present difficulties are resolved.'

'No!' Quest said forcefully, banging his fist on the table. 'I will not allow that. Josef, you've looked forward to visiting these cathedrals for so many years. You leave tomorrow as planned. If I have to carry you both to the railway station.'

'Then promise me that you won't take any foolhardy actions?' said Josef.

'It could be argued that much of what we do is foolhardy,' Quest replied. 'But no, I give you my word that I won't go to Jacob's Island, except as a last resort.'

'I suppose I must settle for that,' said Josef. He turned to his brother. 'Isaac, we could postpone our trip...'

Quest said, 'If you're not on the train tomorrow as planned, I'll go to Jacob's Island just for the devilment of the thing.'

'He would, too.' said Sticks.

Josef sighed. 'Please, my friends, do keep out of trouble while we're away. Try and do innocent things.'

'I have a dinner invitation for this evening,' said Quest. 'I'm dining with Benjamin Wissilcraft and his sister. Where's the danger in that?'

~

Ikey Balfrey ran the best shop for wipes in Field Lane, though there was a lot of competition. His shop, he thought, a cut above that of his neighbour, the unfortunate Colley Rogers, turned off that very day on the scaffold outside Newgate Gaol. He wondered about the possibility of taking on Colley's lease and expanding his little empire. Well, maybe...

Balfrey's dingy windows were filled with pocket handkerchiefs of superior quality, the nicest silk most of them, and not a trace of the owners' initials that once graced them. Every pickpocket around Saffron Hill came to Ikey first, for he was known to pay the best prices. But he only took the finest, the nicest of the daily crop. Many a dip was turned away and forced to sell his wares at one of the inferior shops.

He bought and sold other goods too, though not usually in the front of his shop. Arrangements with burglars and house-breakers were made elsewhere – in the local taverns and drinking dens or sometimes in shadowed rooms in the heart of the nearby rookery. Sometimes he bought and sold the thieves themselves, when the mood took him or the reward became sufficiently high. And for this reason the police left him alone.

Not that the crushers were often to be seen in Field Lane. Or if they were, they came mob-handed. There were places where even the bravest daren't go.

Ikey Balfrey was known, respected and feared for his extensive knowledge of the underworld, his considerable memory and his venomous hatred of anyone who crossed him. He never needed to use violence himself. He had a number of bruisers at hand to carry out such undertaking on his behalf. And though he did sometimes sell his wipes retail, the majority of the purchasers of his handkerchiefs came from the more respectable quarters of the town. They would buy wholesale from Ikey's stock, reselling to little shops in Westminster, Bloomsbury and Piccadilly. It was a most thriving trade.

On this chilly afternoon he was warming his hands at the fire in the back room when the bell over the door rang. He sighed at the interruption, pushed a threatening coal back into the flames and went out into his shop.

A most unwelcome visitor.

He didn't know the man's name and didn't much like him either. A flash gent, smartly clad, with neat fair hair and eyes as grey as the clouds above. The kind of stranger who wouldn't usually last five safe minutes in Field Lane without being robbed or worse. Ikey's eyes lifted to the window. Out in the street were the three toughs who provided the escort for this particular visitor.

The grey eyes were regarding Ikey with a predatory look, the kind of regard a lizard might have for an insect, the moment before its tongue darted out to consume it. His thin lips parted in a humourless smile.

Ikey's fingers wandered to the compartment under the counter where he kept his double-barrelled percussion-cap pistol. A weapon he'd acquired after this man had descended upon him the first time, just over a week before.

It was not often Ikey Balfrey felt fear. But there was something about this particular individual that turned his stomach over... and not just fear. Revulsion too. It was as though the devil had come calling.

The man ran his forefinger across his lips, saying nothing but just staring hard at the fence. Then his eyes darted around the shop, seeming to take in every dingy corner before his gaze came to rest on the pale face of the proprietor.

'I think eight days is quite long enough, Mr Balfrey,' he said, very quietly. 'My employer was disappointed that you failed to send the message we requested.'

'Nothin' to say to you...'

The man took in a long breath.

'I think you have, Mr Balfrey,' he said. 'I think you have a very great deal to say to me. I've given you time to consider the matter. Eight days. My employer isn't usually so patient. But your time is up and I won't be leaving without a definitive answer.'

'Get lost!'

'You know, Mr Balfrey, I do think we are being incredibly generous towards you. My employer recognises your talents and your... how can I put it?... quite encyclopaedic knowledge of the people who frequent this part of the town...'

'What do you want?'

'I told you on my last visit what we want. We want to purchase your little emporium. For a liberal sum. You may continue to run your business as before. We will not interfere. All we ask is that you report back to me at regular intervals. And that the thieves you run, work for us, though, of course, under your immediate supervision.'

'I makes a good living as it is,' said Balfrey. 'Why should I cut you in? Go and jump in the river...'

The man yawned.

'Now I'm getting bored, Mr Balfrey. And I do find boredom quite... nauseous.'

'Well, go and...'

His visitor waved a reproving finger.

'No oaths please. I do so hate uncivilised conversations.'

'If you don't...'

'Fifty guineas, Mr Balfrey. And every day you hesitate, the sum goes down by ten guineas. And if you haven't agreed to our terms in five days, well... life could get very unpleasant. You see, word of your resistance might get out and encourage a rebellious spirit amongst others. And that would be very bad for business, don't you see that?'

'I won't...'

'Think carefully. We would very much like to harness your undoubted abilities, but we might just settle for your shop and the goodwill of its reputation. Nobody is indispensable, after all. Ah, I can see you are agitated. I will trouble you no longer. Send that message, Mr Balfrey. I do urge you to, I really do. Fifty guineas until midnight. Then ten deducted per day. And in five days...'

He gave a slight bow of the head and walked briskly out of the shop.

~

It was going to be a lonely evening without her, the poet thought, though it might enable him to write some verse. That was always the trouble with her. He always felt the greatest need for her body when she was far away.

Well, not that far, really. Just a mile or two across London. He could walk to her front door in a half hour. But he never did. His presence at her home could only lead to complications.

He'd met her briefly, an hour before. Walking along Regent Street. She had imparted to him the bad news, then advised him that he should go away and try and do some writing.

So now he sat in this great empty space. At a little table by a grimy window, overlooking the maddened waters of the Thames. Maddened, yes, a good word, he thought, as he watched the boats struggling against the river's mighty flow as it met an incoming tide. Maddened. A word he would work into his latest verse.

He opened the old ledger and turned to the pages near the back, briefly scanning past work, before he found a blank space for this latest attempt to capture the city.

Four

Benjamin Wissilcraft raised his glass.

'Your good health, Quest!'

William Quest swirled the wine round in his own glass and regarded it for a moment or two.

'What's the matter, Quest? You think I've drugged it? Put in some sleeping potion so that I might have you under my control? Ah! Why is everyone so suspicious of me?'

Wissilcraft eased back his chair to make more room for his great bulk before the dining table.

'You are Queen Victoria's Spymaster,' Quest replied. 'And we all know the lengths you took to fill the vacancy. You can't blame me for being a trifle wary.'

The fat man gave a great burst of laughter.

'I am, perhaps, less conniving than my predecessor....'

'Not so immediately deadly,' said Quest.

Wissilcraft leant forward.

'I neglected to inquire, how is your wound, my dear Quest?'

'It's healed well enough. It was a price worth paying, given the end result. Have I been invited here tonight so that we might discuss that old business?'

Wissilcraft shook his great head.

'Not at all, not really.'

'Not really?'

'Well, we can't pretend that some matters weren't left outstanding, can we? You'll recall that when you left Norfolk, you went away with some property belonging to the State. You made a vow that it would never be returned. I understand how bitter you were at the time, and rightly so.'

'You want the notebook back?'

Wissilcraft leant forward and refilled the glasses.

'I thought, now that several months have passed, that you might wish to reconsider. Our nation is in a parlous position. We are at war with the Russians...'

'You're making a plea to my sense of patriotism?'

Wissilcraft sipped the wine.

'Not altogether. You see, my dear Quest, you hold in your possession a notebook that could bring down much of the Establishment. A document that could imperil the Government itself, even the Royal Family. Writings that would give power to any revolutionaries in our midst.'

'From my point of view, that might be considered a good thing.'

Wissilcraft sighed.

'I'm well aware that you have revolutionary tendencies yourself, Quest. But I plead with you not to exploit the information in your possession.'

'I haven't so far...'

'No, no, you haven't. And my masters are puzzled as to why not? They feel that they're living on a cliff-edge, just waiting for the moment of revelation that will sending them tipping to their doom.'

Quest smiled.

'Then perhaps they should all lead less corrupt lives.'

Wissilcraft shrugged.

'Human nature is human nature. We all have our weaknesses. May I ask if you have perused the notebook?'

'I've read it, yes. Nothing very startling. It just confirms what I've always believed. That the Class is rotten to the core. Our lords and masters deserve to be brought down.'

Wissilcraft patted his hands down on to the table and was silent for several moments.

'And you intend to do so?' he said at last. 'You propose to use the notebook? I'm well aware that the reason you took it in the first place was to protect yourself and your associates. But there's no need, Quest. The Home Secretary has authorised me to issue a free pardon to you and any named persons, absolving you of any responsibility for past... misdemeanours. It's also possible that we might reward you for the return of the notebook. What would be your price?'

'One that would be too high for you and your masters,' Quest replied. 'A redistribution of wealth, perhaps. Extending the franchise to the working people of the land...'

'I don't deal in dreams, Quest...'

'Then we seem to have come to something of an *impasse*...'

Wissilcraft made a temple roof of his hands and rested his chin down on them.

'Then I think we had better shelve our discussion for the time being. Besides, it's nearly time to dine and I want to introduce you to my sister. Have some more wine while I seek her out.'

The spymaster left the room. Like many big men he moved extraordinarily fast. Quest remembered how speedily Wissilcraft had walked across the Norfolk countryside – and how very skilled the man could be at trailing suspects.

He got up and wandered over to the window. Despite the hour it was scarcely dark. He glanced up and down Harley Street. At a first view there were just the usual passers-by. But he knew that out there somewhere was the faithful Albert Sticks, armed with a pair of duelling pistols, a fine dagger, and a lead-weighted life preserver.

And that at each end of the street were stationed two other members of the Monkshood secret society, just waiting to intercept anyone who might be trailing Quest as he made his way home.

He heard footsteps approaching, and came away from the window. A servant opened the door and stood there as Wissilcraft came back into the room. A moment later he was followed by his sister. The door was closed behind them.

'My dear Quest, may I introduce my sister, Miss Angeline Wissilcraft. Angeline, may I present Mr William Quest.'

Quest was surprised at the woman who stood before him. He had pictured a large woman resembling the spymaster. And someone of a similar age. But Angeline Wissilcraft was slim where her brother was fat, fair where her brother was dark, and a good twenty years younger than her sibling. And while the brother's eyes were dark, those of the sister were of an intense and deep blue. For a moment he felt transfixed by her gaze.

Quest bowed.

'Miss Wissilcraft...'

'Mr Quest.'

She was looking right into his face, as though reading the very thoughts in his mind. She smiled and held out a hand. He reached forward to take it, brushing it with his lips.

'We shall be dining in a few moments,' she said. 'It was good of you to come, Mr Quest. My brother has often spoken of you. I was quite intrigued to hear of your adventures last year.'

Wissilcraft looked embarrassed.

'Even spymasters must unload their burden somewhere,' he explained, holding up his hands as though surrendering to some inevitable force. 'And my sister is the soul of discretion.'

'I'm sure,' said Quest. 'I don't believe I've seen you out in society, Miss Wissilcraft?'

'Society bores me, Mr Quest. I have other interests...'

Quest was about to inquire what they might be when the door opened and the servant announced that dinner was ready. But as they turned and left the drawing room, he felt Angeline Wissilcraft's fingers brush the back of his hand.

~

Mrs Bendig wiped the sweat from her forehead.

'Gawd, they're raucous tonight! Are you ready to meet my gentlemen?'

She had excused herself from her position at the head of the great table in the long room of her night house, to cries of despair from thirty or so rather drunken customers, many begging her to come back soon. In the ante-room she had discovered Phoebe watching the proceedings.

'One gent in particular,' she went on. 'There, you can see him at the corner of the table. A gent looking for a young lady, I think, for he can't seem to get drunk, for all he's putting away. You get in there, my sweetheart, and see what you can do for him. A bit of conversation, they likes that. And try and get more champagne down his throat. Then he might not give you such a hard time when you gets him upstairs.'

'Who is he?' Phoebe asked.

Mrs Bendig gave her a knowing wink.

'A Member of Parliament, no less. And a baronet to boot. Used to be in the way of the money-lending trade, but he got virtue of a sort and gave it up in favour of aiding the poor. Waste of bloody time in my book! He's called Sir Wren Angier...'

Phoebe looked through the gap in the curtain.

'He's a handsome man,' she said, following Mrs Bendig's pointing finger.

'He'll get drunk. They always do. Then you won't need to do a lot for him, tonight. Just keep him talking for a few minutes and he'll probably fall asleep. But he saw you earlier and asked for you in partic'lar. Keep him sweet on you, my dear. He's got more money than he knows what to do with.'

~

'I've heard something of your background, Mr Quest,' said Angeline Wissilcraft. 'My brother declares you to be the most dangerous man in London. Is that so?'

Quest smiled. They had finished the meal and he was preparing to leave. A servant had gone to fetch his cloak and walking cane.

'I think your brother flatters me,' said Quest. 'There are a great many people in London who're far more dangerous than I am. He's obviously excluding himself...'

Wissilcraft let out a great gust of laughter.

'Ah, you can't play the innocent, my dear Quest,' he said. 'You have it in your power to bring down the whole of society. What could be more dangerous than that? And as for the secret group that backs you...'

'What secret group would that be?' asked Quest.

'You would have made a great actor, Quest. The way you deliver that line with such an expression of innocence on your face... it would do credit to the Lyceum.'

'I try to leave play-acting to others.'

'Oh, yes, the delightful Miss Rosa Stanton for example?'

'Who is this Miss Stanton?' asked Angeline Wissilcraft.

'A friend of Mr Quest. A very intimate friend.'

'She is your mistress, Mr Quest?'

She asked the question so directly and with such a lack of embarrassment that Quest was quite shaken. Those deep blue eyes held his own gaze with such a power that he had to force himself to look away.

'A good friend,' he replied. 'Someone I've known for a time. And yes, she used to be an actress once. In the provinces and upon the London stage.'

'Was she a good actress?' Miss Wissilcraft persisted. 'Comedy perhaps? Or a tragedian? I'm partial to the drama myself. I may even have seen her perform.'

'I understand that Miss Stanton has performed a great many roles...' Wissilcraft said, giving Quest a sideways glance. 'Though she's not so often to be seen on the stage these days, I think?'

'No indeed,' said Quest. 'She is at present taking a rest from theatricals.'

'A pity!' said Miss Wissilcraft. 'I would so much have enjoyed seeing her. Ah, here's your cloak and your cane.'

She took them from the servant, examining the stick with very great interest.

'A very handsome cane, Mr Quest.'

She drew her fingers along the top few inches of the cane, and then gave the silver rondel a quick twist. The beginnings of a thin but deadly blade appeared. She eased it back into its Malaccan shaft and turned it to close.

'A sword-stick, Mr Quest? I've heard that you're quite skilled with your weapon.' She examined the cane again. 'Was this the sword-stick you used to kill...?'

'I have several,' Quest said. 'I can assure you, Miss Wissilcraft, that this one has never been used in anger.'

'A very clever design,' she said. 'Just looking at it now, you would never believe that anything so potent might be concealed within. A little manipulation often summons up something surprising...'

'I trust it was not intended for protection from me, my dear Quest?' Wissilcraft intervened. 'You are a guest in my house. Even though we have our differences, I wish you no harm.'

Quest smiled.

'Just one of my collection,' he said, putting on his cloak

Wissilcraft touched his arm.

'Please do think on what I've asked,' he said. 'I don't expect an immediate answer.'

'I'll give it some consideration,' said Quest. 'But I fear you may be disappointed. Goodbye, Wissilcraft. Miss Wissilcraft.'

He took her hand to his lips and smiled at her before turning to leave the house.

As the door closed, Wissilcraft looked at his sister.

'You seem to have made something of an impression on our Mr Quest, Angeline. He could scarcely take his eyes off you.'

'He's an interesting man,' she replied. 'Not handsome, but striking in a very rough sort of way. However, I sense that he has not the slightest intention of complying with your wishes. I fear that your masters in Whitehall are going to be sadly disappointed.'

'They'd have him killed if they could,' said Wissilcraft. 'Lord Palmerston said so only yesterday.'

'If the Home Secretary wants someone dead, it usually happens. But then again, his victims mostly lack the capacity to hold the establishment to ransom in quite the same way as Mr Quest.'

'Are you going to take him to your bed, Angeline?'

'Lord Palmerston or Quest?'

'You know perfectly well who I mean. And I happen to know that you've already had Palmerston.'

'I suspect that Quest might have a trifle more vigour...'

Angeline Wissilcraft looked thoughtful for a moment.

'Using my body might be an interesting alternative to the other ways that have been tried. Now that I've seen our Mr Quest close to, I confess it wouldn't be quite the horrendous prospect I'd envisaged. I might well find some amusement there.'

Wissilcraft gave her an expression of concern.

'Please do remember just why we are going through all this, Angeline. Vital secrets are at stake. The State is of more importance than your pleasures.'

She looked straight at his face, her blue eyes slightly hooded.

'My dear Benjamin. Nothing is of more importance than my pleasures.'

Five

'So was she pretty?'

Rosa Stanton nuzzled her head against Quest's bare chest, one hand exploring the nether regions beneath the sheets. Her dark hair spilled across his throat.

'I suppose it all depends what you mean by pretty,' he replied. 'She's a very striking woman in many ways. Nothing at all like her brother.'

'Fair or dark?'

'Very fair, I suppose.'

'What colour were her eyes?'

'A deep blue,' he said, perhaps a trifle too quickly.

'You noticed, then? Most men don't notice the colour of a woman's eyes until they become... better acquainted.'

'Just happened to see.'

They lay in bed in her rooms, just where the road from Tottenham Court arrived in Bloomsbury. The road outside was quieter now, just the occasional rumble of carriage wheels and the whinnying of a horse. A solitary candle burned on the dresser, illuminating a high-ceilinged room filled with rows of theatrical costumes.

'Have I any reason to feel concerned?' she asked

'You mean am I intending to have her?'

'Just so.'

'I can't say I've given the matter a lot of thought. I very much doubt I'll see her again. Wissilcraft and I are hardly on social terms.'

She licked his lips with her tongue.

'Not that I'd be bothered, Quest. You know our arrangement. We enjoy each other's company and we like pleasuring each other. It's fortunate that I can never love you. It gives us both freedom to breathe.'

'Then why would you be concerned if I got better acquainted with Angeline Wissilcraft?'

'Angeline? Is that her name? How extraordinary!'

'Just a name...'

She looked up at him.

'You and I have so many names between us, don't we Quest? Odd ones too, some of them. But Angeline?'

'Anyway, I thought you were intending to leave me to return to the stage?'

'I may well do so. I saw Mr Jolys again only the other day. He's very keen to revive his much lauded production of *The Beggar's Opera*. He said that if he did he would engage me in my old role as Polly Peachum. You wouldn't believe the number of flash gents who yearned for me across the footlights.'

'No, I don't suppose I would.'

She gave a little yawn.

'After all, I can't go on being your mistress for ever? A woman has to make her own way in the world. These performances, these duets, are very interesting but I miss having the applause of an audience.'

'Well, I'm perfectly content to hide away from the world,' said Quest. 'Public exposure would make our secret work quite impossible. And don't you think there's a possibility that someone in your audience might recognise you from one of the many roles you've played for Monkshood?'

'A chance I'm willing to take for fame and fortune,' said Rosa. She gave him a look of concern. 'Tell me you're not really intending to force your way into Jacob's Island?'

'You know about that, then?'

'I saw Josef in his shop this afternoon. He made me promise to hold you back from there by force if I have to. And he's right, Quest. It's a place of death. Not even you could...'

'As I told Josef, I'm not planning to find my way in there in the near future. There's always the possibility that we could snatch their precious King when he's away from the place. I've asked Jasper and Sticks to seek out his haunts. We know he frequents a tavern in Bermondsey. But get him we must.'

'Then leave it to Jasper and Sticks. Please Quest. You're not immortal.'

Quest ran his fingers through her hair.

'Someone took a shot at me, Rosa. Moments later, three bludgers employed by the King of Jacob's Island tried to snatch me. I want to know why?'

'Who is this King of Jacob's Island?'

'When I first heard about him I thought him just a tale, a myth. After all, why should such a lawless place accept such an individual? Why would they need someone to command them at all? But there's no doubt now that he exists. Who he is, though...?'

Quest shrugged.

They lay in silence for several minutes, their thoughts far away. From time to time someone would emerge as a leader in a rookery. Someone stronger. Someone bolder than the rest. A man with a bit more intelligence than was usual. They tended not to last for very long. There was little honour amongst thieves in such places. A blow on the head or a dagger in the guts usually deposed anyone who presumed they were mightier than their fellows.

But the King of Jacob's Island had lasted for two years now. And his power and influence had grown rather than diminished. It was said that he not only reigned over the island but over most of the rookeries south of the river.

And Quest wondered just why he had become the focus of the King's attentions?

'Don't go there,' Rosa said at last. 'You have a very lovely body and I'd hate to hear of it being chopped up and fed to the rats in the Thames.'

She lowered her head beneath the sheets and took him to a paradise that seemed a long way from the hell of the London rookeries.

~

Abraham Anders looked out through the window of his room at Scotland Yard.

A belt of rain had swept in from the west, along the course of the Thames, lashing the midnight traffic in Whitehall Place. He saw his own reflection in the glass, illuminated by the solitary gaslight in the office. Sergeant Berry loaded the small open fire with yet more coals. It was nearly summer but the temperature still felt decidedly wintry.

Anders smiled. He still had a good head of hair, but it was entirely white now. I look bloody old! he said to himself. Too old to be doing this job.

For a moment he considered having his whiskers shaved off. Perhaps? He vaguely wondered at the condition of the skin beneath. Well...

'So that's it,' said Berry, 'an end to the investigation? We can't put your favourite suspect at the scene. And we've nothing else in the way of evidence. Our usual sources of information in the East End have closed ranks. I'm not sure there's much more we can do.' He sat down in the wooden chair and warmed his hands by the fire. 'Do you still think it's Quest?'

Anders considered the question for a while. He sat down at his desk and sipped a mouthful of the tea Berry had made. As usual it was over-strong, the way his sergeant said people liked it in his home town of Manchester.

He shook his head.

'No, in all honesty I don't,' he said at last. 'But I do think he knows more about the killing than he's saying. We get lots of deaths around Shadwell. Men and women stabbed. Stranglings. People bludgeoned to oblivion. But shot with a pistol? It doesn't go with the territory.'

'What does Commissioner Mayne think?'

'He thinks we should put a halt to the investigation. It was, after all, only Bluff Todd, a villainous ponce who was an intrusion on the face of the earth. Mayne's words, not mine. He believes London's a better place without the old rogue.'

'No denying that!' said Berry.

Anders shrivelled up his face at the taste of another sip of tea.

'But it's still an unlawful killing. Plain murder. Or do we only put our hearts and souls into investigating the deaths of people we might have approved of in life? Or members of the Class? No! We shouldn't. Bluff Todd might have been the scum of the earth. He probably deserved a meeting with the hangman a dozen times over. But nobody had the right to kill him outside the law.'

Berry drank his tea with relish.

'But I don't see what we can do, sir? Not unless someone else comes forward. And the locals have definitely closed ranks.'

'Mmm...'

The Inspector looked at him, giving him a smile.

Berry laughed.

'I know, I know. You don't have to spell it out, Inspector. You want me to get down there informally? Ask around a bit? Well, there's something that might be done. Bluff Todd's prostitutes all seemed to go to ground the moment he was topped. Unlikely that one of them did it... not with a pistol, anyroad. But it's hard to believe that not one of them knows anything. They should be emerging from their hidey-holes about now.'

'Exactly so,' said Anders. 'Anything, anything at all. I'll settle for rumour and gossip if I have to. I just want to know why someone's roaming around Shadwell and the Ratcliffe Highway with a pistol, turning off villains. I don't want another Quest in our parish. One's quite enough.'

'The Commissioner won't like it,' said Berry. 'We've still got those hotel thieves to find, not to mention the Kensington jewel robbery. And there's the spate of footpads attacking the gentry south of the river.'

Anders shuffled the papers on his desk.

'And if Mayne asks where you are, that's what I'll tell him. That you're seeking information on all of those cases from your contacts in the underworld. And who knows? You might even gain some useful knowledge down on the ground. But Berry...' He slapped his hand down on the desk. 'Make this rascal with the pistol your priority.'

Berry poured them both out some more stewed tea.

'I'll start first thing in the morning. Get down to where Bluff Todd was killed and work outwards from there.'

Anders nodded approval.

'There's something else, Berry...'

'Sir?'

'Nothing definite, just a feeling,' said Anders. 'Over the last few months, crime seems to have increased on a massive scale in this city. Not just the usual rag-tail bunch of bludgers and burglars, gonophs and magsmen. Something darker, much more sinister. There's been a lot of killings too.'

'These things happen...'

'Yes they do,' Anders agreed, 'but it's as though some territories of villainy are being cleared. In a deliberate and quite calculated way. Three of my regular informants have ended up in the river since Christmas. Well, that's the way these things go. Those who peach often have short lives. But three who almost certainly didn't know each other? Feels odd to me.'

'You think someone's making a land-grab?'

Anders threw out his hands.

'I really don't know, Berry. I've nothing to base such an opinion on. It's just my instinct. That *something* is happening. I might be quite wrong, but I'd rather find out. Better to be safe than sorry.'

Berry nodded. He had a great respect for the instincts of Inspector Abraham Anders where the criminal underworld of London was concerned.

Six

'I d'believe Sir Wren Angier's took quite a shine to you, my girl,' said Mrs Bendig. 'Three nights on the trot he's been round here asking for you in particular. And he drinks a deal before he goes up the stairs. Some of my other gentlemen are getting quite jealous.'

Phoebe frowned.

'I try to do the right thing. But he's so... *demanding*. Wants me all to himself. Though most of the time he just talks or falls asleep. He drinks too much.'

Mrs Bendig squeezed her great bulk deeper into the chair behind the table in her private office.

'And that's why I've asked you to come and see me. To ask about Angier.' She leaned forward confidentially, her great arms concealing the writing slope. 'He hasn't tried to make private arrangements with you, has he, girl?'

'Indeed not!'

Mrs Bendig's smile had vanished.

'Only you'll recall the conversation we had when you arrived here the other day. Other men have come here and taken my young ladies away to be their mistresses. I'd hate to think Sir Wren Angier had made such an approach to you?'

'I swear he hasn't, Mrs Bendig.'

A smile as thin as gruel returned to Molly Bendig's face.

'That's all to the good, then. But you let me know if he tries it on. I won't have my ladies stolen from under me.'

There was a sharp tap on the door.

'What is it?' Mrs Bendig said wearily. She had been acting as hostess until six that morning and was badly in need of sleep. There always seemed to be interruptions during her quiet time.

One of the girls poked her head around the door.

'Gennulman to see you ma'am. Says it's very urgent....'

Mrs Bendig gave a despairing sigh which turned into a yawn.

'Oh, very well. You'd better send him through, Belinda. All right, Phoebe. You can go now but bear in mind what I told you.'

As Phoebe left the room, the girl Belinda showed in the visitor. He stood for a moment in the doorway, all tall and thin, with sandy hair. His head swivelled around the place, seeming to take in all of the details. He put Mrs Bendig in mind of a curious ferret in search of a rabbit. And when his pale grey eyes turned upon her, the lady felt just how that hunted rabbit might feel. A moment later he had crossed to the table and was proffering a visiting card.

Mrs Bendig regarded him for a moment before taking it between two of her fat fingers. She waved him into a chair and read the printed words.

'It says here that you're the honourable Mr Margam Boone, and that you're a lawyer.'

The thin man lowered his head in acknowledgement.

'That is so,' he replied, almost hissing the words. In Mrs Bendig's eyes, the ferret suddenly transformed into a snake. 'And may I say it's an honour to meet a lady of your renown.'

Mrs Bendig spent most evenings listening to such flattering and untrue comments, and took the lawyer's smiling greeting with a very large pinch of salt.

'If you're touting for business, Mister Boone, I fear you've had a wasted journey. I have my own lawyer, Mr Clotdyke of Lincolns Inn. He deals with all of my affairs.'

Margam Boone held up his palms in protest. He gave a beaming smile, with lips that seemed more blue than red.

'Nothing so vulgar, Mrs Bendig, I do assure you. And by the way...' his eyes fixed on hers in a most challenging way... 'it is, for the sake of formality, Mister Margam Boone...'

'Whatever, I've no work for you.'

She looked again at the card.

'You have chambers at Gray's Inn, I see? Not a part of town I'm regularly acquainted with, though some of my gentlemen clients have addresses there.'

'I'm sure they do...'

'But you're not one of my gentlemen, are you Mister Boone?'

'Mister Margam Boone,' he corrected her with a cold smile.

She shook her head, 'No, I believe I'd remember you...'

'I've never before entered your establishment,' said Margam Boone. He looked dismissively around the room. 'I doubt you have anything here that would be an attraction for me.'

Mrs Bendig looked him up and down.

'No, I suspect not,' she said. 'So can we get down to business, Mr *Margam* Boone? I've had a very busy night and I'm looking forward to a restful morning.'

'And that is precisely why I've come to see you, madam. I understand that you have been giving some little thought to retirement – to the sea-side, I believe?'

'Where did you hear that?'

'That really doesn't matter, I think. London is but a village at heart. And full of gossip.'

'I'm not quite sure what business my personal plans are to you, Mister Boone?'

'Mister *Mar...*'

'Or anyone else come to that. I really don't see any advantage to me in prolonging this interview.'

Her hand reached out for the bell on one side of the table. Mister Margam Boone slid his arm forward to block access to that instrument of dismissal.

He smiled again.

'I'm just coming to the advantage, Mrs Bendig. If you will please bear with me. I represent certain... parties, shall we say, who have a very great interest in your, er, establishment. They wish to make you an offer for the property, your young ladies, and the goodwill that would come with such a business.'

'You wish to buy me out?'

'Exactly so. And I'm to tell you that the offer would not be ungenerous. This is a thriving endeavour. Anyone may see that. On behalf of my clients, I'm prepared to begin negotiations... shall we say at a thousand guineas?'

Mrs Bendig gave a great bellow of laughter.

'A thousand! This is the finest night house in London. I've had dukes in here, and royalty. Even a prime minister... If I were to sell. And I'm not saying that I am, I should want a damned sight more than a paltry thousand guineas.'

Margam Boone tapped the table and beamed a smile at her.

'Well, we have to begin somewhere, my dear lady. How if I were to double the offer?'

'And how if I didn't want to sell?'

He looked up at the ceiling for several moments as though deep in thought. He tapped his chin several times with two fingers. And then his washed-out grey eyes sought her own.

'Four thousand pounds,' he said.

'Just who are these clients of yours?' Mrs Bendig asked. 'They seem mighty keen to buy my night house.'

'And as a going concern, Mrs Bendig. There would always be safe employment for your young ladies. And it might be, that in addition to the straightforward purchase price, my clients might be prepared to pay a modest percentage of the profits to you to fund your retirement at the sea-side.'

'That seems a very generous proposition?'

'It is indeed. I think it shows the admiration my clients have for you as a woman of business.'

'And who are your clients again?'

He wagged a reproving finger.

'Ah, my dear Mrs Bendig, you know perfectly well I did not say. Confidentiality is an important requirement of the lawyer's trade.'

She stood up, astonishingly sprightly for a woman of her bulk.

'Then I regret we don't have a deal, sir.'

She reached forward and rang the bell.

He smiled again.

'This has, no doubt, been something of a surprise to you, my dear lady. Perhaps I should have written first, rather than coming in person. You might need a little while to contemplate my offer. I'll return in a few days, Mrs Bendig. To see if we might resume negotiations. I can see you've had a busy night at your work. I will try and call at a more opportune moment.'

'You're wasting your time, Mr Boone. And mine. If you have a serious offer then you bring your clients in person, so I might see who I'm dealing with. I don't do business by proxy.'

Margam Boone stood and bowed.

'I'm sure we may yet come to an arrangement,' he hissed. 'There is usually a solution to any obstructions in the way of business.'

The door opened and Belinda stood there, looking with interest at the visitor.

'No doubt', said Mrs Bendig. 'Show the gentlemen out, Belinda. Good day, Mister Boone.'

~

He was dressed in a disreputable suit of fustian with a stained canvas cap upon his head. In his hand he carried a heavy and dark blackthorn stick. He was unshaven and had a vivid scar down his left cheek. His dark eyes flashed a warning at anyone who dared to take too much of an interest in his appearance.

Not that anyone did very much notice in this rough and rookery-fringed district of Seven Dials. He was a familiar sight in the area, a bludger, a footpad of uncertain temper and rough language. The residents knew very little about him. There were some matters it was better not to go into in any detail. There was a rumour that his close acquaintances called him Bill. Though nobody was certain. Names, in any case, were easily acquired and just as easily disposed of in the Dials.

He paused for a long interval at a corner of Monmouth Street, just at the junction with the narrow alley known as Neal's Yard. He stood tapping the great stick down on the ground, seeming to take a great interest in everyone who came by. Then, as a brewer's dray rumbled by, hiding him from view, he swung into the alley and paced quickly along its cobbles to an anonymous-seeming door in one wall. He took out a key and let himself through.

On the outside it had seemed quite a flimsy door, but on the inside it could be seen as stout, with great iron bolts which he slid across. Some steps led upwards to a tiny landing with another heavy door. He reached into his jacket for another key and entered the room beyond.

Jasper Feedle was sprawled in a battered armchair in one corner of the lurk, his one leg up on a great wooden chest underneath the window.

'Yer late, lad,' he said, 'and I was just startin' ter worry.'

Quest sat back on the bed and began to remove his disguise.

'I went over to Southwark. To see Old Jamie,' he said. 'Given that he used to live on Jacob's Island. But that was in the old days, long before the wretched place gained a King.'

'How's Old Jamie? Still dippin' in pockets?'

52

'Not any more. His hand isn't steady enough. Another candidate for a Monkshood pension. We must remember to tell Isaac when he comes home. Jamie's useful to us. Everyone likes him and he has a rare gift for gaining confidences.'

'So he knew nothin'?'

'It was what he didn't know that was more interesting. He still sees people from the Island. But he says they're as tight as clams. Won't say a word about what it's like now. There's fear there, Jasper. Real fear. Jamie said he could sense it.'

'So we still only hears the rumour and legend?'

'We could dethrone this King where he lives...'

'Now I did hear as how yer promised not to do that. Josef'll have me lites out if I lets yer go wanderin' into that place. It ain't safe, 'specially if it's yerself they're after.'

Quest began to change back into his own clothes.

'You have another idea?'

'There's that tavern. Down in Bermondsey. *The Bold Dragoon,* that rascal who tried ter snatch yer said. We knows his majesty the king goes there from time ter time to conduct his business. Best that I hangs around it for a few days. To see what I can discover.'

Quest sank his head into his hands.

'Could be risky, Jasper.'

'The whole of our lives is risky, Billy boy.'

'I should do it myself.'

'It's yerself they're after.'

'Disguise?' Quest said, looking at the wooden chest that stored the costumes for so many of his London characters.

'We don't know what they knows about yer. Safer that I go. Much safer.'

'Very well, but take no chances, Jasper. I value your neck too much to want to hear of you floating down the river.'

Jasper laughed.

'I values it very much myself,' he said. 'And the river's too filthy for a swim in summer.'

~

Rosa Stanton stood on the stage of the Lyceum Theatre, looking out at the empty auditorium. A few scene-shifters were adjusting the flats for that evening's performance. From somewhere in the distance came the heavy banging of a hammer.

'Miss Stanton?'

The woman's accent still slightly betrayed its German origins, though there seemed a touch of Italian in the rise of the deep voice. The lady was very well-dressed in evening wear, the dark curls of hair showing the first signs of grey. She was near to sixty and Rosa thought she seemed too pale to be healthy.

She gave a curtsey.

'Madame Vestris.'

It was a long time since Rosa had seen the great opera singer and actress up close. The powdered face had hidden the wrinkles from the back seats of the audience.

'Ah, you are a pretty girl, Miss Stanton. My husband, Mr Charles Matthews, recommended you to me, as did Mr Jolys. We do not have a production in mind yet, though I like to keep talented young ladies in mind. Which is the purpose of this interview.'

Rosa bowed her head.

'I'm very honoured, Madame.'

The lady smiled.

'I regret I have not seen you in performance, though Mr Jolys recalled to me your Polly Peachum in *The Beggar's Opera.*'

Rosa felt a touch of embarrassment. She had played at this very theatre in Madame Vestris's *Extravaganzas* only three years before, albeit only in a small role. The great actress clearly hadn't remembered her. Rosa felt herself blushing. Hadn't she lied to Quest on more than one occasion that she had been the leading lady in that production?

'*The Beggar's Opera* is such a beautiful piece of work for the English stage, I think. I am saddened that I have never played it,' Madame Vestris continued.

'But you've performed so many other great roles, Madame. Both in opera and the play. I've seen you so many times. My father brought me to London to watch you when I was quite a young girl.'

Madame Vestris gave her a smile that seemed to light up the whole theatre.

'I fear my days of acting are coming to an end, Miss Stanton. I do not seem to have the energy these days, either to act or to sing. My time is now given over almost entirely to management. These present performances I am rehearsing for will, I regret, be my last upon the London stage.'

'That will be a sad loss...'

Madame Vestris took her by the hand.

'I have been fortunate in my career. But there comes a time when every player must withdraw to the wings. My enthusiasm now is to reveal the talents of other young ladies and gentlemen. To pass on what I have learned and to offer opportunities.'

'That's very kind...'

Madame Vestris looked around the stage.

'I regret that this is a noisy and unpleasant place to conduct an audition. Perhaps one evening, when there is no performance, you might care to come as my guest to the green room at Covent Garden? Mr Matthews tells me that you have a delightful singing voice?' She held her head to one side and smiled again. 'You could perhaps sing something for my guests.'

Rosa was stunned. Invitations to the Covent Garden green room, to people outside Madame's own circle, were as rare as hen's teeth. It was used, to all intents and purposes, as her own drawing room. Madame was known for her restrictions there, curbing loutish behaviour and bad language.

Rosa curtseyed almost to the floor, thinking how to respond.

'Madame...' she said at last.

Madame Vestris laughed.

'Mr Matthews and I are unsure what to do next. We have a new opera soon at Covent Garden, but we favour a play here at the Lyceum. We have been in talks with Mr Dickens about a dramatisation of one of his works. Though I favour a revival of Shakespeare's *Dream*.' She looked thoughtful for a moment. 'Have you ever considered playing Oberon?'

'Oberon?'

'Oh, I know it is a man's part, but I made quite a reputation performing it myself.' She laughed again. 'I've played so many breeches roles. I believe you would be quite divine as Oberon. There is a mischievousness in your expression that is so fetching.

I'm sure that all of the gentlemen in the audience would be quite taken with you.'

'Indeed, Madame?'

'We will see, Miss Stanton. I will go now and sit down there.' She waved a hand towards the auditorium. 'And when I am seated perhaps you might sing for me? You can sing unaccompanied?'

'Well... yes...'

'Then I would like you to sing to me *Cherry Ripe*...'

'But Madame Vestris... that's your very own song.'

Madame laughed.

'All the more important you give an exquisite performance then, Miss Stanton...'

~

The drizzle started again just as Sergeant Berry found himself back out on the Ratcliffe Highway. It had been an unproductive afternoon, difficult to ferret out his informants from the alleys and dives of Shadwell.

Everyone had known Bluff Todd. Nobody had any idea who had brought his life to such a violent end.

But there did seem a nervousness amongst the people he had talked to. Many had tried to slip away mid-conversation. He had held back the majority with the offer of a few copper coins. One or two he had pinioned against the dripping walls of London brick.

And after the first hour or two, he had a curious feeling that he was being watched. As though his presence had been well and truly noted. Three times he'd seen a figure in the distance. Once he thought he caught the reflective light of a telescope pointed in his direction. As he walked up the alley from the dock basin to the Highway, he definitely heard footsteps. Steps that quietened very suddenly every time he stopped and looked back. At one point, he'd turned and rushed back the way he had come.

Just for a moment he thought he heard the sound of someone beating a hasty retreat.

He reached inside his coat and brought out a vicious-looking neddy stick. He drew its lead-weighted end along the alley wall and then rested it over his shoulder like a rifle. Best to let them know you are prepared for trouble. That was always his philosophy in these wild regions of the city.

He stepped out on to the Ratcliffe Highway.

'Almighty God is awaiting you!'

The man held his face so close to Berry's own that he recoiled automatically, holding out the stick in a gesture of defence.

'The Dear Lord is taking the measure of your soul! Repent now before you feel the charring fires of hell!'

He was a little man with a perfectly round face, dressed entirely in black except for the white collar of a clergyman. He held up his right hand almost like a blessing. In his left he clutched a leather-bound Bible. He peered through *pince-nez* at Berry, scanning the sergeant's countenance.

'I see the marks of sin on that face! But it is never too late to seek the blessed deliverance of Our Saviour!'

Berry grabbed the little man by the shoulder and dragged him back into the alley.

'Hasn't the Ecclesiastical Court had you committed to gaol yet, Maggot, you miserable prater?' he asked.

'I know not what you mean, sergeant? I am licensed to preach the good words of Our Lord. I am an ordained priest. And you know well that my name is Jedediah Mooth. I will not accept an insulting moniker that comes from the lowest orders of the street.'

'As I recall, you were unfrocked from the clergy. Thrown out of your parish for helping yourself to the funds. You were lucky to escape the House of Correction.'

'A dreadful calumny! I am an innocent wronged by the libels of the world.' He sighed. 'But it was perhaps all part of our Dear Lord's plan. A test. Nay! a trial of my spiritual strength and commitment...'

'Save the sermon for the gullible, Maggot. I'm too old a sinner to be taken in by it.'

'There are devils in hell waiting to plunge red-hot pitchforks into your guts, Sergeant Berry.'

'No doubt, but until I get there I've a job to do. How many times have we arrested you for your aggressive begging?'

'Even as Our Lord was persecuted and taken up to the Cross, so this innocent has suffered.' He jabbed his knuckles against his chest. 'All of mortal life is a trial of faith.'

'Well, I know a way you can store up some goodwill in the world to come, Maggot. And if you do, I'll make sure that the constables leave you alone in future.' Berry rattled the coins in his pocket. 'And there'll be some financial recompense for the time and trouble taken.'

'You seek to tempt me with the filth of lucre? Mammon rules in this wicked city!'

'Does indeed,' said Berry. 'To the extent of a crown if you're particularly helpful.' He brought out five shillings and held the coin under the rantor's nose. 'Five shillings, Maggot. A whole week's rent for one little transaction. And if you're particularly helpful, I'll give you enough for a roast dinner as well.'

Jedediah Mooth took a step or two away and looked carefully along the alley, and then back out towards the Highway. After a little consideration he came closer to Berry. He took off his *pince-nez* and gave the lenses a furious polishing with a very dirty piece of rag. He replaced them on his nose and looked up at the sergeant.

'And how many innocents am I expected to betray for your pieces of silver?' he asked.

'No innocents, Maggot. Just the guilty. I want to know who topped Bluff Todd and why?'

'And you believe I might know?'

'You haunt every tavern in Shadwell. You hearken to the wicked and the drunkards. There's priests in confessionals that aren't told as much as you. There's not a penny gaff where you're not listening to the gossip in the audience. This place should be alive with rumour, but they won't tell me. Not one of 'em. So squawk, Maggot. Tell me what you know?'

'I won't peach...'

'It isn't peaching, my friend. Just a nod and a wink...'

The preacher looked around once more, and then glared down at the coins in Berry's palm.

'Bluff Todd was shot,' Mooth whispered.

'I *know* he was shot...'

'But did you know he'd been threatened for weeks before? Told to hand over his strumpets? Offered money and ordered to leave London?'

'Who by?'

The preacher shrugged.

'A stranger in these parts, that's what I've heard. A gentleman, they say. Come calling several times to see Bluff Todd. And that's not all. There's others been threatened in the same way. People in the same line of business.'

'Ponces?'

The prater nodded.

'And other businesses too. Shops that - how may I put it? - sell on stolen goods. Most of them in Shadwell have had a visit, and beyond. They say he has spies everywhere, this mysterious stranger...'

'And he's the one who shot Bluff Todd?'

Jedediah Mooth took in a deep breath.

'I think not, sergeant. This man who comes calling is respectable, not a killer. He's others who do his dirty work. There've been many deaths. And warnings. And beatings. Things you crushers know nothing about. There's fear in the air down by the river. The most hardened bludgers are a-trembling. Bluff Todd was very well known. Thought himself cock of the walk. Well, there's a cock that won't be strutting any more...'

Mooth swung his head round quite violently to look back along the alley.

'We shouldn't be talking here,' he said. 'It's not safe.' He patted the brickwork behind him. 'You never know who might be on the other side of a wall...'

'You're safe enough with me, Maggot.'

'Am I, sergeant? They all know you're a jack. Not safe to be seen talking to you. Not at all. There's men and women gone into the river for less.'

'So who killed Bluff Todd?'

Mooth shook his head.

'I know not that. But one day he's warned and the next his blood's spilling out on the cobbles. Tell me there's no connection.'

'Do you know anyone who saw the killing?'

'Well, rumour has it there was a girl...'

'One of Todd's girls?'

'Exactly so, sergeant. A pretty little thing who once obliged me in a nook of this very alley. Not the full works, you understand, but enough for my pleasures. A charming girl, hardly more than a child...'

'The sins of the flesh, Maggot?'

'The Mighty Lord puts temptation in our way so that we may be tested.'

'And you succumbed?'

'Every day I fight these urgings of Satan. When I can resist, I will be allowed at last through the gates of Paradise.'

He looked anxiously along the alley. There were footsteps. Moments later two sailors passed them by, seeking the taverns of the Highway.

'What was the girl's name?' Berry asked.

'Her name? Mmm, I'm not sure I recall...'

Berry sighed and looked up at the drizzling clouds.

Even as he lowered his head, he slammed Jedediah Mooth against the alley wall, causing the prater to gasp with surprise and fear.

'I'm not here to play games, Maggot. I want her name?'

'I am not used to... violence.'

'A pity cos there's a lot of it coming your way if you don't peach. And it'll be the last you'll see of these shillings.'

'Her name is Phoebe. But I don't know any more about her, I swear I don't.'

Mooth's face was wet both from the rain and the sweat of fear.

'Where can I find her?' asked Berry.

Mooth shook his head.

'She left Shadwell when Bluff Todd was topped. I don't know where. I don't know how.'

Berry gripped the white band of Mooth's ecclesiastical collar.

'You're lying!' he said.

Mooth gasped and loosened Berry's fingers with his own.

'Very well. I will tell you what I saw a while before. I was passing through Stepney on the business of Our Lord. I noticed the girl in conversation with someone. A fat woman who comes this way quite often in search of the prettiest tails.'

'A fat woman?'

'She has a drum up west. Near Leicester Square. A place where she entertains gentlemen. A place of light and jollity. A paradise of evil. All who go there are destined for hellfire! And like hell the place is. I went to look once. A long passageway leads up to the doors. She has bruisers to guard it. They bundled me away. I could not pay the price of being in that company.'

Mooth looked sad.

'Not even with all the shillings in your pocket, sergeant,' he added. 'We are talking guineas...'

'What more?'

'That day in Stepney. When I saw the fat woman and the girl. Someone else witnessed that conversation. From along the street. It was Bluff Todd. I could see the anger in his face. And the night he was killed. He'd been drinking in a gattering not far from here...'

'What gattering?'

'A wicked drinking den where only the dissolute congregate. The *Shanghai*. Do you know of it?'

Berry knew it well. A place where the police could only go mob-handed. A gattering where life was cheap. A drinking hole downstairs and an opium den above.

'How do you know Todd was drinking there?'

'I saw him, sergeant,' said Mooth. 'Not a man who ever fell down drunk, the miserable sinner. Bluff Todd only got angrier as he supped the corrupting liquid. I was in the *Shanghai* that night. Seeking to save the wretched, you understand? I look upon these lost souls as my parishioners. I sat in the corner watching Todd. He was cursing the fat woman. Pledging to bring the girl back under his control. And then he went out through the door. And then through the doorway of Eternity.'

'And did he leave the *Shanghai* alone?'

'He left alone...'

Berry noticed Mooth's smile of triumph.

'What else?'

'He was followed, sergeant. By a man who's not quite a stranger to Shadwell, though I haven't seen him for a time. I walked to the doorway and watched him depart on Todd's trail.'

'Describe him?'

'Tall and dark. A scar on one cheek... I forget which. All in fustian, though with a canvas cap. A belcher kerchief round his throat. And clutching a great blackthorn stick as though he'd like to do a murder with it.'

Sergeant Berry felt his own uprush of triumph.

'You know his name?'

Jedediah Mooth shook his head.

'Not his name, exactly, though there's many in Shadwell that fear him. He's a rogue, sergeant. He passes this way when he's got business down by the river. But it's not his neighbourhood. I've seen him elsewhere. In Seven Dials. He's better known there. That's where you should seek him out.'

'Was this man with anyone?'

Mooth thought for a few moments.

'Not with anyone, exactly. Though he did talk to a cripple who was begging on the steps of the *Shanghai.*'

'You know the cripple?'

'An old soldier with one leg. You see him everywhere. His name is Feedle.'

Sergeant Berry felt such a warm glow inside that it expelled all the misery of a late and wet afternoon in Shadwell. An old soldier with one leg. A veteran of Waterloo, where Berry's own father had fought. Not really a beggar, but a screever. A talented writer of Newgate ballads.

Jasper Feedle of familiar memory.

Berry looked up at the rain and felt like punching the air.

Jedediah Mooth seemed alarmed at the policeman's beaming smile. He felt the shillings being pressed into his palm. And while the sergeant was so distracted, he slipped away.

~

Rosa Stanton walked up past the police-offices in Bow Street on her way home from the Lyceum Theatre. She was still humming *Cherry Ripe* and her heart was aglow. What a great day! To be applauded by Madame Vestris herself. And after singing *that* song. The very melody that Madame had revived and brought to a popularity it had never enjoyed before.

And the promise of an engagement in one of her theatres!

It was only when Rosa had stepped upon the stage that she realised how much she had missed the life. And not all the applause of a crowded audience had ever meant so much to her as the plaudits she had received from Madame Vestris.

Fill every glass,
For wine inspires us,
And fires us
With courage, love and joy...

She found herself singing the familiar air from *The Beggar's Opera* very loudly as she wandered up the street. It had never been a song she had actually sung in the play, but she loved it very much.

The men got all the best tunes.

She noticed that passing pedestrians were looking in her direction, some giving her a smile, others nodding their heads in harmony with the tune. She felt again the thrill of drawing in an audience. A few passers-by gathered in a little group and watched as she finished the ditty. There was a kindly clapping at its conclusion.

She gave a little curtsey as they called "More!" and began again with her favourite song from the piece:

...I would love you all the day,
Every night would kiss and play,
If with me you'd fondly stray
Over the hills and far away.

Aware that a larger crowd was gathering, she smiled and bowed and slipped away. Some members of the gathering were bursting into songs of their own. A beggar with a penny whistle was trying to pick out other tunes from the play. A policeman tapped his fingers on the alarm rattle in his belt. It seemed to Rosa that all London had turned quite jolly.

Even the rain had stopped.

She never noticed the man on the opposite side of the road. Never saw the way he hung back, or halted in shop entrances as she made her way back to her rooms in the long street leading to Tottenham Court. Never saw him note the doorway as she entered her home.

When she had gone from sight, the man walked back down to Oxford Street, where a carriage was parked with its curtains drawn. He tapped on the door and muttered a few words to the person inside. A hand came through the curtains and pressed a half sovereign into his palm. Instructions were given. He nodded and walked back the way he had come.

On a narrow side-street not quite across the road from Rosa's rooms, he huddled up against a wall, pulling down his hat and turning up his collar. The rain had gone now and weak sunshine had broken through. But even summer nights seem long when you are stationed in one place for several hours, waiting for something that might never happen.

Seven

'Mr Quest.'

William Quest had been walking through St James's Park, lost deep in thought when her voice snapped him out of his reverie. He had been so far away with his memories, that it took him a second or two to remember just where he was. A hilltop in Norfolk with a line of trees and a great beach on that county's same coast vanished like phantoms. He looked around the familiar surroundings of the park, seeking the source of the challenge.

She was standing a few yards behind him.

'Mr Quest?'

Her head was slightly to one side, the deep blue eyes seeming to draw in his own gaze, her fair hair catching the light of the morning sunshine.

He bowed.

'Miss Wissilcraft,' he said.

'My brother told me you were fond of walking,' she said. 'And so am I. I'd hoped we might meet one day on our various peregrinations. I enjoyed our conversation the other evening. Might we walk together?'

He gave another bow and smiled. For a moment he was unsure how to reply. Those blue eyes held him with a kind of mesmeric force. Her smile showed small but very white and even teeth. It was not that she was exactly beautiful or even pretty. But looking at her face was a bit like beholding one of those country views, he thought, where it becomes hard to tear yourself away, and you can't quite reason why.

They strolled along the broad path.

'Do you like London?' she asked.

He gave the question some thought before replying.

'I'm not quite sure,' he said at last. 'There's a lot about London that I dislike intensely. It has virtues but I feel they are overwhelmed by its vices.'

'The vices to me are objects of fascination. My late mother was similarly interested. She taught me a great deal about nature. I studied under her direction. It seemed to me even as a small child that nature was ruthless and cruel. That there was much about avoiding death. But that the avoidance of a vicious ending couldn't go on for ever. It quite haunted my mind.'

Quest thought back to his own childhood. The deaths and the terrors. The horrors of a youth spent in the rookeries of London. So much dread. So many cared for people gone early to the grave.

'I'm not sure one should dwell on these matters,' he said. 'We all know that such things exist. But perhaps it's better to contemplate the lightness of life rather than the dark?'

'You prefer the countryside?'

'I think I do. I have a home there.'

'Hope Down.'

'Your brother keeps you well informed.' He turned to smile at her. She looked straight into his eyes. 'But then again a spymaster would know everything, I suppose.'

'My brother tells me that Hope Down is quite a modest dwelling. And that you refuse to be a part of the county set. You gave away all of the estate farms and cottages to your tenants. How very magnanimous of you.'

'For once, your brother is misinformed,' Quest replied. 'It was my father who dismantled those relics of feudalism.'

'An unusual thing to do. It's no wonder your neighbours have excluded you from society. They must feel that a most dangerous precedent has been set. And your father, well, shall we say your adopted father, Josiah Quest, was a Radical member of Parliament. A man who in his day trembled the foundations of that very society.'

She slipped her arm through his. He looked again at her and she smiled. They were both silent for a few moments.

'Do you hunt?' she asked at last.

'No, I do not hunt. I feel there's enough blood spilt on the earth without seeking to add to it for personal pleasure.'

She sighed.

'I used to hunt, when I was younger.' She gave a little laugh. 'I got very bored with it. There was too much waiting around. Sitting on a horse outside endless coverts waiting for something to happen. I could never see why it couldn't be all about the chase and the kill. Patience has never been one of my virtues, Mr Quest.

When I want something, I want something. And I don't like to be kept waiting.'

'You remind me of someone else I know!'

'Miss Rosa Stanton?'

He laughed.

'If society were ordered different you could eclipse your brother as a spymaster, Miss Wissilcraft.'

'I've often thought so,' she said. 'I've tried in the past to assist brother Benjamin with his work. My endeavours have not always been appreciated.' She glanced sideways at him. 'Do you intend to marry Miss Stanton, or do you keep her just to warm your bed?'

'Miss Wissilcraft!'

She put a hand to her forehead as though in a gesture of repentance.

'I'm always being told off for being outspoken! But as I've said, I grow impatient waiting at the edge of coverts for the chase to move on.'

'But even so...'

They had reached the Mall and she pointed across to the Palace.

'I fear our Queen is bringing a certain stuffiness to our society. England is changing and not for the better. It was perhaps more interesting during the Regency. People did and said what they liked. Matters were so much more... freer.'

'It might have been so for the minority,' said Quest, 'but not for the general population.'

'Nevertheless, I get my inspiration from those more interesting times. And that's why I'm outspoken. So do you intend to marry Miss Stanton?'

Quest felt an annoyance at her persistence. The tone of her voice made him want to make some waspish retort. But then she faced him again. Her eyes met his. Her smile broke his mood.

'The truth is, Miss Wissilcraft, I doubt very much that she would marry me if I asked. Miss Stanton seems very content with our present arrangement. And if she has ambitions at all, they very much concern the theatre rather than me.'

'Then you are not in love with her?'

For a second he was sent back into a great whirl of memories. Recollections of so many days spent with Rosa flashed through his mind like a whirligig.

He didn't know quite how to answer the question.

Angeline Wissilcraft took his hand.

'It's just that if you're *not* in a settled relationship with Miss Stanton, I would very much like to take you to my bed. I'm attracted to you. I believe that you are attracted to me. Can you think of a better way to spend our time in this miserable world than to enjoy pleasuring each other?'

'Miss Wissilcraft!'

'I really do believe we should drop the formalities. You may call me Angeline.' She smiled at him. 'I don't expect your decision today. I feel sure we'll meet again on our... our peregrinations.'

She gave a nod of the head and walked swiftly away.

~

'And you believe this Mooth to be reliable?' asked Anders.

He and Berry were strolling by the Thames. The weather had improved and the office at Scotland Yard had become stuffy in the afternoon heat.

'Man of the cloth, sir. Well, he was once. He doesn't really lie, not very much. And I can always tell when he does. And what he said does put that old rogue Feedle in the vicinity of where Bluff Todd was slain. William Quest too.'

'So you believe this bludger who haunts the district is Quest in disguise?'

'More than probable,' said Berry.

'But no proof?'

'Well, we know that Quest's a master of disguise. And if he's wandering around the rookeries of London, it makes common sense that he isn't doing it as a gent.'

Anders looked out across the river, watching a sailing barge negotiating the rapid flow of water under London Bridge. A dangerous spot, that arch under the bridge. Men and women often drowned themselves there.

'It makes sense...' Anders agreed.

'So do we collar them?'

'Probability isn't evidence, sergeant. Feedle has every reason to be in Whitechapel and the Highway. And we don't know for sure that this bludger is friend Quest. If we collar them, they're very unlikely to confess.'

'You really don't think Quest did it, do you, sir?'

Anders laughed.

'How easy it would be to put the wrappings on this one if... but no, I don't believe for a moment that Quest topped Bluff Todd. What I do think possible is that he knows who did and is protecting them in some way.'

'One of Todd's girls, then?'

'With a pistol? I could see them poisoning that monster, or stabbing him with a dagger, but a pistol? What your Mooth said about one of the girls being approached by that old witch Molly Bendig... you can look into that this evening, if you will.'

Berry nodded.

'Then what, sir?'

Anders leant on a wall and studied the river for a long while. Sergeant Berry was familiar with these considered silences and made no attempt to interrupt the inspector's train of thought.

'Well...' Anders said at last. 'We know it's very unlikely that Bluff Todd was killed randomly. Someone knew just where he was going to be. So the likelihood is they followed him from the tavern. Or got someone to do it for them. I don't know the place. What's it like?'

'The *Shanghai*? A gathering of the worst sort. A drinkers' kiddly downstairs. But there's a door in the corridor beyond. And a flight of steps leads up to an opium den of the nastiest kind. Not haunted by gentlemen, but used by the lowest of the low. Thieves and rogues. Sailors who've given up trying to get a ship. Those who've got enough money to take the drug, but not enough cash about them to be worth robbing.'

Anders smiled.

'You sound as though you know it well?'

'I was in there once, not long after I came to London. Disguised as a matelot. A lot of fences operate in the downstairs. Worse types in the den upstairs. Opium smoke so thick you can hardly breathe, let alone see.'

'Did you arrest anyone?'

'I wouldn't be here today if I'd tried. Life's particularly cheap in the *Shanghai*. Though the information I got did lead to a collaring a few days later. But go in there and you make an appointment with death. Unless it's your lucky day...'

Anders took in a deep breath.

'So how do you fancy a return visit?' he asked. 'Might be an idea, but you'd better pay a call on Mrs Bendig first. If we can nail that girl Phoebe, our case is closed.'

~

Quest opened the window and looked down into Tavistock Place. The hot air of the afternoon had brought out a number of strollers to this part of Bloomsbury, gentlemen and ladies in all their finery.

He examined the crowds with a practised eye, looking for the easiest marks. As a boy he had survived on the streets of London as a dip, a pickpocket of some considerable ability.

Long before he'd been taken in hand by Josiah Quest and the other members of the secret Monkshood group and been trained up to higher criminal endeavours.

But he could never throw off those early days of living on his wits, easing sovereigns from purses and silken wipes from pockets. Even now, in his occasionally respectable early middle-age, he instinctively sought out the men and women whose valuables he would lift, if he was still engaged in his earlier profession.

And some of the gentry below were making it very easy for an even half-competent dip. The wealthy citizens of London really should know better.

His eyes wandered along the street in search of practitioners of his former art, who might have enjoyed rich pickings that afternoon, but could see none about. Only a very short man with a tall hat gave him any concern at all. A stranger who had been lingering on the street corner since Quest had returned from his stroll in the park.

Quest didn't like strangers so close to home. Particularly gents who seemed to have no purpose, except to give a casual glance up at his windows.

He turned to find Sticks at his shoulder.

'Comp'ny,' the older man muttered. 'I've been watching him for a good two hours. Rank amateur! Been staring up too often for idle curiosity.'

'Seen him before?'

Sticks shook his head.

'No one I've had the acquaintance of...'

'Well, he can't stay there for ever,' said Quest, 'and the moment he goes, perhaps you'd be on his tail. I'd like to know a bit more about that gent.'

'If he goes, someone'll take his place.'

'Perhaps. I'll deal with any newcomer. I just want to know who that one is,' Quest pointed a finger at the watcher. 'Not a crusher. Doesn't have the height for a policeman. He could be something to do with the recent attacks on me. Find out where he lives, Sticks.'

'I'll be on him, the minute he's off.'

~

Mrs Bendig looked across the cluttered desk, annoyed at the interruption. She had been working away at the accounts of her night house for several hours and the numbers were starting to dance before her eyes.

'I said as how I wasn't to be disturbed, Belinda,' she remarked to the serving girl who had poked her head around the door.

'I knows you did, ma'am, but the package is marked urgent.'

She held out a parcel about a foot long, wrapped in brown paper and tied up with string.

'Who brought it?' Mrs Bendig asked.

'A lad, just now. Says as how a gent along the street gave him tuppence if he'd carry it for him. The gent said as how he was in a hurry and wanted to save time.'

Molly Bendig looked at the package with mild curiosity.

'Cut the string and unwrap it, girl. Before I loses me total.'

She looked down at the account book, her pencil hovering over a page, her lips moving as she tallied the final column.

'Oh, and that policeman's waiting outside...' Belinda said as she struggled with a knot in the string.

Mrs Bendig's head shot up.

'Policeman? What policeman?'

'That Sergeant Berry...'

'What does he want?' Mrs Bendig said, half to herself.

'He didn't say ma'am, but I...'

Belinda let out a loud scream, dropping the package on to the desk.

'What the hell's the matter with you, girl?' said Mrs Bendig, half-standing to look.

'It's a rat, ma'am, look, a rat. And I can't abide 'em....'

Mrs Bendig bent over the opened package and looked down. A rat, sure enough, and not long out of the sewers or the river by the state of it, the moisture and filth still evident. She picked it up by the tail and studied it for a moment.

'Only a rat, girl. There's plenty of 'em in London. Calm yourself down or...'

The door swept open and Sergeant Berry dashed into the room.

'I thought I heard a scream,' he said.

'You did,' said Mrs Bendig. 'It was the girl here. Didn't like the look of this rat.' She looked up from the rodent and glared at the policeman. 'And I'll thank you to wait till you're summoned before you comes crashing into my office!'

'You might have been being murdered,' said Berry. 'We usually do investigate if we hear a woman screaming...'

'Gawd knows, there's enough women screaming in this city every day to keep every peeler in London busy. And screams aren't uncommon in this house.'

She dropped the rat back into the cardboard box it had been wrapped in and twisted the paper over it. She glanced at the serving girl.

'Belinda, get one of the lads to throw this rubbish out in the street, will yer? And then bring some tea for me and the sergeant. We'll be in me boudoir...'

The girl looked down at the packet and beat a hasty retreat from the room.

'So, who's posting you rats, Molly?' asked Berry.

She shrugged.

'Perhaps a dissatisfied customer...' he opined.

'All of my customers are very satisfied,' she replied. 'They all come here knowing they will be.'

'Well, someone doesn't like you.'

'If everyone who don't like me sent me a rat, I'd be overrun with a plague of the blessed things. Now, come on through, sergeant and we'll have our tea away from all this paperwork.'

~

The stranger on the street corner hung around for another two hours, seemingly unaware that Sticks was watching him from a hundred yards away.

Quest's house in Tavistock Place had a back yard, abutting on to the similar yard of the premises to the rear. There was no alley between them, giving the impression to the curious that visitors to Mr Quest must have to come and go by the front door. Few knew that William Quest also owned the house at the back of his own, using it from time to time under one of his many aliases. The stout gate between the yards gave convenient access through the separate houses to two discrete London streets.

It was through the second house that Sticks had made his way out into the bustle of Bloomsbury. And there was the spy still in place, pretending now to read a newspaper, but still glancing up at the windows of Quest's home.

Sticks shook his head, more in sorrow than in anger. As someone who'd put the dodge on many a man, observing them at their lurks, and often following his prey clear across London without being detected, he hated to see such rank amateurism.

He pulled up his collar as the rain started, watching as his mark folded away the newspaper. The little man took one last look at the house and walked swiftly away, so fast that he took Sticks quite by surprise. The spy was in Tavistock Square before Sticks came behind him at a safe distance once again.

The rain suddenly eased, and a fog, thick and yellow, crept up through the streets from the direction of the river. But still the man made no attempt to check whether he was being watched. He took no sudden turns, either into alleys or shops as might be the normal course of a man experienced in the watching trade. If anything, he just walked faster, forcing his way through the crowds.

The fog thinned suddenly, the great bank of polluted moisture sweeping onwards as though desperate to corrupt higher ground. The streets becoming clear again as visibility improved, bringing shoppers back out into a dull sunshine.

It was only when he reached the upper end of Whitehall that the man suddenly stopped dead, leant back against a wall and looked all around.

Sticks was on the opposite side of the road, surrounded by a group of workers hurrying home after a long day in the shops and offices of Westminster. He walked very casually in their wake and the little man didn't even give him a fleeting look.

Sticks, halfway down the road now, paused and engaged a street-sweeper in deep conversation about the weather. From the way they chatted, anyone might have assumed they were old friends. As it happened, they were. Sticks knew a lot of the street-workers in London. Old Jeb had been a pal for many a year, a most valuable member of Monkshood. Eyes and ears very close to the capital's seat of power.

They didn't look up as the little man walked past them, once more at a ferocious pace. Sticks gave a nod to Old Jeb and was preparing to move on when the mark turned right into Downing Street.

Sticks sauntered down and watched with interest as the man rapped at a door and entered the residence of the Prime Minister.

~

'Word is, Molly, you've a new girl working here,' said Berry, 'she's called Phoebe.'

'What of it?' Mrs Bendig shrugged. 'I've often got new girls working here. What's my business got to do with Scotland Yard?'

'A lot, particularly when the girl's a suspect in a murder case.'

'Pah! You mean Bluff Todd?'

'He was her ponce,' said Berry.

Mrs Bendig poured out two cups of dark tea.

'Not when he was topped,' she said at last.

'How do you mean?'

'She was working for me for days before someone turned off Bluff Todd. It's all out there in me ledgers, sergeant. And everyone who works here'll tell you the same.'

'I'm sure they will...'

'And the night Todd was killed, well, Phoebe was here. All my people will tell you so. I can even provide the name of the gent she was entertaining.'

'I'm sure you can, Molly.'

Berry leant forward in the chair and sipped the tea. Then he put the cup and saucer down on the table.

'You're a liar, Molly!'

'Oh, sergeant, how long have we known each other? All those years up in Manchester. Then my time down here. And yet every time you comes a-visiting, you calls me a liar.'

'The girl was there, Molly,' he said. 'When Bluff Todd was murdered. I've a witness who can place her at the scene of the crime.'

Mrs Bendig raised her eyes to the ceiling and then looked him straight in the face.

'An' I got fifty who says she wasn't...'

'We both know you're lying,' said Berry. 'I'm sure the whole of your crew'd swear black's white if you asked 'em to, but it don't make it the truth, Molly. I want to see the girl. Right now. Alone, if you'll spare me the use of the room?'

'Whatever...'

Mrs Bendig clambered to her feet and pulled a cord that rang a distant bell.

'You're wasting your time,' she said. 'And mine...'

~

'Downing Street?'

Quest drew the curtains against the night. Sticks passed him a glass of brandy and helped himself to water.

'Makes sense,' he said, 'we know they're desperate to get back that notebook. The little man trailed you after your stroll in the park. Watched long enough to be convinced you weren't going out again. Perhaps it's one of Palmerston's spies that took that pot-shot and tried to get you hauled away?'

'If Raikes was still alive...'

'Well he's not, but there're others...'

'Killing me would be no advantage to them. They know Monkshood would make public the knowledge in the notebook.'

Sticks drank the water in one go.

'But they're not trying to kill you, are they? They wants you snatched. Forced to give up the little book.'

'If they succeed, you know what to do, Sticks? Might as well bring their whole rotten house of cards crashing down.'

'They'd top you for sure, then.'

'Easier said than done,' Quest smiled.

~

She was a pretty little thing, Berry thought, as Mrs Bendig ushered Phoebe into the room.

The kind of girl who'd have broken many a heart if she'd been born into better circumstances. Now all those good looks would go to waste, unless she very quickly tempted the passions of one of Mrs Bendig's more respectable clients and was lured away.

Berry remembered how, so many years before, Molly Bendig herself had been quite a fetching lass. A girl who'd turned many a head. But all those years of drink and debauchery had stolen all that young promise too.

Not that prostitution was the worst of all evils in Berry's view of matters. He'd known girls drift into that way of life and leave with money in their pockets, and sometimes a good husband too. It was rare but it was possible.

Many of the girls who'd taken that path had done better for themselves than the lasses who worked long hours in the northern mills, worn out and exhausted at thirty. Often dead before they reached forty. What a bloody awful world this is for the poor, he considered. Who could blame William Quest for the violence of his crusade?

'Sit down, Phoebe,' he pointed towards Mrs Bendig's ample armchair and leant forward in his own seat.

He glanced up at the hostess. 'Shan't be needing you, Molly. Won't be long.'

'I really do b'lieve I should stay, sergeant.'

He shook his head.

'Don't think so...' he waved a hand towards the door.

Mrs Bendig glowered at him and left the room.

'Now then, Phoebe...' he began.

The girl seemed close to tears.

'Am I in trouble?' she asked.

Berry smiled.

'You're not in any trouble at all,' he said. 'You know why I'm here?'

'I know Bluff Todd got himself topped. It wasn't me...'

'We know it wasn't you, Phoebe. But you were there, weren't you?'

Phoebe was crying now. The various versions of where she was supposed to have been, flooded her mind.

Her rescuers of the night had spent a good hour telling her that she was in *The Three Cripples* near Field Lane with a fat man called Isaac... Isaac... she couldn't even recall his other name, only that he had something to do with the Pauper's Society.

And when she'd related that tale to Mrs Bendig, the hostess had dismissed it out of hand, saying it would be safer to claim that she'd been on her back in the night house, pleasuring a customer.

Mrs Bendig had even introduced her to the man who'd supposedly been taking her, a grinning individual who spoke in a posh voice and was clearly blueing the last of his family's money. Mrs Bendig had promised him several nights' free entertainment if he helped them over this little difficulty.

But as the sergeant looked across at her, she couldn't lose the image of Bluff Todd falling to the ground, a bloody red hole in the middle of his forehead. A look of astonishment on his face, his hand quivering madly in his last moments.

He said something but she didn't hear what it was, for another vision filled her mind. A picture of Newgate with the gallows mounted outside, the hempen rope rubbing harshly against the soft skin of her throat. The fear of darkness as she tumbled through the trap.

If she could be proved to be at the place where Bluff Todd was murdered, then she could still hang. Even if they thought she hadn't fired the shot, they might turn her off as an accomplice.

'I know you were there, Phoebe,' Sergeant Berry said in a very gentle voice. 'I know you didn't kill him. I know what kind of man Bluff Todd was. You've nothing to fear from telling the truth.'

She shook her head.

'You were there, Phoebe. I know you were...'

'I wasn't...' she whispered.

'And someone came along and shot Todd dead. All you need do is tell me what happened. Describe the man who killed Todd. Come on, Phoebe. Lying will only make it worse for you.'

She raised her hand and touched her throat. It must hurt, hanging. Even with the suddenness of the drop, it must hurt. Death must hurt.

She took in a great breath.

'I wasn't there!' she said more firmly.

'I can't help you if you won't help me. You saw Todd shot dead, Phoebe, I know you did. Do you know who killed him?'

'I wasn't there!'

'Was there anyone else there? Apart from the man who shot Bluff Todd?'

'I wasn't there!'

She looked down at the floor for a moment. Then she looked him straight in the face.

'I was here, sergeant. Upstairs working. All that evening. With a man...'

'So Mrs Bendig has told me. And you and I both know that's rubbish.'

'It isn't! It isn't!'

'Do you know a man called Feedle?'

'Never heard of him!' she almost shouted.

'Or William Quest?'

'No!'

'I thought everyone knew Jasper Feedle. Writes ballads about the hangings. One-legged and walks with a crutch. You must know him, Phoebe...'

'Well, I don't,' she yelled. 'There's a thousand cripples in London. I don't know any of their names!'

This little girl's got her courage back, thought Berry. I've pushed her too far and too soon. Never get her back on track now. She's found out that she's got nothing to lose by fighting back. To hell with Molly Bendig!

'All right, Phoebe, all right. We'll leave it at that... for now. But I *will* be back and I'll be asking the same questions again and again until you tell me the truth.'

'I've told you the truth!'

He smiled.

'I've been in this game such a long time, Phoebe. I know when someone's leading me up the garden path. You're not helping yourself. I want you to have a real think about all this. I'll see you again. Meantime, if you have a change of heart, you come down and see me at Scotland Yard. You know where that is? It'll be best for you in the long run.'

He smiled at her again as he stood and walked towards the door. It swung open to let him out, Mrs Bendig beaming a look of triumph at him as she held the door handle.

He'd expected her to be listening, the old witch.

Sergeant Berry put out his tongue as he walked past her.

Eight

'Not goin' ter be easy,' said Jasper Feedle, 'not goin' ter be easy at all.'

'Nothing ever is!' proclaimed Quest.

'And don't we know it!' added Sticks. 'I've a bad feeling about all of this. Like we're punching at shadows. Handy if we could get one of 'em by the throat.'

'Well, as per instructions, I've hung around *The Bold Dragoon* for the past few days,' said Jasper. 'And a fat lot of good it's done me. Never felt so much fear in the air. Didn't see this King bloke, not at all. But he might 'as well have been there. Thieves and villains of every description an' all workin' for him.'

'Did you see anyone you know?' asked Quest.

'I knows most of the blackguards and they knows me. Old friends, some of 'em. But they won't peach or even mutter a rumour. It's like they got the hand of fear round their throat. But the one thing I did get is that his majesty ain't been there for quite a time. Apparently he favours the *Shanghai* these days. Not only favours it, but he's taken it over. That's the only nugget I picked up.'

'You've done well, Jasper,' said Quest. 'At least I'm known at the *Shanghai* in one of my disguises. It would be interesting to meet mine host in his own tavern. And safer to find him there than at Jacob's Island.'

'You'd be running a risk,' said Sticks.

'Not that much of a risk,' Quest replied. 'A variety of custom favours the *Shanghai*, some of them members of Monkshood. And strangers from the ships in the docks haunt the opium den upstairs. Easy to slip in and out. The only real difficulty is that we've no way of knowing when this King's going to be there.'

'Yer'll need someone to watch yer back,' said Jasper.

'We'll attend to that,' said Sticks.

Quest pondered for a moment, looking out through the window.

'Our problem is...' he said at last, 'that it's pointless even going unless the King is there. And we've no way of knowing that. Is he there most of the time, or just a casual visitor? What would be best is if he has a regular day of the week when he visits the premises. I suspect he's too canny for that. Jasper...'

'Yer wants me to go back to beggin' on his doorstep?'

'Something like that. But watch yourself. If he knows enough to want to kill or capture me, then he'll very probably recognise my oldest friends.'

He reached into a drawer and took out a small percussion-cap pistol with a polished wooden handle, and a small bag containing caps and balls.

'Slip this barker away, Jasper. Don't be afraid to use it if you have to. And talk to some of our Monkshood brethren. Tell them you want a drunken riot laid on if you have to get away quickly.'

The old man beamed a smile.

'The old Duke of Wellington would've been proud ter call yer brother,' he said, saluting as he left the room.

'I might hang around there a whiles mesself,' said Sticks. 'These old fists of mine have got a few punches left in 'em.'

Quest nodded.

'Very well,' he said, 'but watch your back. You and Jasper aren't immortal. There's a brother to that pistol in the drawer. You'd better take it with you. In the meantime...'

He pointed towards the street. A very small man with a tall hat was stationed on the far side of Tavistock Place, reading a copy of *The Times.*'

'He's got to be the worst I've ever seen,' said Sticks. 'How obvious can you be?'

'Our friend there's beginning to annoy me,' said Quest. 'I think it's about time we discovered what he's doing. And er... discouraged him...'

'You want me to do it?' asked Sticks.

'I'll trail him this time. When he leaves for the evening. And you follow me at a good distance, to keep away anyone who tries to interfere.

~

'This girl, Phoebe, was there all right,' Berry reported to Anders. 'Not the slightest doubt about that. I know when I'm being lied to. But old Molly Bendig's briefed her well. The girl won't peach. Unless you'd like to have a go, Inspector?'

'If you can't get her to talk, I certainly won't be able to,' Anders replied. 'I don't suppose there's the slightest possibility that the Bendig woman had Bluff Todd topped? Eliminating the competition, so to speak? No! Just clutching at straws. She'd have to top thousands of ponces in London if that was her game...'

Berry studied the glowing coals in the office fireplace for a moment.

'Not Molly Bendig's sort of game,' he said at last. 'But I wonder if there's something in what you say. You recall I told you what Maggot... Jedediah Mooth said to me. About how someone was putting fear into the hearts of all the gentry down by the river. How Bluff Todd was offered money to leave London. Threatened unless he handed over his girls...'

'But who? Like you said there's thousands of ponces in London. It could be any one of them...'

'Not with a pistol, though. Beatings in alleys are more their sort of game. And Mooth told me how others had been threatened. Fences and the like. How a flash gent comes calling, offering to buy them out. Then there's trouble if they resist. I didn't take what Maggot said too seriously, but what if he's right?'

'I don't like the sound of this,' said Anders. 'We've enough trouble with criminals in London as it is. But if they're all at each other's throats, well, then some innocent folk might get caught in the crossfire.'

Berry gave him a grim smile.

'Well, I won't find out sitting here, that's for sure,' he said. 'I'm overdue for a visit to the *Shanghai*. That's where Todd was afore he was killed. It stands to reason he was trailed from there. And I've a feeling in my gut that that's where I'm to pick up a hint of his killer.'

~

The small man left his station outside Quest's house promptly at eight, folding away his newspaper and striding out the way he'd gone the last time he was tailed. William Quest had gone out through the house to the rear of his own and was waiting for the man at the corner of Tavistock Place.

He glanced round only once to make sure that Sticks was in position. The old prize-fighter gave a nod and set off down the street a hundred yards behind Quest.

Quest shook his head in disbelief as he followed the little man through the streets of Bloomsbury and down towards Westminster.

He'd been watched many times during his long career. Followed doggedly in the footsteps of so many observers of his doings. But never, never ever, come across a spy who seemed to care so little about his own safety. The man might have been taking a Sunday stroll through the park, for all he cared about whether he was in turn being watched.

Quest thought it likely that the man was going to repeat his previous journey and walk down Whitehall to Downing Street, but he made a sudden turn before he got there, speeding up a trifle as he crossed Trafalgar Square into Pall Mall.

The street was busy at that time in the evening with gentlemen visiting their clubs. Quest watched as old friends paired up and nodded to their fellows. It seemed that the little man was not unfamiliar to the denizens of clubland, for several passers-by waved a hand to him and wished him good evening.

It was dangerous territory for Quest. His own club was situated in Pall Mall, though he seldom visited it. It was an institution dedicated to political reform, and was a tad out of fashion in these harsh times. But there was always the possibility that some fellow member might call his name from across the street. Quest pulled down his hat and turned his face more to the pavement.

There was a possibility, he considered, that the man was intending to visit his own club. He was dressed well enough to be a member of any of them. And his ability to walk straight into the Prime Minister's home suggested that he was a member of the Class. Quest could hardly walk in to one of these august premises after him. If the man passed through one of the many doorways, the trail would go cold.

And then the man stopped dead outside the *Athenaeum*, his back to the building, looking in both directions and then across the street. Quest pulled back behind a group of gentlemen having a discussion in the middle of the pavement, his hands wandering through his pockets as though he was searching for something. The man wasn't looking his way. He was raising his hat to a gentleman who was approaching him from across the street. A huge individual who towered over the little man.

Wissilcraft!

Well, of course, it had to be, Quest considered. Wissilcraft *was* Queen Victoria's Spymaster, though in reality he was the trusted servant of the Home Secretary, Lord Palmerston, that wriggling mongoose of British politics. The servant who did the dirty deeds that Palmerston wouldn't risk his reputation dabbling with.

The two men were busy in conversation as Quest strolled up to them. Before he could say anything, Wissilcraft looked across at him and smiled.

'You're faster than I thought you might be,' he said. 'But my man here made it so easy for you.'

'A little too easy,' said Quest.

'As for the other day, we thought you might find it interesting when your bruiser Sticks reported to you that Jenkins here had passed through the door of Downing Street.'

'Why not have me followed in a less obvious way?' asked Quest.

'What makes you believe I haven't had you followed more covertly?' Wissilcraft smiled. 'You've fallen into this little trap, after all. Perhaps you're losing your ability to sense danger, my dear Quest?'

'So was it one of your agents who fired a pistol in the direction of my head, and then tried to have me kidnapped by three roughs in an alley?'

Wissilcraft flinched.

'Nothing so clumsy,' he said. 'When did that happen?'

'The other day,' said Quest.

'Then it seems you must have other enemies,' said Wissilcraft. 'Nothing to do with me. If I wanted you lifted, I'd instruct Scotland Yard to do it. Honour bright...'

'Honour!'

'Oh, I do have some, Quest,' Wissilcraft said. 'If I didn't, you'd have been taken in charge long since, wouldn't he, Jenkins?'

The little man beamed a smile.

'So why have your man here follow me?' asked Quest.

'Just to remind you that we are always watching out for you,' said Wissilcraft. 'Suggesting to you that you'll never be able to undertake any of your more nefarious activities without us knowing about it. And while we watch you... and watch yours... your campaigns cannot proceed. Which is all the better for law and order at the end of the day, I suppose.'

'And you imagine I'll simply hand over to you that notebook to bring all of this surveillance to an end?'

Wissilcraft clapped his hands.

'Well, let's just say it would be a start,' he said. 'We might turn a blind eye to your regime of vengeance, as long as the revenge was aimed at carefully selected individuals. But, I fear, those happy days when *you* choose the men you intend to kill are over. Do we have a deal?'

'I think not,' said Quest. 'You represent a rotten society. Your master, Palmerston, claims he's committed to reform, yet all the poor get are crumbs from his table. As far as I'm concerned that still leaves the Class and myself in a state of war.'

'So, no notebook?'

Quest shook his head.

'You realise that if you use the information within the notebook, you are as good as dead?' said Wissilcraft.

'I never expected a long life,' Quest replied.

'And you won't have one...'

'However, I might live long enough to kill you...'

'Others have tried,' said Wissilcraft. 'I'm still here...'

'I haven't...'

'And I thought we were friends!' protested Wissilcraft. 'Only this morning my sister Angeline was insisting we invite you round to dine once again. I do believe she very much appreciated your company.'

'Give her my regards...' said Quest, turning to walk away.

'I will indeed, but think on what I've said,' said Wissilcraft. 'You would be a most welcome addition to my department. The matters we could resolve together...'

'I'm not a butterfly to be pinned in a glass case...' Quest shouted back to the spymaster.

'Not nearly pretty enough!' Wissilcraft laughed.

~

Mrs Bendig was proud of her little house in a street just west of Soho. The property was modest, but had an air of prosperity about it. A good neighbourhood too, with several of the nearby houses owned by widows just like herself. Very occasionally they would come round to tea and applaud her for her good works in the community.

None of them knew of her business interests just a mile away.

In this quiet street Mrs Bendig – as such – didn't exist. Here she was known as Mrs Smythe, a good lady who'd acquired a reputation for rescuing the 'unfortunates' of the town.

Time and again she would bring young girls at moral risk back to her house, accommodate them for a few days, and then pass them on to, well... she would explain to her neighbours that she had found them worthy employment as servants or shop-girls.

The applause from the staid ladies thereabouts was quite deafening.

As often as possible, Mrs Smythe would occupy a pew in the parish church and nod approvingly as the vicar sermonised on the evils of the world. From time to time he would catch her eye and beam a smile. He approved of her doings, being quite a champion of such Muscular Christianity.

Mrs Smythe could often be quite carried away in such spiritual surroundings. It was almost, very occasionally, as if the wayward Molly Bendig had never existed. It was not altogether that she believed in God, but she thought it wise to hedge her bets on his possible existence, and not take any chances.

If necessary, she had long ago decided, she would repent somewhere just on the right side of the Pearly Gates. And wasn't there more joy in heaven over a sinner that repenteth than...?

But back to business. That would be her thought as she wandered away from the Sunday service. Back to the activities that funded such pleasantries.

Mrs Smythe might leave the house and roam towards the more doubtful areas of London, but it would be Mrs Bendig who would penetrate the dismal rookeries. Always on the lookout for girls. Possible employees for her business empire.

The slightly older ones were lured to work in her night house if they were pretty enough. The very young girls were brought back to her other property to spend a few days as virgins. Some were, but the majority weren't, having worked the streets since they were children.

Only very selected gentlemen, rich individuals she'd known for quite a time, and could trust, were ever invited to her private house. Gents with a particular taste for the innocent. Men about town who, either from taste or with a fear of venereal disease, only wanted virgins.

Mrs Smythe would instruct each fresh intake of her young ladies as to what was expected. The fear or nervousness they were expected to show. The cries and screams they were to make as they were taken.

Young as they were, some of the girls had to cast their memories back quite a time to remember how they had behaved on their initial deflowering. The very few genuine virgins did not, at least, have to pretend very much.

The young ladies could only last in this profession for just a few occasions. It was important that Mrs Smythe's gentlemen callers never saw the same faces twice. After a few days, the girls would be taken across town to graduate to the upper rooms of her night house.

In church, Mrs Smythe would whisper a thanks to her Lord that she had been blessed with the opportunity to save so many threatened souls from the disreputable trade of plying the streets.

She would usually walk the mile between her two establishments. Not that she really enjoyed walking very much, but it did give her an opportunity to sink into a different *persona*, and from time to time provided some passing girl who might be seeking employment.

It was very late that night and she was in the depths of Soho on the way back to Leicester Square, in a quiet street just up from Haymarket. She could hear the crowds at a distance as the theatres and dining houses closed for the night. The gaslight gave a yellow glow to the slight mist that had meandered up from the river, suggesting that a fresh burst of rain might not be far behind.

Mrs Bendig looked up at the sky and grunted. She hated getting wet these days, though she'd spent much of her youth being soaked on the streets of Manchester.

When she looked down again the man was staring her straight in the face. A nasty looking individual, too. A pale face covered in spots and scars. The stench of his breath turned her stomach.

'Got a message for yer...' he said.

She reached into her voluminous clothes and grasped the handle of the dagger she kept handy for just such encounters.

'Who from?' she demanded, with no trace of fear in her voice.

'The people what sent yer the present.'

'The rat?'

He grinned, showing a row of blackened teeth.

'Just so,' he said.

'And what is this message?'

'The gent what I works for thinks yer really should go and live by the sea.'

'He said that?'

'He did.'

'This gent what employs you? Would his name be Boone?'

'That'd be telling...' he replied.

She studied him for a moment.

'You got a lot of scars for a young man,' she said.

He grinned again, sending another wave of foul breath in her direction.

'I bin around a bit,' he said.

'You certainly have,' she said, looking him up and down. 'You're a skanky lookin' individual, I'll say that for you. Look like you could do with a decent meal. Like to earn a bit?'

'How d'yer mean?'

'You tell me everything you know about Mr Boone and I'll tip you a sovereign.'

Mrs Bendig noticed the look of interest in his eyes, an indication of greed. The grin became a smile. It took a while before she detected a further emotion on his battered face. Fear came along in bundles.

He almost snapped to attention.

'I'm paid well enough as it is,' he said. 'Now, I'm to take back yer answer...'

She looked him right in the face.

'Go and stuff yourself,' she said.

At first the man seemed bewildered. In all his years of street mugging he'd never had this sort of reaction from a woman. Usually they just surrendered their purses and sped on their way. But this great fat dame seemed almost to be mocking him.

'I'm not here to listen to yer,' he said. 'Yer mark my words. The next time as we meet it'll be nasty. Yer hear that? Yer gets out of London or else...'

'Or else what?'

His scowl turned into a delighted smile.

'He says as how I might hurt yer. Just a little bit. Tear yer hair about or somethin'. Give yer a bruise to remember me by.'

'Go on, then.'

Mrs Bendig glared at him.

'Or are you a coward?' she went on. 'Did you get all those scars from women? Is that it? Nasty little ponce like you. Doubt you could square up to a real man.'

'I can do anythin' I wants,' he blustered. 'Like this...'

He reached out as though to grab her hair, but only a finger touched her before he was overcome with surprise and then a wincing pain.

Mrs Bendig swept the dagger in front of her with a swift and forceful stroke. Her victim caught just a glimpse of its steel in the gaslight before the blade sliced down across his left cheek, parting the flesh and forcing a dousing of blood into his mouth.

As he reached up with his right hand to grasp the wound, the down-strike of the blade cut into the palm and down towards his wrist, sending a torrent of blood spouting towards the gutter. He cried out as he fell to his knees.

Mrs Bendig put her mouth close to his bloodied ear.

'A couple more scars for your collection. And tell your Mr Boone as how he'll get the same if he comes anywhere near me.'

She raised herself and walked on.

'Scum!' she muttered as she passed the now prostrate man.

'I like your rooms,' she said to the poet. 'Discreet, but fashionable. Everything a gentleman's set of rooms should be. It's good that we're able to pay for them.'

The poet sat languidly in his chair, pen in hand, several blank pieces of paper before him.

'They're well enough,' he replied, 'though I simply can't work here. I sit for hours at this table but the words won't come. It's been helpful having the other premises. Dirtier premises. When I'm surrounded by filth it fires the muse. It really does.'

'How extraordinary!'

'Even outdoors is better than here,' he said. 'I use that little notebook you gave me a very great deal. Sitting among the crowds in the fashionable streets. Or on a wall by the Thames. The words flow like the river. But here...'

'There are, of course, the bad areas of town...'

The poet considered.

'Yes,' he said at last. 'I am able to work there, though there are constant interruptions. I daren't write in the streets, though. There are so many unpleasant people about. They might rob me...'

She laughed.

'I robbed you of your virtue,' she said. 'Right here in this very room. You know, I really do feel *I* should be your muse, not the city. You should write verse that immortalises me...'

'You want to be my dark lady?'

'It is a thought,' she considered. 'A puzzle for your readers in the centuries to come. In a world we can't even imagine. A land where what we do is considered normal.'

She moved behind him and ran her hands through his hair.

'If you really can't write today, then we should do other things,' she said. 'Come to bed now. While we still have time. Before the centuries roll over our rotting bones...'

Nine

There was a feeling of menace in the air, no doubt about that. In the three nights Jasper Feedle had hung around the steps of the *Shanghai*, begging for pennies, this was the first time he'd noticed a palpable terror, not just given out by the drinkers and opium addicts who frequented the place, but by the residents in the streets nearby.

Everyone in this dark little world was on edge. As the gentle rain wet the cobbles and the dowdy walls of London brick, Jasper turned up his collar and pulled his tattered old hat even further down on his head.

The door swung open several times as men left the tavern, heavy in drink or dazed by opium. Jasper gave each one a glance before holding out his hand for coins which never came. Not the man he was looking for, so the waiting must go on.

He sighed and gazed up at the dark clouds.

It reminded him of the night before Waterloo, when he'd huddled under a cloak as the heavens opened, wondering whether there'd be a fight the next day. There had been and Jasper Feedle had lost his leg.

And now, once more, he felt the violence in the air.

The door opened and a porky individual emerged, his face marked by the pox, and seemingly long gone in drink. He rested for a moment against the nearest wall and them staggered into the alley, turning to empty his bladder.

'Tonight,' he muttered to Jasper, 'he's comin' tonight.'

Jasper gave no acknowledgement, but waited until the man had turned and walked away, using the wall as a support against his inebriation. Jasper yawned and counted the few pennies in his hand, before standing and walking away, loudly cursing the rain, then singing loudly...

If ever I 'list for a soldier again,
The devil'll be me sergeant,
Poor ol' soldier, poor ol' soldier,
If ever I 'list for a soldier again,
The devil'll be me sergeant...

'Shut yer racket!' protested a bulky man, coming down the street in the opposite direction. 'What yer got ter be so cheerful about, anyways?'

The two men lightly brushed against each other.

'It's tonight!' Jasper whispered to Sticks, as he wandered on his way. 'Old Walter's given the word.'

'Now there'll be trouble,' muttered Sticks. 'See you later...'

The old prize-fighter took a turning out of the alley and then along a street leading up to the Commercial-road.

~

'Same old tricks!'

Sergeant Berry smiled to himself as he watched the supposedly casual meeting between Feedle and Sticks. They're getting too well known in London to pull that one off, he considered. Mr Quest really should bring some new recruits into his regiment of villains. Hopefully, the denizens of the *Shanghai* would be too drunken or drugged to notice.

Berry, from his position at the furthest end of the alley, where he'd pulled under a cornice as though sheltering from the rain, had not heard the words exchanged, but assumed that something must be afoot.

He'd roamed the district for three days now, every so often looking along the alley to the doorway of the *Shanghai*, where Feedle had been on sentry duty. Got soaked by the same bad weather as the cripple, and chilled by the same blasts of cold air wafting up from the river.

William Quest clearly had an interest in that foul den, which suggested that it had some connection with recent events. The fact that Feedle and Sticks had not left together indicated that something was about to happen. Berry's policeman's instinct told him that matters were definitely coming to a head.

He reached into his pocket and took out a notebook and a stub of pencil, writing the words: *Shanghai. Tonight. I'm inside.* Then he left the alley to seek out a busier thoroughfare where he knew there'd be a constable on the beat. Knew because he had arranged that there should be. Only mob-handed did the patrolling constables penetrate the warren of alleyways around the *Shanghai*.

He soon found the constable he was looking for, an old friend and veteran of past adventures.

'For Mr Anders?' said the policeman, giving the note a quick perusal.

Berry nodded.

'Could be dangerous. Might be better to wait,'

'Nothing will happen if we all go charging in,' said Berry.

'You want a loan of my rattle, in case you need to sound an alarm?'

'Bit too bulky,' said Berry. 'They might all be drunk or drugged in there but I fear they'd notice. Got this instead.'

He held up a metal whistle.

The constable shook his head.

'Seen 'em before,' he said, 'but they'll never sound as loud as a good wooden rattle.'

~

In a room above a shop in the Commercial-road, William Quest changed into his outfit of a street bludger: a hardened villain of the worst kind, complete with fustian jacket and belcher kerchief around his throat. Despite usually being very clean-shaven, he'd acquired a few days' growth of stubble and dark locks of hair hung down from under a canvas cap.

'Do the others know what they're to do?' he asked Sticks.

'Jasper's briefed 'em well.'

'Don't want any trouble unless there's no choice. I just want to get the measure of this so-called King and maybe follow him if we can.'

'Might not be as easy as that,' said Sticks. 'He's coming to the *Shanghai* for a reason. It's the wrong side of the river for him, though by all accounts he's making a move north of the Thames. Word is there's a big room at the back of the opium den reserved for his special use. And he won't be alone. I take it we'll be carrying?'

Quest pulled out two pairs of small percussion pistols.

'Two of these each, and I've got this.'

He held up what seemed to be a heavy blackthorn walking cane. Quest flicked it through the air and a small but deadly blade came dagger-like out of the ferrule.

'How many men in the ale-house?' he asked.

'Jasper says twelve, all armed with coshes and life-preservers. The rest of the crowd'll just stand by. Course, we got no way of knowing how many bludgers his majesty will bring with him.'

'Well, let's prepare for the worst.'

'I usually do,' said Sticks.

~

Mrs Bendig sat back in her boudoir and considered her situation. While she quite favoured the idea of retiring to the sea-side, she wasn't going to go at a penny less than her business empire was worth.

Not bloody likely!

And certainly not for the benefit of Mr Margam bloody Boone, or whoever he was representing.

And just who could that be?

Mrs Bendig was no stranger to intimidations, and she regularly made more threats than she received. Mr Boone and his masters had picked the wrong little daisy if they seriously thought she'd wilt in the glare of their extortions. While she was always open to business propositions, she didn't like being threatened. Didn't like it at all.

She looked around the room, which was on the third-floor of the night house. Safe enough; it couldn't be accessed without going past several very rough men in her employ. But she certainly had no intention of hiding away from the world, becoming a prisoner inside her own four walls. Her business depended on her being able to walk the streets at all hours of the day and night. And she fully intended to go on doing so.

Time then to seek out Mr Margam Boone and put the frighteners on him. Two could play at that game. She reflected on the conversation they'd had. Mr Margam Boone, lawyer, of... where was it? Somewhere around one of the Inns of Court. Now, which one? Ah, Gray's Inn, that was it. How silly of the odious reptile to give out his card so willingly. Or how confident Boone must feel about the power and safety of his employers. If the card was genuine, that is...

Mrs Bendig swigged back some more gin.

Well, soon find out. And so very easily. So many lawyers, judges even, came to sample the delights of her night house. Not to mention the politicians. Power enough there to have Boone's business enterprises shut down altogether.

Either legitimately, through the letter of the law, or... well, there were other more unpleasant methods...

Mrs Bendig smiled and then drank some more gin.

~

Quest sat on a bench in a corner of the taproom which occupied much of the ground floor of the *Shanghai*.

A great fog of tobacco smoke filled the air from a dozen or more clay pipes, adding to the stench of forty or more unwashed bodies. The landlord of the alehouse, busily filling tankards from the great barrels on the long table at one end of the room, kept looking anxiously towards the door.

And every time the door opened, numerous conversations would come to a sudden halt, resuming only when a familiar face entered or left.

Quest sipped at his tankard of small beer and waited... and waited. Two hours had passed and the landlord had started to give him peculiar looks. The aim of most of his customers was to get drunk as quickly as possible. Yet, here was this bludger, not unknown to the alehouse, sipping his brew like a lady come for tea. Something not quite right about it...

The same thought was preying on Quest's mind. He simply couldn't sit there and not waste himself like the others. Men of sober habits were not encouraged in the drinking dens of the East End.

To hell with it, Quest thought, swigging the last of his beer in one almighty gulp. He tapped the tankard on the bench, the usual instruction to the tapster that he wanted some more.

Over in the farthest corner a man burst into song, only to be hushed by the mob gathered round him. A couple of opium addicts, limbs contorted, staggered down the stairs from the drug den above, helping each other across the taproom and out through the door. A few of the drinkers followed to empty their bladders in the alley. The tapster put a freshly-filled tankard on the bench next to Quest, holding out his hand for a coin.

Just as Quest was paying his dues, the door burst open and two men entered, bruisers by the look of them, old fighters gone to seed. Both carrying lead-weighted life preservers of heavy wood. They looked around the taproom and then one of them held a door open, giving a nod to someone outside.

The old pugs stood aside to admit a younger man, as dark in looks as Quest himself, black and lanky hair hanging down over his collar. The newcomer glanced around the room and then turned and waved an arm through the doorway.

An old man entered, leaning on a walking stick of discoloured ash; a tiny individual with a pointed nose and chin, with what was left of his hair a chalky white. His three companions nodded their heads deferentially and stood protectively around him as they crossed the room. Half a dozen bludgers followed through the door, trailing after them.

Quest looked at the old man.

The King of Jacob's Island certainly didn't seem to live up to his considerable reputation.

~

They had lifted Jedediah Mooth in Lower Well Alley, not an hour before.

He'd spent the day preaching on the Ratcliffe Highway, scrabbling for pennies, and was returning to his room, when he became aware of the two bulky individuals walking on either side of him. Not initially menacing, but just marching in step. He'd glanced at them through his *pince-nez*, but failed to recognise either. There were heavy footsteps behind him, suggesting a third unwanted companion.

For a while he pretended to himself they were not there. That it was just a coincidence that the little party were marching in step. His hand wandered deep into his coat, feeling for his purse. There weren't that many coins in it. It had been a poor day for prating.

Certainly not enough to warrant getting beaten up or having your throat cut.

If push came to shove, he would hand over his takings. It wasn't the first time he'd been robbed on the streets of London. He seldom got anything worse out of such occurrences than a blackened eye or a punch in the gut.

And this might all be perfectly innocent. But there was really only one way to find out. He turned to the right as if he intended to cross the alley, but the man stationed on that side refused to give ground. Mooth sighed and walked on a little further, aware that the alley was becoming narrower and darker.

He glanced at his companions once more. Three bludgers just for the sake of one old preacher, who struggled from day to day trying to make a living?

He suddenly felt very afraid.

Oh well, better to get it over with. Nothing could be worse than the terror that was seeping down from his head to his bowels. If there was to be a beating, better now than later.

Jedediah Mooth stopped dead, his heart leaping in his chest as someone brushed against his back. The men on either side turned inwards to look at him. Mooth's legs seemed to be folding under him and three pairs of arms grasped him and held him up.

The sweat from his face had misted up his *pince-nez* and he could scarcely make out any of their features. But he didn't seem to know them. The terrifying thought was that they obviously knew Jedediah Mooth.

His lips trembled and he found that he couldn't speak. And, for several horrible moments, his assailants looked down at him without uttering a word.

The man who'd been behind him coughed before he spoke.

'Jedediah Mooth?' he said at last.

Mooth nodded frantically.

'Then yer're comin' for a little stroll with us...'

'Where?' Mooth's mouth was so dry he could hardly get out the word.

'Someone wants ter see yer, and he ain't a very patient man.'

Mooth looked up once more.

'Who?' he gasped.

'The King,' the man replied.

'Why?'

'Aren't yer full of the questions? Yer knows why. Yer've been a bad boy. Openin' yer trap when yer should have kept it shut. Well, the King's heard all about it and he wants an audience with yer. Right now. So let's get along, shall we?'

~

The men in the opium den were strung out on low couches, each one striking a bizarre pose as the smoking drug took hold of them. Some moaned and others sang in low voices. One or two appeared to be dead, though every so often their bodies would twitch alarmingly.

Sergeant Berry had seen it so often before in a dozen foul holes along the banks of the Thames. Watched others heading for mental and physical destruction, just as these individuals were. It was his considered opinion that opium should be made illegal; though as Britain made so much money out of the drug, and its varieties were used in so many medicines, he doubted it ever would be.

Inspector Anders was of a like mind, and frequently expressed an opinion that he couldn't understand why anyone would participate in the first place. But then Anders was even intolerant of alcohol.

Berry had been in the opium den for a good hour, pretending to inhale the drug, but all the time resisting its effects. Not that he needed to actively indulge; the smoke filling the long and narrow room was already having an effect on him; making his eyes water and giving him a thundering headache.

He would rather have waited in the tap-room downstairs, but there was a danger that he might be recognised. Berry was becoming too familiar a face in the East End to get away with such obvious tricks. But up here he was safer. Most of the clientele were sailors, fresh from the ships docked and unloading on the banks of the Thames. There was nobody he recognised. And he had dressed himself as a seaman.

Smoke from the drug wafted over the hard wooden bunk on which he lay, sending a fresh wave of nausea from his brain right down into his stomach, making Berry want to heave. He hoped it wouldn't be long now.

The stout wooden door was slightly ajar, and he could see the entrance to the room that occupied much of the back of these insalubrious premises. Still no sign of the so called King of Jacob's Island.

And who was this King whose threatening shadow hung like opium smoke over the slums and rookeries along the riverside? Berry's mind began a nightmare, where an ogre-like figure wearing a crown was laughing and screaming in his face, deformed claws beating on the policeman's chest.

Good God! The drug must be having an effect on him. He reached inside his jacket and brought out a brandy flask. It was filled only with water. He took a goodly swig to refresh himself and poured the remnants over his face.

Ah, that was better. His mind seemed to be coming back to him. The man in the next bunk groaned and cried out in some foreign tongue, German or Dutch, Berry thought, before beginning to weep very softly to himself. The sailor's right arm stretched towards the filthy ceiling before seeming to reach out towards the door.

Berry looked in the same direction and bit his tongue in anger. While the door to the opium den remained open, the one beyond was now shut, with a bruiser leaning against it.

Dammit! How long had he been under the influence of the foul drug? Long enough; for the bloody King and his entourage must have entered the room without him noticing. Berry reached deep into his jacket to check that the whistle was still there. Deeper down in his pocket was his lead-weighted cosh. He was prepared for anything.

He hoped to God that Anders had arrived and was waiting outside with his reinforcements.

~

'Take off the blindfold.'

The light from twenty candles dazzled Jedediah Mooth's eyes as the dirty rag was torn from his face. But the rope that bound his wrists still rubbed hard against his skin. He could see very little, for the men who had brought him here had taken away his *pince-nez*. He had only the vaguest impression of people sitting at a long table at one end of the room, one separated from the others on a slightly higher chair, like a magistrate in a police court.

He felt hot breath against his left cheek.

'Jedediah Mooth,' a voice whispered. 'Maggot...'

Mooth turned his head and screwed up his eyes to focus. A young man with very dark looks and black hair, his face creased in a smile that bore no humour.

'Here...'

The young man reached out and positioned Mooth's spectacles on his nose.

'There, that's better,' he said. 'Now we can all see each other, can't we?'

He pointed at the old man sitting apart from the others.

'D'you know who that is?' he asked.

Mooth shook his head.

'Say it aloud.'

'I don't know who that is...' Mooth muttered a lie. 'I never saw him before...'

'Yet, you've been talking about him, haven't you?'

'No... no... I don't think so...'

The young man let out a deep breath.

'I think you have, Maggot. And talking to the authorities. To the police.'

'I haven't...' Mooth persisted.

'In an alley... the other day. You were talking to Sergeant Berry of Scotland Yard. You were heard, Maggot. And followed. Berry gave you money.'

'I wasn't in any alley...'

The young man waved an arm around the room.

'You know where we all come from, don't you, Maggot?'

Mooth did know where they all came from, but shook his head furiously.

'Oh, you disappoint me, Maggot. You know perfectly well where we hail from. Jacob's Island... you know that, Maggot, so why bother to lie? And if you know that, well, then you must know who the gent is at the table? Say his name...'

'I don't know his name...'

'His title then?'

Mooth looked down at the floor.

The young man sighed.

'All right, Maggot, say it after me... he is...'

Mooth remained silent.

'I'm losing patience, Maggot.'

The young man reached behind Mooth's back and seized his tied wrists, twisting them upwards until the prater winced with pain.

'After me...' the young man said very quietly. 'He is...'

'He is...'

'The King...'

'The King...'

'Of Jacob's Island...'

'Of Jacob's...' Mooth began.

'Go on!'

'Of Jacob's Island,' said Mooth. He suddenly turned towards the young man. 'Only he ain't, is he? He's Oglow the dip. I've known him since I first come to London. He picked pockets up west till the rheumatics took away his soft touch. You want me to say he's the King, you're trying to trap me into lying. I know your tricks. He's no King...'

'Then who is?'

'You are, you are, you young bastard. I've been south of the river. Watched you build your empire in The Borough and Southwark and Deptford...' the words tumbled out, Mooth feeling a curious sense of power come to him. 'You don't frighten me no more. I knows you of old... and where you come from.'

'Where I came from?'

There was a genuine look of puzzlement on the King's face.

'I know where you come from,' said Mooth. 'And that's why you need me. I've followed your doings since you first come to London.' He looked at the men sitting at the table. 'Do they know? Do they know where you come from?'

'Tell me where I come from, Maggot. Whisper in my ear.'

The King put the side of his face against Mooth's mouth and listened to the whispered words. When the prater had finished speaking, a strange smile crossed the King's face.

'You are most well informed,' he said at last.

'And why shouldn't I be,' Mooth said triumphantly. 'You know my background. I know yours. Harm your reputation wouldn't it? If I told?' He glared at the men sitting along the table. 'You want to know how your King started out, do ye? I'll tell ye. I'll tell ye. Every last one of ye. He's...'

The King brought his fist crashing into Mooth's face, sending his *pince-nez* flying across the room. He reached out with one hand and seized the prater, dragging the little man's head backwards, forcing him to look up at the ceiling.

'Look up, Maggot, look up. See what I've got waiting for you.'

Mooth screwed his eyes and tried to focus. Something dangling down from a hole through the rafter. He couldn't quite make out... but then the King reached upwards and grasped the end of the rope, the stretch of hemp tied in a hangman's noose.

Suddenly the reality and desperation of his situation touched the mind and the gut of Jedediah Mooth. His stomach turned over and he felt his lips trembling uncontrollably. He wanted to talk, to shout and tell all in one great burst of vocal revenge, but the words he uttered were pleas for mercy.

The King drew the noose over Mooth's head, pulling the harsh rope hard against his throat. He waved an arm as a signal to the two bruisers holding the other end of the rope. They gave a great heave and then secured the rope over a hook above the wainscoting.

The King looked up just those few feet to where Mooth was dancing in the air, giving out a loud and very peculiar groan, his head nodding frantically as though it might edge its way out of the rope's grip.

Raising an arm in the air, the King gave a great yell and then a burst of laughter as he caught the terror in the eyes of the hanging man.

~

There was a sudden silence in the taproom of the *Shanghai,* as first Mooth's groan and then a near hysterical burst of laughter seemed to burst through the floorboards from the rooms above. The drinkers put down their flagons and looked at each other. Some, members of Monkshood, looked towards Quest, their hands reaching inside their jackets for concealed weapons.

Quest gave a nod to them and then charged up the stairs, aware of the heavy feet of his men behind him. Something was happening and it was time to bring matters to a conclusion.

Two men were fighting in the corridor between the opium den and the closed door of the back room. One, a heavily-built individual who looked like a broken prize-fighter, had his hands around the slighter man's throat, and seemed impervious to the blows being rained down upon his head from the short cosh in his victim's right hand.

Fighters were used to taking a lot of punishment, was the thought that fleeted through Quest's mind as he waded into the battle.

He slammed the weighted end of his blackthorn stick hard across the side of the bruiser's head. The fighter pushed his original adversary hard against the wall and shook his head, gasping and cursing. After a moment, his hands free, he charged at Quest, pulling back his right arm and then forcing it forward in a mighty punch.

Quest pulled his head away from the incoming blow and waved the blackthorn through the air, releasing the dagger from its secret compartment.

But, before he had a chance to use the blade, a hand reached over his shoulder, palm open, and stopped dead the attacking fist. Sticks held and twisted the man's hand, then brought his own heavy punch into the bruiser's face, once, twice, thrice...

The man groaned as he crumpled to the floor.

'I knows you,' said Sticks. 'You always was a clumsy oaf, Catbells. I beat you the same way that day at Richmond, when the Runners raided the match afore I could finish you off.'

Quest looked down at the fighter's victim.

'Damn you, Berry,' he said, before throwing his weight against the closed door.

The sergeant gave this rough individual only a glance before putting the whistle to his lips and giving a blast of sound that made his head ring. Still dazed by the combat and the whistle's reverberating sound, he picked up his cosh and followed Quest and Sticks through the broken-open door.

The body of Jedediah Mooth was swinging across the room, his feet only inches from the ground, the hempen rope creaking on the huge beam.

'The birds have flown,' said Berry, looking over Quest's shoulder.

A ladder led to a trap door in the ceiling. The dark of the night sky could be seen beyond. Somewhere below were the shouts of policemen crashing into the *Shanghai*, forcing their way through an obstructing force of riverside villainy and the members of Monkshood.

'It's all your bloody fault!' shouted Quest. 'If you'd left it to us we could have saved that poor devil and caught the men that did it to him.'

Sticks had crossed the room and was lifting Mooth upwards by his legs, his head against the little man's chest.

'This 'uns not dead yet,' he said. 'He ain't been swingin' for long enough. Cut the rope someone while I gets him down.'

Quest swept the dagger in the blackthorn stick through the air, slicing through the rope with little effort. Sticks lifted Mooth on to the table and eased the rope away from his throat. He put two fingers into the prater's mouth to stop Mooth choking on his own swollen tongue.

'Will he live?' asked Berry.

'Hard to say,' said Quest, rolling back one of Mooth's eyelids. 'Depends how long he was hanging before we got into the room. He needs a doctor and fast. Men have swung for a while and survived. He might yet.'

'Doctor Hillaby's nearest,' said Sticks. 'Just a street away. If anyone can bring Mooth back, he can.'

He left the room at considerable speed, knocking aside the policemen who were crowding into the doorway.

'Put the cuffs on that creature,' ordered Berry, pointing at the groaning Catbells. 'The only bird left in the cage.' He turned to Quest. 'Perhaps I should have you shackled as well?'

'I d'believe my men outnumber yours, Berry,' Quest replied. 'And this is a neighbourhood that's hostile to you peelers. So you may keep your cuffs in your jacket. You'll do better with Catbells there. He's partial to gin. Pour enough of that down his throat and he'll trill like a skylark.'

'And why exactly are you here, Mr Quest?' Inspector Anders entered the room. 'Your disguises might fool the wretches who haunt Thames-side. They don't me.'

Quest gave a mocking bow.

'Sometimes you have to blend in with the scenery, Inspector,' he said. 'And I think my costume for the night has the beating of Sergeant Berry's here. If opium hadn't dulled the wits of the inhabitants of this rat-hole, your sergeant'd be floating in the river with his throat cut.'

'Who's he?' asked Anders, pointing at the man stretched out on the table.

'Mooth, sir,' said Berry. 'My informer. The villains tried to top him with a rope. Didn't give him long enough before we all came charging in. He might live yet. We've sent for a doctor.'

Anders nodded.

'He'd better,' he said. 'I want to know exactly what's been going on here, and why these rogues thought this Mooth needed hanging?'

He looked across at Quest. 'And I think that on this one occasion you should tell me everything you know, Quest. Or I might break the habit of a lifetime and arrest you. Whether it upsets Lord Palmerston or not.'

Ten

'Mooth's alive,' reported Sergeant Berry. 'They've taken him to the London Hospital. I've put half a dozen men on guard and got him in a room to himself.'

They were all sitting in Quest's library at Tavistock Place, for he had flatly refused to accompany Inspector Anders to Scotland Yard.

Quest was no longer the dangerous looking bludger Anders had encountered in the room at the *Shanghai*, but a slim and refined gentleman who looked as though he might live entirely in a world of books and study. The change in appearance caused the policeman to hide a smile.

'What about this villain, Catbells?' Anders asked.

'On his way to Clerkenwell in a closed wagon,' Berry replied. 'I thought it best to get him right out of the district. Too many shady characters down by the river.'

He looked at Quest with a grin.

Anders waved an arm in Quest's direction.

'Our friend here still denies he knows very much about the slaying of Bluff Todd,' he said. 'I know you know much more than you're saying, Quest, but I'll let it go for the moment. I'm more interested in this character from Jacob's Island. We can take him at least for the attempted murder of Jedediah Mooth.'

'How exactly?' asked Quest.

'Go down to the island with as many men as I can muster. Pull them all in for questioning.'

'And you seriously imagine you'll nab this King?' said Quest. 'The place is a warren, with so many hideaways and passages that you'll never get near him. The residents of Jacob's Island live in a world of crime and violence. They won't be threatened, however many men you take in.'

'You go in and you'll find nothin',' said Sticks. 'I knows men – aye, and women, who've resided there. It'd be more than their lives are worth to betray anyone, let alone this man you're after. And if you do pull in their King, there'll be a hundred come forward to claim he was in a tavern in Bermondsey or wherever when Mooth was attacked. You can put 'em all in charge, burn down the wretched place. You'll still not get near him.'

'I think Sticks has it right,' said Berry. 'Our best hope is to get this Catbells drunk enough to turn Queen's Evidence. At least then we'll be in with a start.'

'He's a demon for gin,' said Sticks. 'Pour enough down his great throat and you might get a whisper. At least some hint as how you might catch this King out on his own.'

'And he'd be a fish worth catching,' said Berry. 'We've all heard the tales of how people are being intimidated. Forced out of their trades. Even the criminal underworld is succumbing to some sinister figure from that side of the river. And Mooth hinted to me that it all emanates from around Jacob's Island.'

'I've heard rumours about Kings of the Underworld before,' said Anders. 'But rumours are all they usually are. There's always villains trying to muscle in on someone else's patch. But I suspect that's all it is. If this King exists I doubt his power extends much beyond his own particular rookery.'

Quest gazed out of the window. A deep fog had swept up from the river. He could scarcely see the opposite side of the road. After a moment he became aware that the others were all looking at him.

'You know the underworld better than most, Quest,' said Anders. 'What do you think?'

'I think there's something unpleasant in the air,' Quest replied. 'There's always fear in the poorer areas of this city. But now I sense more than that. You may be right, Anders. I hope you are in so many ways. But I suspect your sergeant is bang on the mark. There's more to this than a little local villainy.'

'So what do you suggest?' asked Anders.

'What's clear is if you take your men down there and assault the place as though you were the Grenadier Guards, you'll grasp a great many by the neck, but not the man you want. This needs a more considered approach...'

Sticks caught the look on Quest's face.

'Oh no you don't,' he grumbled. 'You gave your word you'd not go down to Jacob's Island. There are...'

'Word to who?' interrupted Anders.

'Never mind,' said Quest. 'That was then. This is now.'

'They've already tried to top you once, lad...' said Sticks.

'What's this all about?' inquired Anders.

Quest told him about the shooting and the roughs in the alley.

'You should have reported it to the police,' muttered Berry.

Quest laughed.

'There's only one way to root out a rat and that's to send in a rat-catcher,' he said. 'Just one...'

'Don't be a fool, boy!' roared Sticks. 'You might get near him, but you'll never get him out of there. They'll be on you like nothin' else, and you'll be floating face down in the Folly Ditch in minutes. That's unless you're thinking of just topping him?'

'Oh, no,' said Anders, 'I'm not letting you add this man to your list of victims, Quest. Run through with a swordstick and a noose thrown down on the ground. I want this man in the dock at the Old Bailey.'

'That might not be so easy...'

'The only way,' Anders replied.

'For the sake of argument,' asked Quest, 'if he attacked me, would I be allowed to defend myself?'

'It would depend on the circumstances, and...'

There was a furious rapping on the front door of the house. Sticks went down and admitted a police constable, out of breath and red in the face.

'What is it, constable?' said Anders.

The policeman swallowed deeply.

'The villain we took at the *Shanghai*, sir. They got him. He's dead, sir. He's dead.'

~

It was not the first time that Catbells had been inside a closed and barred police wagon, but rarely one that sped along so swiftly through the streets of London. He could hear the crack of the whip and the cries of the policeman on the seat above, urging pedestrians out of the way. Through the little barred window, he could see the crowds looking on to see what all the hurry was about.

They had cuffed him before bundling him into the wagon. Then fastened a leg iron to his ankle, attaching it to the metal bar that ran the length of the wagon's floor.

Well fastened, for Catbells had given the chain several hefty tugs as soon as the door was secured. Pity, for the door itself would have presented few problems for a man of his considerable strength.

Despite all of these inconveniences, Catbells had great faith in the King. He'd fought hard to give his leader an opportunity to get away.

The King would not forget him.

They went back a long way.

Catbells knew so much about him. Could tell so much. He'd been at Jacob's Island the day that young man had arrived two years before. When the man who was to be King had been a lot chattier. Catbells had been amazed at the story he'd been told, but he didn't think much of the new arrival until he'd witnessed the King's particular brand of ruthlessness.

In all his years in the London underworld, Catbells had met nobody like the King. A man so calculating, so clever, so... so vicious. And he knew that other secret too. He knew where the King went on his own, when he wasn't at Jacob's Island. Knew who he met and what he did.

And the King knew that Catbells knew.

He peeked out through the little window again. The wagon was near the end of the Ratcliffe Highway now. He'd heard the three policemen atop mutter that he was to be taken to the gaol at Clerkenwell. Catbells grinned. He'd freed himself from that House of Correction once before. And he doubted the King would let him travel so far before intervening.

His liberation came suddenly, just before the wagon turned out of the Highway. There was a sudden shout, a wild whinnying from one of the horses, and a screech from the wooden block that braked the wheel. The wagon skewed across the road and swung sideways, crashing into some object with a mighty bang. For several moments there was absolute silence. Then he heard groans from one of the policemen.

There was the familiar sound of a jemmy forcing the door open, then a sudden burst of light as the gas-lamps illuminated the interior of the wagon.

There were four of them, hoods up and masks across their faces. He could tell who one of them was by his slim form and the swiftness with which he moved.

Catbells gave a broad grin. He hadn't expected the King to come in person. It showed just how much he was valued. Catbells held up his darbied hands in a gesture of triumph. He gave a welcoming cry, half-yell and half burst of laughter. But in a second, felt his throat tighten and his stomach loosen.

He saw the four pistols being aimed in his direction. Watched the flashes from the percussion caps and the smoke from the barrels. Heard the dry barks from the pistols even as the lead balls tore into his great chest. He fell forwards on to the floor of the wagon, his last sensation being the scent of sweat and piss from previous occupants.

Then only darkness.

~

The letter had come with the early morning post, and Rosa Stanton had studied the unfamiliar handwriting on the envelope for a good five minutes before she opened it. She read its contents several times before giving a triumphant yell at the ceiling, putting on hat and cape and dashing out of the door.

Her first thought was to walk very speedily across town, though the letter had specified that she had two hours' grace before the appointment. But on reflection she decided that she would look a little less flustered at her destination if she took a *cabriolet*. Consequently, she was far too early at the Lyceum Theatre, and was obliged to walk up and down Wellington Street and the Strand for a good hour. But it was a fine morning and there seemed to be gaiety in the sunny air. She looked at the little watch on her lapel.

It was time.

Madame Vestris was standing alone on the stage as she was ushered in through the wings. The older lady looked at her and positively beamed a welcome, taking Rosa's hand in her own.

'My dear Miss Stanton, how good of you to come at such short notice,' she said. 'It is always a delight to give good news to a young person of talent.'

'There is nowhere I would rather be...' Rosa began.

Madame Vestris looked thoughtful as she studied Rosa.

'You have a rare beauty, my dear,' she said. 'I was saying as much to Mr Matthews and Mr Jolys only last evening. We all agreed that I should write to you at once and have you here at this dear old theatre this very morning.'

Rosa gave a little curtsey.

'I'm honoured, Madame. I take it this will be a supporting part in your next production?'

Madame Vestris shook her head vigorously.

'No indeed! No indeed! We have something much more ambitious in mind, Miss Stanton. A leading role in a revival no less, though the performance run will be of a short duration, I fear... though I have plans that... oh, I'm running ahead of myself!'

Rosa smiled.

'I'd be very happy to perform any role for you, Madame,' she said.

'Quite so, quite so...'

'You indicated a revival?'

'A familiar piece for you, Miss Stanton. Mr Jolys tells us that you were such a delight as Polly in *The Beggar's Opera*. And having heard you sing the other day, I was so entranced. And it would help us out of a little difficulty...'

'Difficulty, Madame?'

'Well, we have in the course of preparation a new *Extravaganza*. But we will not be able to stage it here quite as early as we thought. To fill in the gap in our schedule, we intend to revive *The Beggar's Opera*, Miss Stanton.'

She took Rosa very firmly by the hand and walked with her to the footlights.

'It is always such a popular piece,' she continued, 'and we can think of nobody better to play Polly than your good self. Oh, I know it is but a revival, and a temporary piece at that, but... oh, my dear Miss Stanton would you do us the great honour of giving our audiences your Polly Peachum?'

Madame Vestris looked down at Rosa, an appealing look on her face.

'For me, Miss Stanton. And who knows what other parts it might lead to? I am still firmly of the opinion that we should produce the *Dream* with you. You might have been born to play so many roles in the *Dream*...'

Rosa suddenly felt quite faint, as she looked out at the huge auditorium. She could almost hear the applause from the stalls and the cheers from the boxes and galleries.

'It would be... such an honour!' she smiled.

~

'I take it Commissioner Mayne wasn't in the best of moods?' said Sergeant Berry, as Anders came back to their little office at Scotland Yard.

Anders hurled a fresh piece of coal on to the fire and bashed it with the poker, rather wishing it was the Police Commissioner's head.

'We'll be pounding the beat as constables in uniform if we have any more ill-luck,' he said. 'And why not? Perhaps we might both be a damned sight happier. No worries except during the hours we work. Home at a set time. Regular nourishment. No commissioners breathing down our necks...'

'But boring?' ventured Berry.

'Perhaps... do you remember last year? When Inspector Gurney of the Norfolk Constabulary suggested we join his little force? After the morning I've had, I'm bloody tempted!'

'Ah, but all that countryside, sir. Sinister place the countryside. I find alleys and rookeries so much easier to deal with. You know just where your enemies are coming from.'

A glimpse came into Anders' mind of the downs and woodlands of Wiltshire and so many boyhood adventures. So different from the crowded rush of London. He thought that he might take off to the countryside on holiday, as soon as this wretched business was finished with.

'What did Mayne say?'

Berry's words snapped him out of his reverie.

'Mayne finds it hard to believe that a police wagon can be ambushed with such ease, three constables beaten, and a prisoner shot dead,' said Anders. 'He dreads what the newspapers will say. He wants us to bring to book the people responsible.'

'You mean he wants us to march down and take this wretched crew on Jacob's Island?'

Anders shook his head and bashed the lump of coal once more.

'That's the last thing he wants,' he said. 'He fears a bloodbath if we go in mob-handed.'

'Never thought Mayne would agree with the sentiments of our Mr Quest.'

'Not sure that he does,' said Anders. 'The Commissioner is more concerned with how it might look in the newspapers and dreads the thought of having the Home Secretary fend off embarrassing questions in parliament.'

'So what do we do now?'

'Well, we've still got Mooth. Might be a good idea if you went down to the London Hospital and see if he's come round. They must have been swinging him for a good reason. He knows something or they wouldn't have been trying to silence him in such a dramatic way.'

'I thought Mooth knew more than he was telling.'

'Whatever happens, Berry, I want the crown knocked off the head of this King. We can't have the underworld of London controlled by such a creature. It would be even more dangerous than...'

'More dangerous than Quest?'

Anders laughed.

'I don't want either of them! But if I have to choose, then I'll take Quest to our side and depose this riverside villain.'

~

Mrs Bendig poured out two glasses of sherry.

'Your good health, Sir Wren.'

Sir Wren Angier raised the glass in salute to his hostess and smiled at her before taking a sip.

'And yours, dear lady,' he said.

'You've always been one of my most favoured customers,' Mrs Bendig said. 'And I'm pleased to see you coming more and more often over recent days.'

'There's nowhere quite like your rooms in the whole of London,' he replied. 'So relaxing, and in so many ways. I'm most taken with the new addition to your house.'

'Little Phoebe?'

'Exactly.'

Mrs Bendig glanced around her boudoir, sipped some more sherry, and beamed a broad smile that made her huge face wobble.

'You're making my other young ladies quite jealous.'

'I take it you have no objection, Mrs Bendig? I find Phoebe so easy to talk to. As you may be aware, I've been at something of a loose end since winding up my business enterprises.'

'Money-lending wasn't it?'

'Not a reputable trade,' he said. 'Not for a gentleman.'

She gave him a look of bewilderment.

'Seems honourable to me,' she said. 'If I had the time I'd invest in such an industry myself.'

She noted the thoughtful look on his face. He was still handsome and slim, though nearly forty. A baronet and a member of parliament. And he visited the House of Commons much more often these days. She'd read the speeches, puzzled as to why this one-time exploiter of the poor had seemed to have acquired compassion. Could it be religion? It did happen, and even bishops had come a-whoring in her night house.

Yet this man had changed in the past year. Thrown off some doubtful associates. Given up dubious business enterprises. And Phoebe had let slip that he was as keen to talk as much as share a bed.

But he'd done Mrs Bendig some favours in the past, and could always be trusted to be discreet.

'I think my Phoebe's quite taken with you, Sir Wren, but you know I've a very strict rule...'

'Rule?'

'One of the great difficulties in running an establishment such as mine... with the most beautiful young ladies in all of London... is that now and again, my gents become attached in a more personal way to a girl than is good for the business.'

Sir Wren nodded.

'Become attached in an emotional way,' she continued. 'I've even had gentlemen fall in love with my young ladies...'

She screwed up her face as though she'd sucked on a lemon.

'I suppose it must happen,' he ventured.

'Well, it does. And that's not what this business is about at all, don't you see? Temporary passions is one thing. But something more long-lasting? I'm afraid I can't really permit that. D'you know I've had my girls lured away to become mistresses...' She took in a deep breath. 'Even on one occasion a wife!' She raised a hand to the ceiling. 'Can you believe such a thing?'

Angier finished his sherry.

'I suppose the world has to change,' he said.

'Ah, it doesn't really, Sir Wren. Not deep down. There'll always be a need for night houses like mine. It's in the nature of mankind, don't you see?'

He shrugged, wondering just where this conversation was going. Mrs Bendig looked thoughtful for a moment or two before she enlightened him.

'Have you ever, by any chance, Sir Wren, encountered a lawyer named Boone? Margam Boone of Gray's Inn? Looks like a viper in ill-fitting clothes?'

'I think not,' he replied. 'Is he a customer of yours?'

'Heaven forfend! Anything but. To be frank, Sir Wren, he's threatening me.'

'Threatening you?'

She related her encounter with Margam Boone, the arrival of the rat, and the scabby villain that she'd had to fight off. She pointed out the likelihood that these events were connected.

'How deeply unpleasant,' he said.

Then a wave of memory swept over his mind and conscience. These were just the tactics his own hangers-on had employed against victims during his former days as a money-lender. Before his conversion to better things at the hands of a man clad all in black, who had appeared mysteriously in his set of rooms at Albany.

The man who'd made him re-examine what had become a miserable existence.

'You've done me some favours in recent months, Sir Wren,' Mrs Bendig continued. 'You're in parliament and know people in the law. I need to know about this Boone. Who's paying him and what I can do to fend him off?'

Angier rubbed a cheek and considered.

'Finding out about this Boone won't be difficult in itself, Mrs Bendig. Lawyers can hardly conceal themselves or their reputations. Finding out who his client may be is immeasurably harder.'

Mrs Bendig poured out more sherry.

'Yet it might be that pressure might be brought to bear on this Boone... from higher up?'

'It could... lawyers rely on the goodwill of the Class to survive...'

'And you're not without influence, Sir Wren...'

'I could make inquiries.'

She put a beringed hand on his.

'I do wish you would,' she said. 'You've always been a great favourite of mine. And, well, should you have a notion to steal away my little Phoebe, I'd be prepared to let her go with my blessing.'

'That would have to be her decision, Mrs Bendig. I've become fond of the girl, I admit that. But one of the lessons I've learned in life is that people must be allowed to do things willingly.'

'Naturally...'

'You leave this matter to me,' he said. 'I'll see what I can find out about this Margam Boone.'

~

'I don't know where he is,' said the doctor, 'but he's not back with us yet.'

Sergeant Berry was at the London Hospital looking down at the prostrate body of Jedediah Mooth. The little man lay on his back staring up at the ceiling.

'His eyes are open,' said Berry, hopefully.

'Not unusual,' the doctor replied. 'This man's in a state of deep unconsciousness. It's possible that the inability to breathe during the time he was hanged has damaged his brain. And even if that's not so, the trauma of the experience might have sent him out of his mind.'

'Do you mean he might never be able to tell us anything?'

The doctor sucked in a breath.

'It's far too early to tell,' he said. 'We can only hope for the best. But it might be as well to leave a man by the bedside. It's not unusual for such victims to talk aloud even when unconscious. Just as we sometimes do in our sleep. He might say something relevant.'

'Very well,' said Berry. He turned to the doctor. 'Lives may depend on what we learn from this man. We really do need him to talk.'

Eleven

Ikey Balfrey was just about to close his shop for the night when he looked up to find the lawyer Boone on his doorstep.

Balfrey wished he'd closed the door a tad earlier.

'What d'yer want?' he asked.

Boone stepped inside the shop.

'You know what we want,' he said. 'I really do think my masters have been most generous, Balfrey. They made you a very good offer. And you threw it back in their faces.'

He sighed.

'Now, I've just come to make one final attempt to get you to see reason. There are still ten guineas on the table. And you will be left to run both your shop and your thieves on our behalf. For which you will receive a certain amount of commission, and a guarantee of a long and safe life.'

Balfrey reached underneath his counter and produced a long, lead-weighted life preserver. He slammed it hard down on the wooden surface.

'Why don't yer...'

'No curses please, Mr Balfrey. I really don't like curses.' The lawyer waved a hand through the air. 'Very well. If you really do not wish to sell, then so be it.'

He raised his hat and stepped out of the shop, pulling the door behind him. The sound of the bell seemed to jangle in Ikey Balfrey's head for several minutes.

The fence tidied up the wipes hanging in the shop window and hid the money he had taken in the secret compartment under the floorboards.

It had been a good day.

The dips who worked for him had had a productive time picking pockets. Lots of good quality silk wipes, only needing the initials of their former owners picking out. Four purses filled with coin. Three fob-watches, two of them gold. His boys and girls had served him well.

The bell jangled again.

'Who is it now?' he muttered, as he stood up.

It took him a moment for his eyes to focus in the dim gaslight. Two figures stood in the doorway. One wearing a crape mask and with a hood over his head. The other unmasked, a face that Ikey Balfrey knew only too well. A grinning man with dark hair. Someone he knew from a while ago.

'What now?' he asked, then grunted with fear.

The two intruders gave out a burst of laughter as they each raised a pair of pistols. Balfrey raised an arm in front of his body, and the pair laughed again.

He heard the ringing laughter as four pistol balls cleaved into his chest, sending him crashing against the far wall of the shop. His hand gripped a cord of hanging handkerchiefs, dragging the silk wipes with him as he tumbled to the floor.

~

'You can't be serious,' said Quest.

'Perfectly serious,' Rosa replied. 'Madame Vestris has offered me the part and I intend to take it. You didn't raise any great objection when we discussed it the other day.'

'I said, if you recall, that there was a danger of someone recognising you from our other activities. And there is. You've been playing the actress too long as a member of Monkshood to get away with it on the public stage.'

She flounced towards the window.

'That's absurd,' she said. 'I've donned a few disguises and costumes in the course of our work. Mostly for the benefit of people who'd never go near the theatre. And my disguises have been good. There's little chance of anyone identifying me at a distance across the footlights.'

Quest put down his copy of *Lavengro*.

'It only needs one, and that could mean a noose round your neck,' he said. 'You came into this enterprise in the first place because you said you were bored with theatricals.'

'Well, now I'm not bored. I came to London to go on the stage. Long before I ever met you. And I was successful. But you wanted me to work alongside you and... and to share your bed from time to time. And I did and it was amusing. But can't you see, Will, it's not enough anymore?'

'Not enough?'

'The years are going by. We're all getting older. There's only a limited time when I can play these leading roles on the stage. And Madame Vestris has offered me a whole new world of possibilities.'

'Possibilities!' he muttered.

'Yes, possibilities, Will. Some sort of security. Knowing when I wake up in the morning, I might still be alive when dark comes. Not hearing the crashing of a locked door in Newgate in my mind. Doing something that gives me joy.'

'I thought we'd found joy together?'

She knelt beside his chair and took his scarred hand in her own.

'And we have,' she replied, 'and we can have a future of such joys. But for now, just for now, I want this. Can't you see that? This isn't an option I'm discussing with you, Will. This is a course of action I intend to take. Monkshood doesn't need me. You have lots of people who can do everything I do.'

'But none of them are you...' He looked at her in such a pitiful way that her heart turned over.

She took in a deep breath.

'A lovely line, Will. And delivered by possibly the greatest actor in London. I've seen you perform too, out there on the streets and in the rookeries. If I thought you meant that line, if I believed it was spoken with sincerity...'

'It is.'

'I'm not convinced,' Rosa said. 'You've said you loved me, but I've never really believed your words. I'll tell you what I think. I believe I'm just a habit. As comfortable for you as taking down a beloved book from your library shelves. Read again and put away until you yearn for it once more.'

'I do love you...'

'Then prove it by giving me your blessing.'

'It's too dangerous.'

She stood and walked across to the door, resting her hand on the door-knob and swinging it open a few inches.

'It's not dangerous at all, except in your mind.'

She looked back at him for a long while before she spoke again.

'I remember the first time I set eyes on you, Will. That day in the park, when you were sitting against a tree and looking as if you had the whole weight of the world on your shoulders.'

He looked up, an appalling look of sadness in his eyes.

'I remember it too,' he said. 'You took me home and to your bed. It seemed to solve a lot of my problems. I wish...'

'What do you wish?'

'I wish we could live ordinary lives.'

'We can...'

He shook his head.

'It's too late,' he cried. 'I can't stop any of this now...'

'A great tragedy was inflicted on you when you were very young. Then you were involved in events that... can't you see that you'll never change the world? Your adopted father expected too much of you. Nobody can do what you do and be undamaged. You were never meant to be this killer, this nemesis... you've been fighting against your nature...'

He pointed a finger towards the window.

'But look out there, Rosa. Out in the streets. At the cruelty and injustice. When will it ever stop... unless someone is determined to wipe such brutality from the face of the world...'

'But it doesn't have to be you!'

'Who else? Are we to wait a hundred years for parliament to bring about justice? The poor and the vulnerable don't have the luxury of time on their side...'

'They don't, but I'm tired of fighting everyone else's battles.'

'Somebody has to.'

'Then go on with it if you must. And who knows? One day I might be there to help you again. But right now, I have my own destiny to follow.'

As she looked down at Quest, he seemed to shrink into the armchair. She wanted to go back and take him in her arms. Wanted to draw the curtains and block out the world and make everything the way it always was.

She gave a nod to him, a half-smile and walked out of the door.

~

There was a chill in the air, despite the brightness of the morning. An occasional swift breeze swept up the dust from the road, to the annoyance of the pedestrians wandering up and down the Strand. The lads and old men who brushed away the detritus from the road and the pavements muttered curses under their breaths, touching their caps as the gentry passed by. Not all their curses were about the mud and the dust.

Sir Wren Angier was quite enjoying himself, though he hadn't had much sleep during the hours of darkness. He'd spent a few hours in parliament in a deep discussion with several Radical MPs, and shared a tumbler of rum with Lord Palmerston, the Home Secretary. He'd feigned an interest in the matters of the day with an old acquaintance of his in the Lords. It hadn't taken him long to acquire the needed information.

He'd left the House at around three in the morning, making his way through the streets and alleys of the city. A dangerous time for a gentleman to be abroad in some of them. He'd had a few glances from yawning whores, but turned his eyes away from them.

Some bludging villains had taken an interest in his passage through the night. Angier had been obliged to draw out a few inches of blade on three occasions, causing them to back off.

Soon after dawn he'd found himself in the vicinity of Gray's Inn. His informants had told him that the lawyer Margam Boone was a rising star in the legal profession, a man specialising mostly in the conveyancing of land and complicated matters of inheritance. He was more than efficient in that line of work, if not over-friendly with other members of the profession.

It seemed that many of those Angier had talked to, respected Margam Boone, even if they didn't appear to like him very much. The man himself lived above his chambers, very close to the Inn of Court. Nobody seemed to know anything at all about his private life, except that there were no obvious scandals. Apart from what he did for a living, Margam Boone appeared to have little in the way of personality at all.

And there he was, walking along the Strand, not fifty yards ahead of Angier. An early-riser by all accounts, for Angier had scarcely been waiting ten minutes before Margam Boone appeared.

For a good hour, the lawyer had wandered aimlessly through the streets, with no apparent fixed purpose. Angier considered the possibility that the man was aware that he was being followed, but rejected the notion. Margam Boone was walking speedily, arms flung out with every step. This fast walking must be his exercise regimen, that was all.

After that hour, Margam Boone had retreated into the Temple Gardens and occupied a bench for fifteen minutes, apparently doing nothing but taking in deep breaths. Not something I would do myself, Angier considered. The stink from the Thames was particularly bad on the morning air. It had been foul the night before as he wandered through the corridors of parliament. The stench seemed to cast a dreadful miasma across so much of London, and not just on warmer days.

More than one kind of miasma over London these days, Angier considered. He thought back a year, to the days when he'd added to the sum total of all the misery in this city. A craven, cowardly figure who'd ignored the results of his actions. A pathetic individual who'd got others to do his dirty work. And now...

And now...

Now, Angier knew all the answers. Respected the man who had set him on a different course in life. An individual not unlike himself in so many ways. Someone who chose not to lead a selfish life. Now Angier's remaining peccadillos were played out in Bendig's night house. Time to bring that to a halt too, time to...

Margam Boone had got up from the bench and walked speedily up to the Strand, and the excitement of the chase had banished all thoughts from Angier's mind. Now the lawyer seemed to have a fixed purpose, as though he was on a definite course. Margam Boone paused only once, to look at the time on his pocket watch. He scarcely glanced at the street around him before walking on towards Charing Cross.

Angier held back a little more, for the crowds seemed to have dispersed. But Margam Boone appeared have no interest in such matters. He must, Angier thought, be about legitimate business, not caring whether anyone was taking any interest in his movements. If so, the whole expedition would be a waste of time.

There would need to be other days of early mornings. Angier had enough of his old character left to find the prospect dismaying.

Then, not far short of Charing Cross, Margam Boone turned suddenly into an alley leading down to the river. A short journey from a prosperous world into one of drudgery.

Wren Angier knew it well, for he'd visited the place once before as part of a parliamentary commission. Some of the neighbouring streets had been rebuilt two decades before, and this dark passage was a remnant of the factories and slums that were once crammed in to a relatively small area of space.

Now the sweatshops had gone, though the ruinous buildings seemed haunted by memories of crying children forced to labour, and the poor going hungry on the cobbles of the alley. The stink from the Thames was almost overpowering.

Angier found a little stone bay in a crumbling wall, holding back in there, lest Margam Boone turn and look back. But the lawyer seemed preoccupied with his mission.

Margam Boone walked down to a building of some five storeys, over-hanging the filthy waters of the Thames. He examined his watch again, then took his first good look around before rapping on a stout wooden door. Angier waited, counting long moments and thinking that the lawyer's demand for admission wouldn't be answered. Indeed, it took a good two minutes before the door was swung open. He watched as Margam Boone entered, the door slamming shut behind him.

Angier timed five minutes on his pocket watch before he began to walk down the alley in the lawyer's footsteps.

~

'Another man who's no loss to law and order in this place.'

Inspector Anders looked down at the corpse of Ikey Balfrey. 'I'd like to believe there's no connection with what's gone before, but we know there is. Too much to hope that it was just a straightforward robbery?'

Berry shook his head.

'A drawer full of money, and more on the body.'

He waved an arm around the shop.

'And all these wipes are worth something. No, not a robbery. Besides, the local villainy bludge their victims over the head, strangle or stab. They don't use pistols. Ikey Balfrey's been shot four times. It was his business they were after.'

Anders rubbed his forehead.

'Well, perhaps the best thing we can do is wait and see who takes over and bring them in,' he said. 'Seems to me that whoever's responsible for this land grab is having too easy a time. We can at least keep an eye on this shop.'

'I'll see to that, sir. But they'd as like put someone in to run the place who's as clean as...'

'No doubt. But I don't see what else we can do. You know the difficulties. If we storm Jacob's Island, we'll nab everyone but this King. We don't know anything about him. Who he is or where he comes from. We know nothing of any associates he might have. Anyway, Commissioner Mayne is opposed to us assaulting the place. And if we did, this King'd just slip away and establish himself somewhere else.'

Berry looked again at the body.

'Sounds to me, sir, as if we might have to give Quest a free hand. He's the one man who might be able to slip into that vile place and account for this menace.'

'You know we can't let him do that.'

'But on his terms, sir. Bringing the King out alive to face trial. Only despatching him if Quest's life is threatened.'

'Don't like the thought of it,' said Anders. 'Not one little bit. Quest might shoot him dead and then claim it was in self-defence. Who would ever know the truth?'

Twelve

He'd walked all night, not really noticing where he was or where he was going. On the occasions that he stopped moving for brief moments, the memories came flooding back.

At first, Quest had journeyed the short distance between his house in Tavistock Place and Rosa's lodgings in the road up to Tottenham Court.

He'd stood outside her door for several minutes, looking up at the lighted window, his hand reaching out for the brass door-knocker in the shape of a fox. Each time his fingers touched the animal's mask, and every time he drew his hand away.

The feeling of loss he was experiencing, quite surprised him. He and Rosa often had rows, and so many times had she stormed out, occasionally throwing something at him or slamming a door. And always with a great yell of anger. But this time she had been positively cold and unemotional. As though something between them had perished irretrievably. Something lost that might never be found.

He had been unreasonable, he knew that from the second Rosa had left his house. There was, in reality, very little chance of anyone recognising her across the glare of stage-lighting.

Rosa had donned disguises for much of her work with Monkshood. She was known to be Quest's mistress, but what of that?

To most of society, Quest was known only as quiet and retiring, with a small circle of friends and not usually noticed anywhere he went in London. He was a minor landowner at Hope Down with a reputation for benevolence. A man who was known for his love of books and *penchant* for long country walks. Who he took to his bed was nobody's business but his own.

As the darkness fell completely and the lamplighter took his journey along the road, illuminating the hissing gas-lamps, Quest took one last look at the door and set off in the direction of Oxford Street, forcing his way through the late crowds like a ship crashing through waves.

The problem with spending so much time in one place was that you couldn't eliminate the past, he considered. He'd first worked

Oxford Street as a pickpocket, a young boy escaping from a nightmare in the lonely countryside of Norfolk.

Quest had lived not so far away in the foul rookery of St Giles, a place where the poor led very short lives. Where criminality was forced on to people just so that they might acquire the basic necessities of life. He had been rescued from such an existence, educated, turned into a gentleman by Josiah Quest and his associates. Come to be a leader in the Monkshood secret society. Forced into the kind of activities that had now caused the rift between him and Rosa.

And the alternative to that life?

No doubt at all. If he'd continued with his boyhood life he would probably have died very young; from hunger or disease, as most did who lived in the St Giles rookery. Or been transported to Botany Bay for theft. Perhaps strung up outside Newgate Gaol for worse crimes. Quest had nearly died in Norfolk with his father and brothers. It was pure good luck that he hadn't. Pure good fortune.

So William Quest hadn't died. But as he stamped from Oxford Street and into Soho Square, he wondered if he'd actually ever really lived?

There were days off from the world, days when he might enjoy a peaceful walk, or spend time in his study reading a book. When the injustice of the land and all that had to be done about it was put away for a precious few hours. But always there would come a tap on the door or a voice hailing him across a meadow. A jolt back into the reality of England.

He sat for a long while by a water pump on the edge of Seven Dials, chained up to prevent use after the last outbreak of cholera. Quest had used it often enough as a boy and survived. He sometimes considered the possibility that he had been meant to die in such a way. Whether his survival was an aberration. But what in hell was the use in thinking like that? You had to deal with your life as it was, and just looking at the paupers on the street in front of him showed how necessary it was to fight against greed and injustice.

And Rosa?

He would give her a day or two and then go and see her and apologise. He'd done it so often before. She had not always been right in the past when she'd stormed out, but she was now. Quest thought back to their first meeting. The lady novelists often referred to the concept of love at first sight. He wasn't sure that that had been the situation between them, though there was lust and liking in their initial moments, and those feelings had never gone away.

Quest had often considered what his life might be like without Rosa. He found that he couldn't even imagine it. He'd lost a lot of people he cared about, mostly through death. His life was diminished with their passing. There were just a few who were very close now. And the danger of the days meant that any one of them could be lost to him at any time.

Where was the peace of mind, once you knew that?

Quest set off again, on a long ramble through Covent Garden, and then to the river at Westminster, following the Thames right up to Chelsea. It was well into the morning before he returned to Bloomsbury.

The street outside his home was busy with pedestrians. A knife-sharpener was busily grinding blades outside the house of a neighbour. A street-sweeper, a member of Monkshood, who kept an eye on the neighbourhood around Quest's house winked an eye, nodding to a man across the street who was watching Quest.

Quest gave a little nod of thanks as he climbed the steps to his front door. He reached into the deep inner pocket of his coat and felt the wooden handle of the little pistol he kept concealed within. He was aware that the man had crossed Tavistock Place and was approaching him.

Someone familiar, smartly dressed, with a walking cane that looked as though it might conceal a sword-stick. A man he'd met once before, though it took Quest a moment to remember just where. He eased back the hammer on the pistol, even as he turned to face the man.

'Are you seeking me?' he asked.

'You are Quest?'

The man looked as tired as Quest felt, as though he might have been wandering the streets for most of the night as well. He was handsome in a rakish sort of way, though the fine lines around his eyes suggested a wearied body and soul.

'I don't think I've had the pleasure of your acquaintance,' said Quest.

'Oh, I believe you have,' said the visitor, 'though you weren't quite dressed as you are now. Much more formal. You were all in black with a dark cape round your shoulders.'

'I don't quite...'

The man gave a nervous laugh.

'You sat in a chair in my set in Albany. A chair in the corner of the room. You kept my own pistol trained upon me. I fear that your hand is placed even now on the stock of a similar pistol. You came to my rooms with the intention of killing me. We had an interesting... enlightened conversation. You spared my life, which in some cultures means that it is still at your disposal.'

'I don't believe in such debts,' said Quest.

'Nor do I, but in any case, I come to beg a favour, not to grant one. I can tell from your eyes that you know me. You are the one man in London who might be able to provide the advice I need.'

Quest looked the man up and down again, eased his pistol deeper into his pocket and brought out his hand from his coat.

'You are Sir Wren Angier,' he said.

Angier gave a bow.

'My title's but a baronetcy, inherited not earned. It ill-becomes my character these days. Do call me Angier, as I might call you Quest.'

'May I ask how you found me?'

'Not so difficult these days,' said Angier. 'You've made a mark in those dusty rooms at Westminster, where the likes of Lord Palmerston is wont to engage in gossip.'

'Palmerston sent you?'

Angier shook his head.

'Merely complained to me about you. As it happens, the Home Secretary would quite like you dead, Quest. But there's the matter of a certain notebook...'

'You've come for that?'

'Not at all,' said Angier. 'As I've indicated, this is a personal matter. A friend of mine's in trouble and I don't know how to render assistance. From my own experiences of you last year, I do believe that you might be able to help.'

Quest pondered for a moment, then took out his key.

'You interest me greatly, Angier. Perhaps you'd care to step inside?'

Quest unlocked the door and pushed it open, smiling at Sticks who was standing to one side of the doorway, a heavy cosh held in both hands.

~

He sat on the edge of the bed looking down at her, her long hair was draped across the pillow. The late morning sunlight seemed to turn the leaves on the tree brushing the window a very bright green. Outside he could hear the carriages working their way through the streets of this very select part of Chelsea and the conversations of the people on the pavement below.

'Exciting enough for you?' he asked.

'You or our recreation? Let's start with you,' she replied. 'You... please me enough. As for the other matter, well, I'd be a fool not to enjoy it. But we still have a long way to go.'

'I think I've done rather well,' he said. 'Getting so many to trust a complete outsider wasn't easy. When I first heard your plan I thought it a tad ambitious. I was wrong, I admit. But if we can carry it through, well...'

He gave a great burst of laughter.

'By the way, my book of verse is published tomorrow,' he said. 'I'm to do a reading tonight at the home of my publisher, Mr Murray. I do hope you may be able to attend?'

'Poetry bores me...' she yawned. 'Tell me, do your family approve yet?'

'I don't think they consider the writing of verse to be anything but an amusement. They expect better things from someone with my background and family connections.'

'Snobs!'

'Indeed. Are you sure you wouldn't care to attend? Mr Murray has great hopes for my reputation as a poet. His father published Byron, you know...'

She sat up in bed.

'Well, when I said I didn't like poetry, there are exceptions. I very much admire Byron, the man perhaps more than the verse. I always regret not living at the same time as him. I'm told he was so wonderfully entertaining in so many ways.'

'And I'm not?' he asked.

'Well, my dear, you're only just starting out. If you do the things I suggest, who knows where you might end up? I've every confidence in your abilities. Now, come and take me again. I have an appointment for luncheon and I really mustn't be late.'

~

'I confess to being puzzled,' said Quest. 'While I appreciate the efforts you've made to walk away from your previous life, I hadn't quite expected you to set yourself up as a champion of the persecuted. To be honest, it's hard to think of that old witch Bendig as a victim at all.'

'I can see why you might dislike her,' said Angier.

'In her own way she's brought considerable misery to a lot of people. And she's not averse to selling information on individuals to the police. Desperate men and women have been gaoled and transported on her word. So you can see why I'm not terribly sympathetic to any threats to her sordid little empire.'

'Then I must find out more about this Margam Boone myself,' said Angier. 'You might consider that Mrs Bendig is not perhaps his only victim.'

Quest looked across at Angier. Less than a year ago, Monkshood had decreed that the man must die, and that Quest should be his assassin.

But at the last moment, what should have been Angier's final few seconds on earth, Quest had changed his mind. He'd received a great deal of criticism for his act of mercy, but had been proved right. Angier had changed his ways, and now he was demonstrating a desire to go further.

'This building by the river? You're sure it's deserted?'

'Well, Boone went there. He was obviously meeting someone.'

Angier stood and took up his sword-stick.

'You intend to go there?' asked Quest.

'It might hold the solution to Boone's associates.'

'But it might not. You say that this man is a lawyer specialising in the conveyance of property? Is it not most likely that he might just

131

have a legal interest in this building? He might be helping to assure its sale.'

'There was no indication that the property was for sale,' said Angier. 'I happen to know from my work in parliament that all of that area is marked out for a re-development. It's probable that a new railway station will consume that very alley.'

'With respect, Angier, you've followed Boone for just a day. These are considerable speculations to make on just one outing. My friends and I often follow men for weeks and still find little real evidence of what they are about.'

'I don't know what else to do,' said Angier. 'It would be difficult for me to follow Boone on my own. I have a feeling that this building by the river is worth examining.'

Quest looked across the room at Sticks.

'No good looking at me!' said Sticks. 'You know damned well you're going down there!'

'I am indeed,' said Quest. 'You'll accompany me, Angier? And be assured I'm not doing this for that dreadful woman. I'll examine this building because I believe your story sounds familiar to me. Others have been threatened in London, some killed. There's probably no connection, but we have to grasp at the slightest straw.'

'We're to go now?' asked Angier.

'Why not? There's a possibility that Boone might still be there. And that vicinity is safer in daylight than in the dark.'

~

Jedediah Mooth stirred on the bed, his eyes rolling and a horrible gurgling sound coming from his throat. His right arm thrashed the harsh wool blanket, seeming to have a life of its own.

'Is he dying?' Anders asked the doctor.

The medical man smiled.

'Not at all,' he replied, 'rather he's coming back to life.'

'But that sound, doctor? Like a death rattle...' said Berry.

'You must understand, gentlemen, this patient sustained a very severe constriction to the throat, not to mention the bruising around his neck. The trauma of the experience of being hanged might well have caused him to become deranged.'

'Given those injuries, will it be physically possible for him to talk when he becomes fully conscious?' asked Anders.

The doctor shrugged.

'Far too early to tell,' he said. 'But the man's not dead. You say he was a preacher?'

'Of a sort,' said Berry.

'Then he can presumably read and write. Even if he can't talk, he should be able to note down answers to any questions you care to put to him. That may be your best hope, though there's no physiological reason why he won't be able to talk in time.'

Anders nodded.

'Very well.' He turned to Berry. 'I want two more constables stationed here, sergeant. Your best man at Mooth's bedside to note down anything he might say. But above all I don't want him left alone. Not for a moment. If the man who had him hanged discovers that he's alive and conscious, who knows what might happen.'

~

'I doubt the door's been left unlocked,' said Quest. 'Otherwise the place'd be crammed with every poor wretch without a roof over them. No, I thought not...'

He turned the handle, very carefully.

'You intend to go in through the front door?' asked Angier.

'Why not? Your man Boone does, so it's probably the safest entrance for us. It's the little entrances around the back of such places that tend to have traps set around them. The main entrance might be watched, but it's seldom set for the more unpleasant kind of ambush.'

'Quite a stout lock, that. And new by the look of it,' said Sticks. 'Why would someone put a new lock on a hovel like this? Best get the Bettys out...'

He reached inside his fustian jacket and produced a small package, which he handed to Quest.

'Bettys?' asked Angier.

'Picklocks,' said Quest, showing him the collection of wires and rods. Heaven knows why they're called Bettys. I was taught to use them when I was very young.'

He knelt down and examined the lock before selecting one particular picklock, thicker than most of the others.

'There's no key on the inside,' he said, 'so let's hope nobody's at home...'

He eased in the picklock, seeming to feel around inside the lock. Angier saw Quest smile and give a nod to Sticks. Then Quest gave a rapid rightwards twist. There was a dull clunk from within the door.

'The showier the lock, the easier it opens,' muttered Sticks. 'They never learn...'

'Could be bolted,' suggested Quest.

'Only if there's someone in there,' said Sticks. 'I reckon they'll think that fancy lock is enough. Are we all going in?'

'Well I am...' said Angier.

'The two of us should be enough,' said Quest.

'Then I'll just hide mesself over in the corner of the wall yonder,' said Sticks. 'Blow on yer whistle if yer needs my assistance. I'll start singing like a drunkard if anyone comes a-walking down this alley.'

'Be ready with your swordstick,' said Quest to Angier, as he eased open the door.

It took them a while for their eyes to get used to the dimness, for the windows were all shuttered. The long room must at some time have been a workshop. There were tables set around the walls and three occupied much of the middle of the room. A few broken chairs lay scattered around. A thick layer of dust covered all of these and the floor.

'Looks deserted,' said Angier.

'Not quite,' said Quest, indicating the bare boards of the floor. A narrow path had been created through the filth, winding round the tables and leading across the room to a flight of stairs. There seemed to be no doors at ground level to anywhere else.

'They obviously don't use this room,' said Angier.

'Too easy to access,' Quest replied. 'A mob could crash through that door with little warning and be on anyone in here. Notice how those big heavy tables have been arranged to force men to go round them to reach the foot of the stairs. That would buy them some time to get away, if they were in the rooms above.'

Quest reached inside his coat and brought out his pistol.

'Better to be prepared,' he said, as they wound their way through the tables to the steps beyond. Quest held up a hand and stopped then for a good three minutes. The timbers of the old building groaned in the slight breeze from the river. They could hear distant shouts from vessels out on the Thames.

Quest noticed the inquiring look on Angier's face.

'It seems quiet enough,' Angier whispered.

'Let's see just how quiet it is when we get up the stairs,' said Quest. 'Be ready for anything...'

But the next floor of the building was just as deserted. It was obviously another workshop like the first, filled with furniture and broken tables. The dust indicated that nobody recently had bothered to even enter the vast room, only along a narrow path leading to the next flight of stairs.

The next two floors were much the same. Yet more abandoned workplaces, with a decade of dust and cobwebs across the floor and tables.

'I fear I've wasted your time,' said Angier.

'You seem disappointed?' said Quest.

'I like to know the answers. I wanted this matter of Boone resolved once and for all. I thought this place might produce a solution.'

Quest waved his pistol in the direction of the final flight of steps.

'It might yet,' he said.

He took in a deep breath and began to ascend. When his head came level with the floor of the storey above, he peered over. Angier saw Quest smile.

'A busier place, anyway,' Quest whispered, going up to the top of the stairs.

The room was narrower than the workshops below, occupying perhaps just half of the old building. There were three closed doors in the far wall, suggesting that the rooms beyond might have been the offices of this riverside enterprise.

A solitary table with a dozen serviceable chairs around it, occupied the centre of the room. Both men noticed that there was no dust on the floor or furniture here. As though the top room of the building was regularly swept. Along the far wall, below narrow but un-shuttered windows looking out towards the Thames, were a line of narrow tables, with a desk in the far corner piled with ledgers and loose papers.

Angier pointed towards it.

'They may repay reading,' he said, dashing across the floor towards the desk, evading Quest's attempt to restrain him, a look of triumph in his eyes.

'Angier, no!' Quest cried out, but too late.

Angier was just two yards in front of the desk, when the wooden boards parted. A huge trap door fell away carrying Angier with it, out of sight.

Quest heard the man's cry of fear, as he dashed across the room to the edge of the trap door. He rested his pistol on the floorboards and looked down. Angier was hanging by his fingers from the end of the trap, his face white.

This edge of the building hung over the river, where the stakes and piling of some ancient boat landing pointed upwards. If Angier fell away from the outside wall he would end up in the Thames. But more likely he would be impaled on the wooden points below. Angier looked down and then back at Quest, a look of terror on his face.

Quest reached down and tried to grab the man's hand, but the trap door was too long. However much he stretched, even at the risk of his own safety, left him a good foot away from being able to grasp Angier's hand.

'Hold on,' Quest said.

Hurriedly taking off his coat he lowered it towards the dangling man. Angier, whose fingers were sliding off the rotten wood of the trap door, grabbed the cloth with a sigh of relief. Quest wrapped his end of the coat around one shoulder and began to pull the desperate man towards him.

But so much was Quest's concentration on Angier's desperate predicament, that he neglected to even glance back across the room.

If the attacker hadn't yelled, he would have succeeded in sending both Quest and Angier tumbling down on to the wooden stakes or into the river.

But his mistaken triumphant cry made Quest look away from the peril of the trap door. Gave him a precious moment to reach out for his pistol with his left hand. Quest heard Angier gasp as the coat slipped downwards, but he managed to hold it fast even as he raised the weapon.

The attacker was dressed like a stevedore, burly, with a huge round face. He held a wide-bladed old military sabre above his head and was now only a yard from Quest. The weapon was starting a downward path towards Quest's head when the pistol barked.

Quest hadn't had a chance to aim, but at that distance there was no risk of missing. The ball hit the man on the right hand side of his chest, but it didn't stop the impetus of his charge. His legs crashed into Quest, and the attacker screamed as he fell forward through the trap, colliding with Angier as he plummeted downwards.

In a second, Quest twisted back round to see Angier hanging from the coat by one hand, the other hand waving about. Quest reached forward and seized it. With a great shout he heaved Angier upwards and hauled him out of the hole and on to the floorboards.

As they both gasped for breath, they looked back down through the trap. The stevedore lay across one jagged wooden piling, his body almost broken in two. A great cloud of blood was turning the filthy waters of the Thames a vivid red.

Angier tried to say something, but no words came. He steadied himself and drew in a great breath. His cane lay nearby on the floorboards and he used it to lever himself back on to his feet. He looked back down through the trap.

'That could have been me,' he said at last.

'But it wasn't,' said Quest, 'and a miss is as good as a mile.'

'How can you be so calm about it?'

'I'm never calm,' said Quest, very seriously.

'Then you're used to it?'

'I suppose I am...'

'I hope to God I never get used to it,' said Angier. 'I've always had my adventures second-hand, and I...'

He followed Quest's eyes which were now looking away from him and across the room. Three more roughs had emerged through an open door on the far side.

One was armed with a cutting hook, the kind of instrument used to open crates down on the docks, the others carried heavy coshes. As they watched, the three men began to advance towards them around the table.

Out of the corner of his eye, Quest noticed Angier looking at him nervously. He reached down and lifted up his coat. Fortunately, his second pistol was still in the deep pocket. He brought it out, pulled back the hammer and held the weapon in front of him.

The three dockers hesitated for a moment.

Then the stevedore with the cutting hook brought his other hand from behind his back and produced a pistol. He levelled the weapon at Quest.

'We've a shot each,' Quest shouted across at him. 'You drop me and I'll certainly drop you before I die.'

'Works the other way,' grunted the stevedore. 'In any case, there's three of us and only two of you. Yer'll both die and two of us might live.'

Very slowly Angier withdrew his sword-stick out of its protecting cane.

'I hope you knows how to use that?' grunted the stevedore.

'Well enough,' said Angier.

'But then he won't have to,' said a voice from the stairwell.

They all turned their heads at the same time. Sticks was standing on the steps, covering the three roughs with a pair of pistols.

'Three shots an' all three of you drops,' said Sticks. 'Now, who wants to be the first dead hero?'

The three stevedores glanced at each other. The man with the pistol slowly lowered the weapon.

'It'd be wise if you all put your weapons down on the boards,' said Quest. 'We'll let you live, but I want to know just why you're trying to kill us and an awful lot about the man you work for.'

'Not bloody likely!' muttered the man with the pistol.

'Your friend in the middle's very bold,' said Quest. 'It'll probably be the death of him. But neither of you others have to die. I'll not only let you go, but I'll give you a bag of sovereigns to help you fund a new life away from London.'

Quest could see the look of defeat on the faces of the other two men, saw the coshes slipping down through their fingers. He saw something else too, greed at the very mention of gold coins. One of the coshes fell to the floor.

'What d'we have to do?' muttered the rough who'd been holding it.

'You keep your bloody trap shut!' yelled the man with the pistol. 'You peach and it's death for us all.'

'I'm not dying for him!' proclaimed the other rough. 'He wouldn't die for me! And if this man gives us gold we can be so far from London he'll never get us.'

He looked across at Quest.

'You mean it? You'll give us money and not hand us over to the crushers?'

'You have my word,' Quest replied.

'Then I'll...'

The man took a step forward.

'No, you bloody won't!'

The other stevedore pressed the pistol against the man's back. The sound of the shot seemed to fill the room, the crash of the echo bringing dust down from the ceiling to mingle with the smoke.

Even as the dying man tumbled forwards, both of Sticks' pistols barked, one shot catching the armed stevedore in the side of the face, the other tearing into his chest. He swirled round, smashing against the table before falling across one of the chairs and then down to the floor.

A terrible noise seemed to fill the room. It took Angier a moment to realise that it was the sound of the third and youngest stevedore screaming. The man had dropped his cosh and was holding a protective arm in front of his face.

He seemed to be rooted to the spot, then suddenly dashed forwards towards Quest and Angier, seeming not even to see them. He paused for only a second before flinging himself out through the trap door. The outward momentum saved him from the splintered pilings beneath, and he hit the brown waters of the Thames with a mighty splash.

Quest and Angier studied the river, but could see no sign of the man surfacing.

'Could he have survived?' asked Angier.

'He missed the pilings, but it's a long way down and he was in a state of panic.' Quest shook his head. 'I can't see a trace of him. Perhaps he couldn't swim.'

'I'm a thinking we should get out of here,' Sticks said, looking over their shoulders. 'Who knows how far all that shooting might have carried?'

'I agree,' said Quest. 'But we'll take the papers from the desk with us. One thing's for sure. This isn't some innocent building that Boone has a legal interest in. Those three watchdogs were here for a purpose. That villain had a good quality pistol. One he'd never be able to afford for himself. Let's grab those papers and get out of here.'

Thirteen

'How do you cope with it?' asked Angier. 'The peril, I mean, and the killing?'

He and Quest were sitting in the study in Quest's house in Bloomsbury, drinking brandy and looking out of the window at the last of the evening sunlight.

'You don't,' said Quest. 'No rational man could ever cope with experiences like that. You just bury them deep inside. But even that's no answer. The darker moments tend to resurface when you least expect them. In the dead of night, or in the quiet moments of a country walk.'

Sticks poured out more brandy.

'Best not dwell on 'em at all,' he said. 'They were men who were going to kill you, and would have done it without anything preying on their consciences. We've done the old world a good turn by sending them to hell.'

Angier sipped his brandy and looked at Quest.

'Last year... you were going to send me to hell,' he said. 'I know the life I led. There are still days and nights of shame in what I do. Pleasures that exploit others...'

'You've come a long way...' said Quest.

'Not far enough. Today... even today... I followed Boone and went into that building with you as some sort of lark. I didn't do any of it for the reasons you would have.'

'Few do have my reasons.'

'I envy you, Quest,' said Angier.

'What for?'

'Your courage. I could hardly move today when they attacked us, I was so scared.'

'Fear is natural.'

'But you weren't frozen to the spot.'

'There was a time when I would have been. It's a horrible thing to admit, but you get used to it. And that's the most terrible thing of all. The real question, Angier, is would you be prepared to do it all over again?'

'I'd like to believe I might. There's still the matter of Boone.'

'Well, given what happened to us down by the Thames, there's no doubt the man's dishonest. Those men weren't just hired watchmen. They were killers.'

'Then we have more work to do? You've told me about this King of Jacob's Island. Do you believe there's a connection between him and Boone?'

Quest considered.

'They are certainly both in the same line of work,' he said. 'Threatening dubious business empires like Bendig's night house. Trying to seize control of criminal enterprises. It seems likely to me there's a connection.'

'So we go on?' asked Angier.

'Are you game for it?'

'I'm still shuddering with fear... but I won't duck out now.'

'Very well,' said Quest, walking across to the writing table by the wall. 'Let's have a look at these papers we've snatched.'

~

'What the devil's happening?' asked Anders. 'It's as though a war's broken out in London.'

'A couple of Thames watermen reported seeing the body on the pilings. When the constable went into the building he found the two men upstairs, shot dead.'

They were walking down the alley towards the old riverside building. Darkness was starting to fall and raindrops were pattering on the cobbles.

'You've seen the bodies?' asked Anders.

'The two upstairs. They're still trying to prise the man off the pilings. Completely impaled. Not pleasant work. I don't recognise the men. They look like stevedores, but then stevedores don't usually end up being shot. Do you think this has anything to do with the other business?'

'Yes, I do,' said Anders. 'If they'd been knifed or beaten around the head, I might believe it's a dockyard brawl. But pistols? Since when did stevedores get involved in fights with pistols? What is this building?'

'It used to be a blacking manufactory. The company moved its premises to Stepney three years ago. It's stood empty since then.

The whole area's set for demolition. There's to be a new railway station and substantial changes to the waterfront.'

'Probably for the best,' said Anders, 'the building's rotting away. I thought the stench from the river was bad enough at Scotland Yard, but it's almost unbearable here.'

Berry pushed open the door and they entered the old building.

'I want to know who owns this, Berry? And before these bodies are taken away, I want you to get the constable to bring a selection of local dockers and stevedores here to see them. I want to know just who these men are?'

~

'What's it all mean?' asked Sticks, watching Quest turn over the pages of the ledger. 'Just accounts from the old manufactory that was in the building. Nothing of use at all.'

The loose papers proved to be just advertisements for a blacking company, one of the ledgers was completely unused, and the other held a list of financial transactions, no more than a commonplace profit and loss account.

'Nothing at all to do with any shady business,' said Angier. 'Not unlike the books I used to keep...'

Quest turned another page and then thumbed towards the back of the ledger.

'I'm not so sure it's that simple,' he said. 'Where is any indication that these are sales made, or products bought? No customers or suppliers listed. Just amounts in money alongside random letters.'

'You think it's a code?' asked Angier.

'I do. If you were keeping the accounts for some illegal enterprise, you wouldn't list the names of the people you were threatening. You'd give them an identifying letter or number in your ledger and keep the cipher somewhere else, supposing you didn't know it by heart.'

'And these payments out?' asked Angier, running his finger down a column.

'Payments for employees,' suggested Quest.

'Employees?'

'Why not? A racket on this sort of scale would demand the employment of a great many roughs, such as the ones we encountered today.'

'It's possible,' said Angier, turning slightly red.

Quest guessed that Angier was remembering the men he'd employed to chase the debtors of his money-lending business.

He turned over more pages of the ledger. It was about three-quarters full. Then there were a number of empty pages. He examined them carefully, concerned that not a clue should be missed.

And then, near the back, the pages were filled with writing in a neat hand.

'Our book-keeper's a poet!' exclaimed Angier.

On the last few pages were fragments of verse, some odd lines, differing versions of the same poem. Some had a diagonal line drawn across them entirely, with a fresh attempt made underneath. Occasionally a single word was crossed out, with several alternatives listed below.

'He takes his work seriously,' said Quest. 'What do you think?'

'I loathe poetry,' said Angier. 'A good sensational novel's more my thing.'

'Well, I've seen worse,' said Sticks, looking down at the verse, 'though I prefers a good novel myself, Mr Borrow or Mr Dickens maybe. Something with a bit of life about them.'

'One thing's for sure,' said Quest. 'These verses are in the same hand as the one that's kept up the business transactions in this ledger. I wonder if he's published. He has a distinctive style. If he has been published, we might be able to track him down.'

'I've some acquaintances in the publishing world,' said Angier. 'Tear me out one of those pages and I'll see if anyone recognises his hand.'

~

Wissilcraft was sitting at the table in his dining-room, not even seeing the documents piled in front of him. Night had fallen and the gaslight was in a stuttering mood. It was long past time to eat, but he'd told his servants that he was not hungry and that they might retire to bed. He heard the front door open and close. A minute later his sister entered the room.

'Where are the servants?' she asked. 'I had to let myself in.'

'I dismissed them for the evening. I wasn't sure you'd be back tonight.'

He looked at her curiously.

'Why shouldn't I be?' she said.

'Sometimes you are and sometimes you aren't.'

'I've been to a reading of poetry, at the home of Mr Murray the publisher.'

'Poetry!' he almost spluttered. 'When did you acquire an interest in poetry?'

'I've always liked poetry.'

'You have not! I remember well our father trying to interest you in verse. Apart from that dreadful Byron, you took no interest at all.'

'Byron was not a dreadful poet.'

'He led a shameful life.'

'Shame can be very poetic. And what you call shame might be someone else's pleasure. Why are you in such a disputatious mood, brother?'

'I've spent much of the day with Lord Palmerston...'

'Not the most pleasurable way to pass the time, I admit. He's such a bore. Especially in bed.'

'It's a pity he didn't fatally succumb to your passions, Angeline. It would have spared me an awful day.'

'If you really wanted him to succumb, well, I'd be willing to try again. For a substantial reward. He wouldn't be the first to die in such a way.'

'One day they'll put a rope around your pretty neck...'

'Undoubtedly...'

She stood behind him and massaged his shoulders.

'So, what's the old mongoose done to grieve you, brother?'

Wissilcraft gave a great sigh.

'The usual matter...'

'The notebook and the mysterious Mr Quest?'

'Exactly...'

'Quest has a political agenda. He wants to overthrow everything you and Palmerston hold dear. What I can't understand is why he doesn't publish the information in the notebook? He could achieve many of his aims in a week.'

'But once he'd let slip his dogs of war, he knows we'd have him. His possession of the notebook is his only safeguard against arrest for his many other crimes.'

'If it achieved his ends, do you think he'd care?'

'Then why hasn't he?'

Angeline Wissilcraft dug her fingers harder into her brother's shoulders.

'It would be interesting to know,' she said. 'Even if he didn't go as far as that, he might blackmail individuals. He could end up a very rich man. Powerful too.'

'Wealth and power are the least of his motivations.'

'How strange...'

'The problem is I can never anticipate Quest's next move.'

She drew a hand across his brow.

'Would you like me to find out?' she asked. 'It might be amusing to try.'

'Mr Quest seems to have resisted your charms so far.'

'So far isn't far enough,' she said.

~

Rosa Stanton looked around her room, at the theatrical costumes lining the walls and the empty bed. She glared at herself in the mirror, not quite liking what she saw. Rosa felt like smashing her hand into the glass but decided not to do it. It was a lovely long mirror and might be hard to replace.

It had been days now and still he'd not called to see her, damn him! They had had plenty of rows in the past, but they'd never lasted very long. Their desire for each other usually overcame any temporary difficulties.

Three times Rosa had dressed to go out, intending to make her way to Tavistock Place. She'd even thought of renouncing all theatrical ambitions if that's what it took. Three times she'd taken her hat and cape off again and returned to her upstairs room.

Why hadn't Quest come to see her?

It reminded her of a time in her father's country vicarage, not that many years ago. One night after evensong, Rosa had announced to the old parson her intention to take up the acting profession. She had never seen such a look of absolute horror on his face before.

Her father had stared at her for a very long time before replying with the words, 'I think not!'

Then he had looked down and started to read his Bible, not even acknowledging her presence in the room.

She knew her words had hurt him. Every night of her life Rosa had lain in bed, last thing at night, and listened to his footsteps on the creaking wooden stairs. Every night of her life he'd said 'Good night, Rosa, and God Bless!' through her door as he passed her room.

That night he didn't, nor any night that followed. Worse than that, he had scarcely spoken to her in the three weeks before she finally left home.

Being under-age, Rosa had waited until she knew her father would be away for the day – a meeting with the bishop in the nearby cathedral city. She had written a long letter the night before, and left it in his study.

The servants were away for the day, and the only person at home was her younger brother, Daniel.

Rosa had told him everything, for despite his youth they had always shared confidences. Daniel had wept and begged her not to go. He was a keen reader and devoured the works of Mr Dickens. London was such a dreadful place. She would almost certainly be exploited by villains, he exclaimed...

And in some ways, she thought, she had been.

But only villains of the best quality, she mused, and quite a while after she'd at least worked on the stage. And there had been William Quest, and she missed him, but...

Rosa suddenly felt a wave of anger at herself. She was almost on the verge of succumbing to sentimentality. And that would never do...

Two days only before her next appointment with Madame Vestris. An informal meeting to meet the other players. Rehearsals were still a week or two away. But how she relished the prospect of them. And as for Mr William bloody Quest, he could roast in...

'Damn you, Will!'

Rosa hurled a hairbrush at the reflection in the mirror.

~

'I can see it's not good news,' said Anders.

Berry slumped into the office chair.

'No news at all,' he said. 'I spent all day trooping dockers and stevedores past the bodies in the manufactory. Nobody knew them and certainly nobody had worked alongside them.'

'They *looked* like stevedores.'

'Might have done, sir, but not from any dock or wharf in London, unless half the river workers are born liars. I've had most of the constables in the force down there as well, workhouse guardians and parish priests. Unless they're all part of a conspiracy, these men aren't local.'

Anders shuffled the papers on the table.

'Best circulate descriptions to other constabularies. Given the way they died, these men must be known to someone. Go through their clothes again. They can't have just appeared from nowhere. Now, what else have we got?'

'Only Jacob's Island,' said Berry.

'Well, as it happens, I've been talking to a friend of mine, Higgins at the London County Council, about that wretched place. Our lords and masters certainly intend to have much of it demolished. It took them all a while to acknowledge its very existence.'

'What about the residents?'

'Not as many as you might think,' said Anders. 'Apparently the cholera outbreak last year put a lot of them underground. For a while it was more or less deserted, though Higgins said there's been a drift back in recent months.'

'Heaven knows why. The Thames is as filthy as ever and the little river Neckinger's no better than an open sewer. A place of death. I only went in there once, that time we took Mr Dickens. The stench was over-powering.'

Anders reached across to the bookshelf alongside his table, taking down the bound parts of *Oliver Twist*.

'Dickens must have been there before his visit with you, when he wrote this. And he certainly didn't exaggerate. Higgins says it's improved since then...'

'Perhaps the King's brought some sort of order to the place?'

'Not the sort of order I'm keen on. We'll have to go in there, I'm afraid, whatever our blessed Commissioner thinks. We might have to rely on the services of Quest and his villains. I don't know yet. Is there anything we can do now?'

Berry scratched his chin.

'Only Molly Bendig,' he said. 'Whatever she says, I think someone's threatening her and her business empire. I told you about the rat? Yes, and one of her women who keeps me informed, says that she's had a menacing visitor.'

Anders looked askance at his sergeant.

'You've a spy amongst her whores?'

'Not one of her whores exactly. Her servant as it happens. I slip her a few coins from time to time. Much of what she gets is just gossip, but she did tell me that this gent had come a-calling and disconcerted the old haybag.'

Anders shook his head.

'Might not be connected,' he said. 'Her night house might be immoral but it's hardly a criminal enterprise like these others we know about. And it's a step from the river. Still, if we've nothing else. You'd better go and have a word, and don't be too gentle about it. Money or threats. Whatever you think will work best.'

'Money or threats? Better not let Commissioner Mayne get wind of either,' said Berry.

~

How beautiful it could be, thought the poet, as he wandered across Westminster Bridge, admiring the Thames and London in all its splendour.

These parts of the city that offered the finest aspects to the human eye stood apart from anything else in his experience. But even Westminster had its slums and rookeries, its corners of unpleasantness, though it was harder to see them from this vantage point.

Wordsworth had been a crashing old bore in his poetry, so very much of the time but he'd got that right. His poem of the view from Westminster Bridge was still one of the poet's favourites, though he would never admit it to his fellows.

It was a wonderful view, he considered, as he looked across the Thames to Whitehall, despite the disruption of the present works in hand.

The new parliament building was still under construction, following the disastrous fire. The builders shouted and yelled, yet they couldn't take away the magic of the setting. They'd been at work now for over ten years and there was still a great deal to do.

Sad that he couldn't quite see the view known to Wordsworth, but that was the past. Building works were sweeping away much of the London he'd known as a boy. This transformation was the subject of the great poem he was writing. He'd read the first two cantos at the home of Mr Murray, his publisher. There hadn't been many people there, but he'd been cheered by his reception.

His was a new kind of poetry, he had abandoned romanticism and brought what he hoped was realism to his verse. He had seen how, initially, it had shocked his audience – and then enthralled them, as they understood his portrayal of a London they already knew.

One day he would write a better verse about the view from Westminster, and about the sadness of the bridge itself. They said the bridge had begun to subside and was expensive to maintain. One day there would have to be a new bridge, but it wouldn't be the same. It just wouldn't. So much history would go with its demolition. Even the memories of William Wordsworth.

The poet sighed. He would have to write an elegy to Westminster Bridge. Such a poem might seal his reputation as the coming man in English literature. Reference, but elbow aside, the poets of the dead age that had gone before.

There was a chill in the breeze that swept down the river but the poet felt warmed by the prospect. Darkness was falling, but there was time to write more of his destiny on this old city.

Fourteen

The crowds were pouring out of the theatres in Haymarket, well-dressed gentlemen being accosted by the better class of street whores.

Ladies hurried into their carriages, dragging their husbands behind them, pretending not to notice these other forms of London entertainment. There must be at least three hundred prostitutes working the street this night, Quest thought as he pushed through their ranks.

Ever since he was a boy he'd found this part of London to be quite fascinating, this almost sanctioned coming together of those who sought sin and those who sold it. Quest had never succumbed to its temptations. He'd never had a need to. But he knew many a gentleman who did, many who spent an hour or two in the streets all around before going home to their wives.

There were others, bachelors and married men who had an excuse not to go home at all, who would party and play the night away at one of the night houses. But that was a very expensive recreation. No wonder the awful Mrs Bendig could be considering retirement in a villa at the sea-side.

Quest had found the need to go for a walk. Only in motion could he really clear his mind for thinking. He had tapped on Rosa's door as he wandered down from Bloomsbury, but there had been no response. Whether she had heard him or not, he didn't know. There had certainly been a light on in her rooms. He liked to believe she hadn't heard him knock.

But the possibility that she had heard his cane rapping on the door and ignored it, upset him. When he left his home in Tavistock Place, he had told himself that he had no intention of seeing Rosa. He knew in his heart it was a lie, that his need for a perambulation through the streets of London was just an excuse. He had wanted, somehow, to make things right between them. But the rapping on the door, increasing in volume, had been ignored...

Quest felt a heaviness in his chest and his stomach, a feeling he often experienced when he couldn't advance matters in any direction. He felt tired too, tired of London with its heaving streets and alleys. This was no place for a walk. He yearned for the deep woodlands and airy tops which might be reached from his country home at Hope Down. The peace of sitting in his favourite country churchyard, listening to the rooks in the trees. Watching the robin working the hedgerows in the meadows thereabouts. Feeling the peace that always came upon him on country walks.

He felt a wave of anger that he was trapped in London for the foreseeable future. The streets which had once promised adventure and mystery, had now become oppressive, claustrophobic. And every corner reminded him of exploits with Rosa.

Quest felt the heavy feeling again in his chest. He wondered if he was sickening for something. The reality was, as he knew too well, that the illness originated in his mind and not his body.

Her hand was on his shoulder, but not Rosa's hand he noted, as he saw it out of the corner of his eye. He knew her hand so very well. Quest thought for a moment that he was being accosted by one of the street whores. He turned swiftly, angrily...

'You walked right past me, Mr Quest,' said Angeline Wissilcraft.

Even in the gaslight, her eyes seemed almost unnaturally blue. Her lips parted as she smiled.

'You seem to be in a great hurry,' she said. 'Do you have an urgent appointment?'

Quest looked around expecting to see her brother with her, or at least a companion.

'This isn't a safe time for a lady to be about unaccompanied,' he said. 'Nor a safe place.'

Angeline laughed.

'Isn't it risk that makes life so delightful?' she asked.

'Not here. Not now. I'll walk you back to your home, if you care?'

'Now that would be a disappointment. London is such a place for an adventure, don't you think? And we haven't had any sort of adventure together yet....'

'Do you think it appropriate that we should?' he asked.

'Life is very short.'

They walked up to the top of Haymarket. The silence that had suddenly sprung up seemed like a physical barrier. Quest really wanted her to go away, so that he might be alone with his thoughts.

But then she slipped her arm through his and he changed his mind.

'Do you still work with your brother?' he asked.

'Work with my brother? I'm not sure I know what you mean?'

'Just something he said last year,' said Quest. 'I was lying wounded in a tavern in Norfolk. Your brother had taken a trifle too much brandy. He told me that you supported him in his work as a government spy.'

He felt her arm tighten against his own.

'Only in the sense that one family member might support another,' she said at last. 'My brother has no wife. I do what I can to make his few restful hours more pleasant.'

'He implied more...'

'There's no more to tell,' she said.

She was leading him across the road, dodging through the line of carriages that were taking people away from the theatres. They were moving rather swiftly, as though Angeline Wissilcraft had some definite destination in mind.

'We're going somewhere?' he asked.

'I know a little place in Soho where they don't mind the spectacle of an unattached man and woman sharing a drink,' she said.

'It would be most inappropriate, Miss Wissilcraft,' he said.

'Inappropriate, but fun.'

'Where is this place?'

She named a premise in Frith Street.

He laughed.

'I think not, Miss Wissilcraft.'

'Why not?'

'Because it's a most notorious house of assignation.'

'Then you've been there before?'

'Not within its doors,' he said.

'I assure you it's a very respectable place... of its kind. And I'm very much in need of... refreshment.'

'You know there's been cholera in Soho?' he said.

'There always is cholera... somewhere. But not where we are going.'

The streets were narrower now, some busier than others, the area populated by a strange mixture of the very poor, their faces pinched with hunger, and colourful gentlemen, smartly dressed, many of the latter carrying stout walking sticks, or canes which looked as though they might conceal a blade.

On one street corner an artist sat on a stool, painting colourful daubs of the passing scene. A group of well-dressed boys, mollies by the look of them, Quest thought, were laughing and carousing as they rushed through the crowds. As he watched he saw one of the bolder lads embrace the fellow nearest, and two or three more touching hands.

As they walked deeper into Soho, he saw more than a few familiar faces, though none who knew of him as William Quest. He'd first walked these streets as a pick-pocketing boy called Billy Marshall, and more recently as Bludger Bill, the tough from Seven Dials that nobody dared to cross.

They walked on and the air around them and the tall buildings thereabouts suddenly seemed to shudder. From the sky there came a great crash. Quest looked up, the stars and moon had vanished. There was only blackness.

'A thunderstorm,' he remarked.

'Splendid!' said Angeline. 'There's no more fascinating sight in nature.'

'You are not alarmed?'

'Should I be? You're not, so why should I be? But I do think we should hurry to our destination before the rain commences. Neither of us is dressed for rain.'

The crowds had hurried away by the time they reached the southern end of Frith Street. There was a sudden stillness in the atmosphere. They could hear little but the distant clop of horses. The thunder crashed again.

She swung round in front of Quest, her hands encircling his neck, those blue eyes gazing into his own. She reached up, her tongue parting his lips, beginning to explore his mouth. He stood there for a moment, unsurprised, for surely their adventure was bound to lead to this. But even so...

He pulled back his head, disengaging himself from her embrace.

'This isn't a good idea, Miss Wissilcraft.'

She shrugged.

'I think it's a very good idea, Mr Quest. But in any case, you can hardly abandon me now, not in the middle of Soho.' She held out a hand, palm upwards. 'And now the rain really is starting. The premises I mentioned are just a few yards away. We might at least seek shelter there until the storm has passed.'

A large man with a great dyed moustache greeted them as Quest pushed through the stout wooden doors. Was it his imagination, or did he see a flicker of recognition as the host spotted Angeline Wissilcraft? The man beamed a smile. He had teeth like gravestones.

'Sir... Madam?'

'We're in need of refreshment,' said Angeline.

'Yes, indeed, ma'am.'

The host glanced out through the high-set windows.

'A terrible storm,' he remarked. 'The rain is really quite heavy. You are wise to seek shelter.'

He waved an arm to draw them further into the entrance hall.

'Would you care for a compartment or a room?'

'A room, I think,' said Angeline.

'Miss Wissilcraft...' Quest said.

She put her mouth close to his ear.

'The compartments here are so dreadfully cramped. And all very close together. Conversations can so easily be overheard. Are you frightened for your virtue, William? Surely that should be my fear?'

Quest didn't like the expression on the host's face. Something too smug, too knowing. He felt a terrible desire to punch him. Quest really wanted to walk out and back into the storm. But some instinct was telling him to remain.

'I can recommend the brandy,' the host said.

'Excellent,' said Angeline. 'Please have it sent up to the room at once.'

The host snapped his fingers. A fair-haired, pallid boy appeared from a corridor at the back of the room, holding a pewter tray. He held his head to one side as he looked up at his master.

'Sir?'

'Brandy, Cain. Take it up to number twelve straight away. Quickly, boy, quickly. Our two guests mustn't be kept waiting. And make sure the fire is lit...'

Cain gave a little bow and vanished at great speed.

'I don't believe you've been here before?' said the host, looking directly at Quest.

Quest shook his head, noticing that the question seemed to be directed only at him and not Angeline Wissilcraft. He glanced at her, but she seemed to be studying the ceiling, the way people do when they are impatient and bored.

'Might I take your hat and cloak?' the host said to him. 'They'll be quite safe in my private parlour. Perhaps your cane too.'

'I think not,' said Quest. 'I may wish to depart very quickly if the rain stops.'

The host rubbed his hands together and gushed an even broader smile.

'Sir, once you've felt the warmth of the fire and enjoyed the comfort of the room, not to mention tasting our best brandy, I doubt you'll ever want to leave at all.'

He gave a hideous little laugh, and blinked at his customers.

'Now, if you'd care to follow me...'

He led them along the corridor through a double-row of wooden compartments, several already filled with carousing customers. Quest could hear loud conversations, the squeal of women and the laughter of men. Great clouds of tobacco smoke seemed to permeate through the cracks around the doors. As they approached the staircase Quest heard a woman cry out, though it was hard to tell whether with it was with fear or passion.

The host turned and gestured outwards with his hands, as though he was embarrassed by so blatant a noise.

'If you would follow me,' he said, leading them up the narrow staircase, on to a landing and then along an ever narrower corridor.

'Our private rooms are quite proofed against noise,' he said. 'Listen...' He held an open palm against the back of his ear. 'Even the din of the storm is quite vanquished.'

The door of room number twelve stood wide open, the boy emerging just as they reached it. The lad stood to one side of the corridor as the host led Quest and Angeline Wissilcraft within.

'This room is at the back of our premises,' said the host. 'Much quieter! Not even the sound of people and horses from out in the street. Ah, I see that young Cain has undertaken his duties with his usual efficiency.'

A fire was starting to blaze in a small black-leaded grate. A tray bearing two glasses and an open bottle of brandy stood on an occasional table. There were two armchairs and an ottoman, covered with a bright green blanket, was set just below a window of stained dark glass. Taking up the length of the wall furthest away from the door was a bed of wide proportions, with immaculately clean sheets.

'Well, if there's nothing else?' the host bowed and pointed to a bell rope. 'Please do ring the bell, should you require my services...'

He left the room.

'He seems to know you quite well,' said Quest.

'I've been here once or twice,' she said. 'There are very few places in London where a woman of my class might seek refreshment. This might not be ideal, but...'

Quest gazed through the darkened window. It was hard to make out anything below. A solitary gas-lamp struggled to illuminate a court leading out into an alley. The noise of the thunder seemed further away now. A solitary flash of lightning suggested the backs of buildings in the next street.

He turned to Angeline.

'Miss Wissilcraft!'

She stood there, completely naked. How she could have stepped out of her clothing with such quietness and speed baffled him. Despite her natural fairness, her skin seemed a darker, yellower brown in the gas and fire light.

Angeline Wissilcraft took the few steps towards him and wrapped her arms around his shoulders.

'My dear Mr Quest. You and I together could conquer the world,' she said. 'We are a match made in...'

Her mouth sought his and, almost unwillingly, he felt himself responding. His hands began to explore that almost too perfect body. He felt a deep stirring within himself, and then, suddenly, what felt like ice on the back of his neck.

Quest pulled away.

'What is it?' she asked very gently. 'Your first time for a while without the actress? She doesn't deserve you, William. She really doesn't...'

'This is a mistake...'

'It isn't,' she replied, 'it really isn't.'

She indicated her naked body.

'I've shocked you, William? I always do things in undue haste. We should have talked first. Got to know each other a little better. Discussed those other matters we have in common...'

'Other matters?'

She ignored the question.

'That fire is taking such a while to warm up,' she said. 'And this room is rather cold, don't you think? I'll pour us some brandy.'

As she crossed the room, he wrapped his cloak around her shoulders. He watched as she poured the drink into the two glasses.

'I really rather hoped we might get better acquainted,' she said, handing him his brandy. She took a sip of her own. He drank down half the glass, feeling a fire within that banished the ice of that initial encounter.

'What other matters?' he asked again.

She smiled and shook her head.

'You won't be pleased if I tell you,' she said. 'And this is a room for pleasure and not business. My brother warned me against cultivating you in this way.'

'Wissilcraft!'

'My dear, slow, honest brother. He really has no idea how to progress matters. He believes you to be a man of some honour. I believe you to be just a man.'

The realisation gripped Quest. He sank down the rest of the brandy. She took the glass and eased him backwards on to the edge of the bed.

'So this is your brother's way of getting the notebook?'

'He wasn't entirely against the idea.'

'And he's prepared to ponce his own sister?'

'My idea, not his,' she said. 'And we needn't include brother Benjamin in any of our negotiations, need we? Have you considered the power and wealth there is that little book? What you and I might do with it?'

'Your brother would be horrified at the very suggestion.'

'He would indeed.'

'And I always draw the line at blackmail,' said Quest. 'I really do believe we should leave this place, Miss Wissilcraft. I'll escort you back to Harley Street as I promised. It would be wise if we didn't see each other again.'

She drew her hand down the side of his face.

'Such a pity,' she said. 'You're a very dashing and handsome man, William. We could have played this game with such enjoyment. And I don't believe you're in any condition to leave here at the moment.'

'I'm used to brandy,' he said. 'And...'

Quest tried to stand, but his legs were no longer there to be controlled. His mind seemed to be drifting away from his body. The room dissolved into a glaring yellow light. Her beautiful figure was dancing away from him. Quest saw the floor rushing up to meet him, the crimson carpet burning into his face.

It must be death, he thought, it must be death...

He could almost taste the scent of her naked body as she put her face so close to his. The yellow glare within the room was absorbing the bright fairness of her hair.

Quest felt nauseous. He put a hand against the carpet and tried to force himself up, but there was no strength there.

And then there was only darkness.

Fifteen

'So tell me about him, Molly?' said Berry, leaning back in the chair in Mrs Bendig's boudoir. 'Tell me about this character who's putting the drop on you?'

Mrs Bendig yawned.

'Don't know what you're talking about.'

'Oh yes you do. I know about the rat in the parcel. I was here. And I know you've had this man around trying to force you to sell. Who is he, Molly?'

'Nobody's putting the drop on me. Who d'you think'd dare to?'

'That's what I want to know. As far as I'm concerned, I don't care what happens to you and this foul establishment. It can be burned to the ground for all I care. And if someone wants it so desperately that they're prepared to buy you out or scare you off, well, so be it.'

'Then why are you here?'

Sergeant Berry got up and paced over to the window. The thunderstorm had died away but the night was very dark. He turned at last and looked down at her.

'You and I go back a long way, Molly. All the way to Manchester. When I walked the beat and you were a two-penny whore on the streets...'

'I was *never* a two-penny whore!' she yelled.

'All right, better than that, but still a whore. And I turned many a blind eye where you were concerned. I have ever since. But I need your help now. There's others being threatened. Some have even been topped. You could be next if there's a connection. I don't know. But I need to know who this man is. I really do, Molly. I can see it's no good offering you money any more. You must be one of the richest women in London. But for your own safety please...'

She shuffled her great body in the chair.

'Who told you about this man?' she asked.

'So there is a man?'

'Who told you? Which of the treacherous little sluts is betraying my secrets to the crushers? And how much are you paying them to sell me out?'

Berry leaned over her.

'People always think I've got informants everywhere,' he said. 'When much of what I do comes from putting two and two together.'

She looked up at him.

'You couldn't possibly have guessed!'

'Who is he, Molly?'

Mrs Bendig folded her arms and stared obstinately at the fireplace.

'I could do this the unpleasant way,' Berry went on. 'Station constables right outside your door. Raid the place of a Saturday evening. Carry some of your clients off to the local police station. Perhaps with a newspaperman or two in tow. Would you like that, Molly? Would you like me to be indiscreet?'

She looked up at him with a challenging expression.

'It's been tried before,' she said. 'The League of Purity's attempted it a dozen times. I'm still here.'

'It's not been tried by me,' said Berry.

'You know you can't threaten me, sergeant,' she said. 'I've got customers who could put you back on the beat. Out of the job altogether, if I chose. Even the Home Secretary, Lord Palmerston himself's been here on a Saturday night to dip his wick...'

Berry sighed and returned to his chair.

'What you say's true, Molly. But you know what? I don't care. I became a policeman because I believe in the rule of law. I might bend the rules a bit... I've done it often enough on your behalf... but only so the rule of law prevails.'

She waved a hand in the air.

'It's Friday, not Sunday. Spare me the sermon.'

'Better that you hear *my* sermon than have some parson mouthing words as he throws dust down on your coffin lid. And that's what'll happen, Molly. Come on, have you been threatened?'

'Go away!' she said, remembering the man she'd defeated in the alley.

'I can see it in your face, Molly. I can see the fear there. Tell me, and I can help you.'

'I've already got someone helping me,' she spat out the words in haste. 'Better than the police too. Someone who really knows his business...'

'There's nobody better than the police...'

'Oh, there is... there is...'

'Where's the harm in it, Molly? Telling me the name of this man who's been threatening you? I can sit here all night, Molly...'

She looked at him.

'You would as well, you bastard!'

'His name?'

'His name's Boone. Margam Boone. He's a lawyer.'

Sergeant Berry reached over and patted her on the wrist.

'There... that wasn't so difficult, was it?' he said.

~

Quest woke into darkness and thought for a few moments that it was just another bad dream. He felt nauseous, his limbs ached and were incapable of movement.

He'd had dreams like this before, when he'd woken suddenly, feeling that all of his personality was trapped within his body. As though his soul had awoken but his body was somehow dead, no longer under any control of the motivating force which usually fired it into life.

As a child the experience of this apparent death in life had frightened him. But then he had learned the trick of escape. Put all your mental energy into animating just one small part of your limbs, a thumb perhaps. Then the hand, then the arm. That usually enabled him to jerk awake.

But as he tried to move his fingers and then his hand, he recognised that the force holding him down was external, and not in his mind. As he juggled a wrist he felt the harsh texture of hempen rope.

Quest had been tied with rope several times before in his career. After a slight struggle he recognised that these ropes had been tied by an expert.

As he opened his eyes, a fresh wave of nausea seemed to consume his body. He felt sick and lay still until that unpleasant feeling had gone away.

Breathing deeply for a few minutes, he opened his eyes again. As his vision focussed, he could tell that he was in the same room in the house of assignation, tied flat out on the bed. As far as he could see through the darkened window it was still night. The gaslight on the wall was turned down low and the fire had burned down to embers.

'You slept longer than I thought you would,' Angeline Wissilcraft said. 'You must have been very tired as well.'

'The brandy?' he asked.

'The brandy.'

'You really are very good, Miss Wissilcraft. I usually watch when a stranger prepares a drink for me. I didn't see you put any sort of philtre in the glass.'

She knelt down by the bed and put her face close to his.

'A philtre in the strictest sense of the world should be a love potion. Perhaps what I gave you was one of those? As for my skill at *legerdemain*, well... a talent of mine since I was quite a small child. And I don't like to think of myself as a stranger. More a friend...'

'My friends don't usually drug me and tie me to a bed.'

'What dull friends you must have... some might say that such actions bring a friendship to a new level of excitement.'

The feeling of sickness had passed away. His head was clearer. He noticed that there was a very tiny scar above her right eyebrow. But somehow it added to rather than detracted from the classical perfection of her face.

'You do realise that I still won't let you have the notebook?' he said.

'Your friends might,' she said.

'They won't.'

'That little boy, Cain. The boy who served the brandy. Even now he's running with a letter to your home. The letter states that I intend to cut your throat at nine in the morning unless the notebook is produced before then. I've stationed a carriage with very fast horses in the Strand. That's where the notebook is to be taken.'

'You assume the notebook is in London? It might be miles away. It might not be possible to produce it by dawn?'

'That would be most unfortunate...'

'Do you really imagine that my associates are going to oblige you in this? They know the importance of what's in the notebook. It's worth far more than one life.'

'Even yours?'

'Especially mine.'

She sighed.

'Such a pity!' she said.

She leaned over further and touched his lips with her own.

'Such a terrible waste,' she said. 'I really do believe that sharing a bed with you might have been one of the more memorable experiences in this very boring existence.'

'I could shout for help...' he said.

'Shouts are not uncommon in this place. They are part of the background of any house of assignation. These rooms are particularly designed to stifle screams. As for the people who work here, well... they work for me. I own this house, dear William. The creatures who work here are all mine. And somehow I doubt if you've ever shouted for help in your life.'

~

He read the *Review* again, as if he hoped the words might have changed from the dozen times he'd scanned it before. But the words were just the same. The poet felt a heaviness in his stomach and a twisting pain in the right side of his head.

Had it been a publication he despised, the critical appraisal of his volume of verse might have been easier to accept. But he had taken the periodical since boyhood, admiring the clarity and perception of its reviewers.

All such notices were anonymously written, but it was well known in literary circles just who the reviewers were. Each one had an individual style. The man who had penned the words was one of the finest poets and critics of the age. The poet admired him very much, cherished his regard. The critic had written him a fine and encouraging letter some years ago, praising his juvenile efforts and pressing him to continue.

And now?

The poet wanted to kill his critic. He really did. And he considered how he might bring his death about. What pain he might inflict on the man. How he could cut off the hand that had written these offending words. He studied them again:

This work is largely derivative, and brings little that is new to the muse. What there is in this slim publication is not worthy of the reader's time. Moreover, there is a callousness and sense of obscenity in much of the verse. We have occasionally publications to peruse and enjoy at the fireside. These poems are only really fit for the fire.

The words seemed to float in front of the poet's eyes. At last he threw the copy of the *Review* across the room. He had seen the critic there at the poetry reading held only days before at the home of Mr Murray, his publisher.

He'd noticed then how quickly the man had retreated from the parlour as soon as the reading was finished. How he had left the premises without a word. Without a handshake or an encouraging pat on the shoulder. Saw him raise his cane in farewell to Mr Murray. But not a word to the poet giving the reading.

Yet Mr Murray had been encouraging. He really had. Compared the poet to Byron. But had that been merely damning with faint praise? Byron had fallen out of favour in these new puritanical times. Was Mr Murray politely trying to warn him that he was swimming against a literary tide?

Murray himself was no longer publishing verse on a regular basis, unless it was by some writer of renown. He might put his imprint on an occasional publication, but only then if the funding for its printing came from elsewhere. The poet had used up much of his allowance on the production of this little volume.

And for what?

Copies had been circulated over the past four months, in advance of publication. Yet the *Review* was the only periodical to give it any notice. And the *Review* was the most influential critical monthly in the land.

In a few lines the poet had found his reputation damned.

He was breathing with such a struggle now that he began to wonder if his heart was failing? There was a blackness in front of his eyes and a pain deep in his chest.

He had a moment's romantic phantasy that this might be how his body would be found. Lying on the floor in his pleasant rooms in Chelsea, clutching the publication that had damned him so. A tragedy, perhaps a subject for artists. Immortalised in death by his passing, if not his actual work.

An absurdity. He gained back breath by recognising that what he knew was the pain of rage, not ill-health. He was a young man, with so many aspects to his life. If he could not pursue one at the moment, he would follow another. And then he would make sure he triumphed as a man of literature.

He really would.

But for the moment he just wanted to kill somebody.

~

Sticks handed Jasper Feedle the note. It had banged through the letterbox only a few minutes before. He had read it very quickly, then opened the door to see if he could see who'd delivered it. Tavistock Place was quiet, though a young lad was running along the pavement towards the square.

'More trouble!' muttered Jasper. 'Where the hell can he be?'

Sticks threw out his hands in a gesture of despair.

'I told him not to go out on his own,' he said. 'They've tried before. This time they've succeeded. And we ain't got a clue where to start looking.'

'Our best hope's this coach in the Strand.'

'Are you thinking we could follow it, mebbe?'

Jasper grimaced.

'More like as how we should grab who's inside and hold a blade at their throat. We can make 'em talk, sure enough. Tell us as to where they was meant to take the notebook if they got it.'

'They might top Will before we get to him...'

Jasper nodded.

'They might at that, but what more can we do?'

'The one thing we mustn't do is what they want. Will was determined that should this happen they weren't to get that bloody notebook.'

'Then they shan't,' said Jasper. 'We'll see 'em in hell first. But we'll need a fair run of Monkshood folk to seal off the Strand.'

'Then let's get on with it,' said Sticks.

There was a tap at the door. Sticks opened it and found Sir Wren Angier standing there, a look of excitement on his face.

'Is Quest here?' he said, as he entered the hallway.

'You'd better come in,' said Sticks.

~

Wren Angier had spent a thankless time visiting publishing firms and literary critics, with a page of poetry from the ledger. All to no avail.

Nobody had recognised the handwriting. He was on the verge of giving up, sad that he couldn't report better news back to William Quest. He found himself in Pall Mall and decided to seek refreshment at his club before returning to Quest's home in Bloomsbury.

After ordering a brandy, he sought out his favourite armchair looking out through the window to the street below. Busy people were rushing by; members of the Class going to their businesses or their pleasures.

A few more dubious characters who appeared to be watching the passers-by with a tad too much interest. Crossing-sweepers waiting for a pause in the traffic, so that they might brush mud and horse-droppings out of the way of pedestrians.

He looked down again at the suspicious wayfarers in the street. Pickpockets, he supposed, or villains of some description. A fancy in his imagination posed the idea that one of them might be William Quest in disguise. The sort of thing he might do. Quest had mentioned that he was a member of a club here in Pall Mall.

I wouldn't put it past him to linger outside its august doors, posing as a street rogue, thought Angier.

As he sank back the brandy, he suddenly realised how good he felt, fully alive for the first time in years. His mind drifted back to his former life in usury. The days wasted as an indolent member of parliament. A progression made in his life because he'd been jaded and come into his money much too early. Every day of that life he'd been bored. Every night of that life he'd had to bring himself to a state where he could get off to sleep by drinking or whoring.

But these last few days with Quest.

Wonderful, quite wonderful. He'd even slept like a log the night after that terrifying experience down by the Thames.

And this very day, frustrating though it had been, traipsing up and down through literary London, had been a positive joy.

It was as though he was seeing the city with new eyes and a completely refreshed mind. Noticing every little detail of the streets; the habits of the rich, the way they pretended not to even notice the poorer members of society; the way street beggars shuffled into corners, desperate for money but seeming scared of being noticed; the tactics of pickpockets who huddled in little groups, watching and discussing the pedestrians they might rob.

There was such a lot wrong with this city, so many divisions based on poverty and injustice. All through his life Angier had only ever viewed this situation from his own privileged side of the fence.

On the occasions when he'd bothered to turn up, the Commons had sometimes debated these folk, often described as the 'unfortunates' in society.

He'd sat there while gentlemen around him had referred to the appalling poverty in the land. But even then, some members had risen in the house to comment that it was pure want of hard work that kept the poor destitute. Yet at the same time claimed that God had ordered whether a man or woman was born with wealth or not.

To his own shame, Angier had often cried out "hear, hear" as the words were spouted.

And it was such nonsense. It really was. But it had taken that brief incident the previous year, when Quest had threatened and then spared his life, to make him realise the truth about the state of this wretched country.

Now he was seeing it with those new eyes and refreshed mind.

Wren Angier smiled to himself. More of this and you'll be sitting alongside the Radicals in the House. But then, why not?

He took the paper from the ledger out of his pocket-book, reading the verse again, though he now knew it by heart. He didn't realise that he was saying the words aloud, albeit very quietly.

'Such rot!'

He glanced across to the armchair on the opposite side of the window. Old Lord Brough was sitting there, his mutton-chop whiskers whiter than ever. He was shaking his head with a vigour that belied his age.

'Absolute rot!'

'My lord?' said Angier.

'Never heard such demmed drivel in all me days. And I know a demmed lot about poetry as well. Knew 'em all in me day. Byron. Wordsworth. Coleridge. Even Shelley, though the least said about that firebrand the better.' He pointed a finger at the piece of paper Angier was holding. 'But that is absolute rot...'

In all his years at the club, Angier had never heard Brough say quite so much.

The peer was well over seventy and never spoke in the Lords these days. He'd had a colourful past during the Regency, notoriously fought three duels, had a country estate he seldom visited, and spent most of his time dozing in an armchair at his club.

'I only read a few lines, m'lord,' said Angier. 'Would you care to hear some more?'

'Don't need to...' Brough muttered. 'Heard the fellow read it himself only the other day...'

Angier felt a surge of excitement.

'You know the poet?'

'Wouldn't say I know him,' Brough replied. 'Know him to speak to. That's about all. Saw him though. At Murray's literary *soiree*.'

'Murray?'

'John Murray, the publisher. D'ye know nothing, boy? Printed me memoirs a few years ago. Not that anyone much bothered to read them, but...'

Angier waved the paper.

'This poet is published by John Murray?'

Brough gave a little laugh.

'Wouldn't go so far as to say published. Printed them, used his imprint. I suspicion the boy had to pay him to churn out the rubbish.'

Angier took in a deep breath.

'What's the name of the poet?' he asked.

'Young Boone, of course,' Brough replied. 'Randal Margam Boone, son of the peer. Though the family's fortunes have declined since the grandfather used to cavort through London with me. They keep their heads up by being distant cousins of the mongoose – Lord Palmerston. Apparently, Palmerston's promised that if he becomes prime minister he'll get the boy a seat. Can't see it mesself. If his politics are as poor as his poetry, well...'

Angier leant forward.

'Is there a brother? A lawyer?'

'There is, but I'm dashed if I remember his name. Oily looking chap. Conveyed some property for me cousin. Met him once. Can't say I took to him. Seemed peeved he had to work for a living...'

'This younger Boone, Randal...'

'Properly Margam Boone. Got the Margam from the mother's family. A condition of inheritance, I b'lieve.'

'Do you know where he lives?'

Lord Brough shrugged.

'Not a clue. They used to have land in Hampshire. All gone now. The father gambles. Not a very clever man. You should never gamble unless you're clever... or demmed lucky. The old boy lives in Brighton in some small villa. I say, where are you going?'

Angier had jumped to his feet.

'Must dash, m'lord. Urgent sitting in the Commons. A pleasure to converse with you. Must do it again soon. I'll have some brandy sent over to you. My treat....'

~

'Margam Boone?'

'So Molly Bendig says,' said Berry. 'I took the trouble to look him up in the lists. A practising lawyer, true enough. We've

170

nothing against him. He must have the least colourful legal career in London.'

'A property lawyer, you say?' said Anders.

'And not much else, though he's regularly retained by members of the aristocracy. Must make a bob or two. He does have some interesting family connections...'

'Such as?'

'He's Lord Palmerston's cousin.'

Inspector Anders gave a humourless laugh.

'So the chances are if we drag him in, we'll have the Home Secretary on our backs. Probably the Prime Minister as well. Commissioner Mayne will love us for that. But what I don't understand is why, with the connections you say, he's helping to take over criminal enterprises across London?'

'We could feel his collar and ask him...' Berry suggested.

'And we will!' Anders said determinedly. 'Whatever the consequences. But as far away from Scotland Yard as possible. Find me a police-office in an obscure little corner of the city, Berry. Somewhere with just a sergeant and a few constables, where nobody'll be in any hurry to ask questions if we turn up with a prisoner. We'll nab this Margam Boone and take him there.'

Berry walked to the window and pulled back the shutter.

'Dawn in an hour and a fine looking morning it's setting up to be,' he said. 'The gent'll probably be at his office for nine. We can pull him there.'

'Discreetly, Berry. No constables in uniform. Just the two of us, with a carriage waiting close by. We don't want half the legal minds of Gray's Inn rushing to his defence.'

'Or telling Palmerston.'

'Nor that, either. You go and arrange our transport and...'

There was a fierce knocking on the door.

'Yes?' said Anders.

Cooper, a constable of the detective force, stood in the doorway.

'Thought you'd like to know, sir. Word's come from the London Hospital. That Jedediah Mooth's fully conscious at last.'

~

Randal Margam Boone had left his rooms in Chelsea at midnight, following the river downstream to Westminster. The thunderstorm passed away even as a thousand church clocks across the city tolled the dead of night.

There was a slight mist above the waters of the Thames, but otherwise the weather seemed to be setting fair. He crossed the river by Westminster Bridge and took a circuitous route down into the Borough, where he kept on another set of rooms that only one other person knew about.

Boone had liked the Borough from his first visit as a gawky lad fresh up from the family's old home in Hampshire. He'd read about the place in a host of books by his favourite writers from Defoe to Dickens. Throughout its long history, the Borough had been a place somehow beyond the legal limits of the rest of London. A place where miscreants would lurk. A haven for thieves and debtors, for renegades, and individuals leading a double life.

He remembered how he'd been viewed, that first time. A well-dressed boy, clearly in funds, well worth robbing. The men and women who'd looked him up and down had frightened him. Even now in his memory he could recall how his fancy had thrust dirty hands into his pockets, brought the blade of a knife across his throat.

Then, that first time, Boone had found a smarter street, leading to a market, its stalls stacked with fruit and vegetables. There were more respectable characters in this part of the Borough. Honest traders come to buy stock for shops across the city. Pedestrians with a better style of dress. Police constables walking the street.

Safer, but somehow not quite as exciting as the threatening areas he'd left behind. On his return to the family home, across the bridge in Westminster, Boone had written up his experiences in his commonplace book. His experiences had fired his imagination, words tumbled out as poems and stories. He'd returned to the Borough, again and again, until he knew every street and building. It was the first part of London he got to know really well. And the folk in the Borough had got to know him too.

But not as Randal Margam Boone.

No, that would have been too dangerous, given the dark hours he wandered there. He'd taken to dressing in the rough fustian favoured by the denizens of that wild place. A canvas cap pulled down on his dark hair. His own accent submerged into the rougher tones of a youth brought up on the London streets. In a disreputable tavern he'd struck up acquaintanceships with many of the criminals who worked the Borough. Invented the legend that he was a thief on the run from a distant part of the city. For a young man with a vast imagination, it was all very simple.

On his first journeys into the Borough, he'd intended only to gain knowledge and write down his experiences into a novel. A work of imagination that would eclipse the offerings of Defoe and Dickens.

Boone had come home one day and found his older brother reading and grinning at the dozen finished chapters. Taller though his brother was, Boone had given him a sound thrashing. Smiled and felt a sense of power as his brother crawled into a corner and begged him to stop.

A young man learned a great deal about dirty fighting in the darker corners of the Borough.

His room was above a slop-shop in the next street to the church. A modest little hideaway where he kept a change of clothes and assorted weapons. Where he could, in privacy, complete the change from Randal Margam Boone to his other persona. He owned the shop beneath and the shopkeeper worked for him, earning a profit from the poor and keeping a watchful eye on the room above. The shopkeeper gave a salute and a bow as Boone glanced in through the window.

Boone climbed the narrow flight of stairs and unlocked the door, shutting and bolting it behind him. For a room in that particular street, it was immaculately clean. The bed was freshly made with good, clean laundry. A desk stood beneath the window, for he would often write here, finding that the neighbourhood inspired his muse. He seldom wrote at all now in his rooms in Chelsea. The words were more likely to fly from his pen here, or in the manufactory down by the river.

And as to that...

There was a note propped up on the desk. He picked up and unfolded the paper, read the words several times and grunted with frustration. Important news, but not the letter he was expecting. Had her plan gone awry?

Nonetheless, it was interesting information. Something that needed to be acted upon, even if it meant a swift walk down to the river. And he really did feel quite in the mood to murder someone that morning.

Anyone would do.

He had one particular individual in mind.

Sixteen

Jedediah Mooth was sitting up, a police constable in the chair beside the bed. Another constable was stationed by the door, armed with a percussion pistol and a neddy stick. The prater was so alert, his eyes shining so much with life, that it was hard to believe he'd been unconscious for so many days. He seemed excited to see the two detectives.

'You're looking better than you were, Maggot,' said Berry, as he and Anders drew up chairs beside the bed. 'We quite thought you'd journeyed to the pearly gates.'

Mooth waved a reproaching finger.

'And so I did, Mr Berry, so I did. Though I wish as how you didn't use that silly moniker. I'm a man of the church and it's disrespectful to refer to me by other than the title... reverend.'

'You've no more right to call yourself reverend than I have,' said Berry. 'You were unfrocked...'

'Once a man has been called, only God can take away the title. You knows that, Mr Berry.' He looked at Anders. 'Who's this?'

'This is Inspector Anders,' said Berry.

Mooth reached out and grasped Anders' wrist.

'Have you been saved, my friend?'

'Not exactly,' Anders replied.

'Well you should have been,' said Mooth, 'for God is merciful and loves a sinner come to his understanding. Oh, and I've come to mine! Indeed, I have! For look at me now, risen from the dead to bring the word to a miserable world and...'

'Stop spouting that nonsense. We're a lost cause,' said Berry.

'Oh, Mr Berry...'

'Time to talk, Mooth,' said Anders, 'and I don't want words of religion. I want to know why the King of Jacob's Island tried to string you up at the *Shanghai*?'

'I'm not quite sure as I remember exactly why,' said Mooth.

'I think you do...' said Anders.

'And just suppose I did know why? If I was to give you a reason. What's to stop his highness hangin' me all over again?'

'What's to stop me putting you away in Millbank Prison until you do decide to be obliging?' said Anders. 'And the lost souls in there hate the sight of praters.'

'You are a fallen angel...' Mooth began.

'Or we could just release him on to the streets,' said Berry. 'Let the King have another shot at stringing him up. Get our wagon outside to drop him off right by Jacob's Island, eh?'

They both saw the fear in Mooth's eyes.

'You wouldn't dare. You...'

Anders nodded.

'I don't think that's a bad idea, sergeant. Get these two constables to carry him down to the street.'

'For the love of God...' said Mooth.

'On the other hand, we could tip you a reward, Mooth. Ship you out of London to some distant place. Give you letters of introduction. Life would be so much simpler if you cooperate with us. Just think of the reward, Mooth. Guineas. Golden guineas.'

Mooth looked at them slyly.

'You'd do that for me? Honour bright?'

'We would,' said Berry.

'It'd have to be speedy,' said Mooth. 'He's the very devil. He sees everything and knows everything.'

'Tell us now and I'll have you out of London before the clocks strike midday,' said Anders.

'How can I trust you?'

'You'll have to,' said Anders. 'You know the alternative.'

'Come closer...'

Mooth beckoned them.

'I know...' he whispered. 'I know who the King is...'

Anders leant forward.

'How would you know that?' he asked.

Mooth looked round the room, staring at the door as if his would-be killer was standing there. Then at the windows as though somebody might have clambered up a hundred feet from Whitechapel High Street.

'Many years ago...' he began, then suddenly stopped. 'Send the constables out...'

'Why?' asked Berry.

'Constables talk too much,' he said, under his breath. 'I trusts you, Mr Berry. And I can see this Mr Anders is a gent, but....'

Anders turned to the constables.

'You two can have a half-hour to yourselves,' he said. 'Report back here then.'

Mooth watched as the two men left the room.

'Better... that's better,' he said.

'You'd better not be playing games with us, Maggot,' said Berry.

'Ah, it's worth the hearing, Mr Berry.'

'Get on with it,' said Anders.

Mooth sat up higher against his pillow, glancing again at the window. He put a finger up to his lips, his head moving up and down as though he was deep in thought.

'It was years ago,' he began. 'I was a very young man, not long out of theological training in Salisbury. I was poor... so poor. But I got myself a curacy in Hampshire. A tiny parish, not far from Fordingbridge. Small village, and all the peasants worked for the squire. For the big house owned all the land thereabouts...'

'What was the name of this parish?' asked Anders. He knew that part of Hampshire quite well.

'It don't matter,' said Mooth, 'in any case it's not hard to discover. The squire had to sell up. Bet his money away. A manufacturer of silk gowns has the estate now...'

'Get to the point,' said Anders.

'Well, the old squire took a liking to me. When the vicar died sudden, he made sure I got the living. Put his own money into my purse.' He looked angry. 'When the estate changed hands the new master cut off that stipend. Said I should live off the tithes and the chancel tax. But you couldn't do it, Inspector. Not there. Not in a place with so few people. And so much money having to go to preserve the fabric of the building.'

'So you helped yourself to the fabric fund?' suggested Berry.

Mooth looked down at the harsh woollen blanket.

'To my shame. But even a servant of God's got to eat and drink.'

'Go on...' said Anders.

'Before that... the old squire... he had two sons. Never got on with the eldest. A cold creature. But the younger sang in the choir and would come round of an evening to read my books. A warmer creature than his brother, though he'd have terrible bursts of temper. He was artistic, that lad. Would paint and draw some fine landscapes in the parish. But his real gift was the writing of poetry. Not my kind of thing, for I prefers Mr Tennyson. But I could see he had some sort of gift.'

'What's this got to do with anything?' said Berry.

'One night, after evensong, the boy came round to the parsonage. In a terrible temper, he was, and he hadn't been to the service, which was unusual. Said his father had lost all their money, excepting an allowance he was to get from an aunt. He was in a black mood, sure enough. Kept beatin' his fists against the wall. I tried to comfort him, but he just grabbed me. Pinned me up against the door with his hands on my throat...'

Mooth's own hands had gone up to his neck, rubbing the flesh that still bore the marks of the hanging rope.

'I thought as how he was going to kill me, Mr Anders. I really did. But then he just threw me to one side and stormed out into the night.'

'Did you see his father about it?' asked Anders.

Mooth shook his head.

'His father had left the parish by the next morning. Went to a villa at the sea-side. Some relation took pity on the old man and provided him with a home and a small offerin' to pay the bills. I never saw him again. Nor the boy...'

'Until you came to London?' said Anders.

Mooth rubbed his forehead.

'I couldn't believe it, Mr Anders, I really couldn't. I'd heard about the rise of this man who's been taking over the underworld. But I never dreamed... I thought it was some riverside rough. It was a while before I set eyes on him. Then one night he was there, at a tavern in Bermondsey. He didn't know me, of course. I must look older than when I knew him as a boy. And for all he knows, I'm still a vicar in his father's old parish.'

'So when did he recognise you?'

'Not till he was a-stringin' me up. I whispered in his ear. Then he knew. It alarmed him so much, he punched me in the face to keep me silent. Then had me hauled up by that rope.'

'But why should he care if people know?' asked Berry.

'He poses as a rough, you see. Best bit of acting I've seen for a long while. There's an artistic talent for you. They're all taken in by him. Frightened to death of what he might do to them if they disobeys.'

Mooth gave a humourless chuckle.

'There's some'd be mighty angry if they know he really lives in a full-rigged gaff in Chelsea. Lives on an allowance. Writes his poetry and mixes with the toffs in his spare time...'

He leant forward, a malicious smile on his face.

'And there's some as might cut his throat if they find he's a cousin of Palmerston. Might b'lieve he's peachin' to the Home Secretary about all their doings. Playin' a double game.'

'You're sure he isn't?' said Anders.

'That young master sees it as a way of coming into wealth again. He's in this only for himself. Though they do say as how he has a partner in crime.'

'Who?'

'I don't know that,' Mooth replied. 'Only that they go on killin' sprees together. More'n like another lad like himself. He has others. Men he puts forward as the King if he's in a public place. But he can't fool me. I knows 'em all. I knows him.'

'What's his name, Jedediah?' asked Anders.

'Our deal holds good?'

'It does.'

Mooth whispered the words.

'His name's Boone. Randal Margam Boone.'

Berry waved a hand.

'You got that wrong, Maggot. We know of Margam Boone. He's a lawyer. Nothing like the creature you've described. He might have an interest in these doings, but he's definitely not the King of Jacob's Island.'

Mooth looked smug.

'I did say, Mr Berry, as how there was an older brother. He's the lawyer, what gets the barony when his old father shuffles off his mortal coil. Randal is the younger boy. Margam is the elder. And every king has a lawyer. Mark me if this one don't.'

~

'It's dawn already, William,' she said very quietly. 'It comes so early at this time of year.' She glanced up at the ceiling and sighed. 'Inevitable is the dawn. It will be interesting to see if your death is inevitable.'

'Rest assured it will be,' said Quest, 'if the price of my life is that notebook.'

'Now, you're being very stubborn!'

'It's a fault of mine.'

'A fault that you have only an hour or two to correct.'

'One dies with all one's faults.'

'That would really be very silly... I mean, what did you intend to do with the notebook, William? Were you just intending to hide it away until the names therein are all dead and the information is valueless? What would be the use of that? Perhaps you were plotting some acts of individual blackmail?'

'Perhaps we were...'

Angeline Wissilcraft sighed.

'Then why not do it in company with me?'

'Because you would blackmail for money and position.'

'What else is there?'

'We would blackmail for better reasons,' said Quest. 'We'd use the information to make sure that acts of parliament were amended. To speed up the pace of reform. We'd use this knowledge to ensure that the printed press took notice of the many injustices in our society.'

She yawned.

'How very boring!'

'I can see it wouldn't appeal to you, Miss Wissilcraft.'

'Angeline, please... let's have a little informality and pleasure in these early hours of the morning.' She drew her fingers down his cheek and across his lips. 'This is really such a waste, William.'

'What will your brother say when he finds out you've cut my throat?'

'He won't be surprised,' she said. 'Time and again I've done his dirty work for him. All those little employments he was too sensitive to deal with himself. All those prisoners who wouldn't talk or cooperate. Benjamin always relied on me. He has such a sensitive nature, don't you see? He really is in the wrong profession. Very good at handling meetings with politicians or trailing suspicious characters around the countryside, but, well, really, not very good at the cold, hard and brutal side of the business.'

'You're not that good at it yourself, Miss Wissilcraft,' said Quest. 'If you were, you'd cut my throat right now. There's no point in waiting for the allotted time. You are not going to get the notebook.'

'We'll see...'

'I assure you.'

'Oh, William... what a partnership we could be...'

'We could never, ever be that. You see, Miss Wissilcraft, I've expected to die every day since I was a small child. Death holds no fears for me. But I suspect you enjoy living too much to have such an absence of terror. You'll kill me and my associates will kill you. Sooner than you think.'

'But they don't know who I am...'

'You think not? You know I work for an association of revolutionaries? Men and women dedicated to changing this sin-sick world.' Quest indicated the window with a shake of his head. 'They're out there, Angeline. Thieves and dips, the men who drive the cabriolets, the women who sell flowers, the lads who sweep the street crossings.'

'So?'

'Even I don't know all of them. But they all know me, Angeline. I can't walk across London without my movements being noted. My friends'll know where I am. And how long I've been here. They'll have observed just who I arrived with. If my time on this earth is limited, well, so is yours.'

She smiled, 'I don't believe any of this. I really don't. And it's too early in the morning for such bedtime tales. I will kill you, William, if my messenger fails to bring that notebook. Oh, and in such a painful way. Cutting your throat will come very late in the proceedings.'

~

Randal Margam Boone walked out of the darkness and into the dawn, through the wharves and docks of the south side of the river.

A wild-looking character dressed in fustian, waving his heavy stick through the air with every step. His neat dark hair was unkempt now, the long locks sprawling below his canvas cap were blowing in the slight breeze that swept down the Thames. His face was dirtied with the grime of the city. A stevedore unloading a cargo at a wharf just in from the river glanced up, wondering whether or not to challenge the right of this intruder to be there.

But one look at those dark eyes persuaded him to remain silent. The stevedore knew who this man was, for he lived on the fringes of crime.

He'd seen the King of Jacob's Island holding court at a tavern in Bermondsey. Knew full well the punishments meted out to those who questioned this particular intruder's right to rule and roam. The stevedore glanced down river. He could just see the rooftops of the rookery that was the dominion of this particular ruler. He turned away and lifted more cotton bales into the nearby warehouse.

Boone walked on, the stench of the slums disgusted him, but the thrill of power brought him back there again and again.

At last, the wrecked buildings of Jacob's Island came in view, a place Boone had first heard about in the pages of Dickens. It had changed since that author's day. Attempts had been made to part-fill the ditches which gave the wretched place its name. Some of the strung-out buildings had been demolished. The place was not only derelict but partly deserted. The scourge of cholera had killed some of the population and driven many of the others away.

Only the villainous and truly desperate remained.

Those that still resided there lived in a huddle of filthy rooms, grime black and over-hanging the muddy ditches. Lost souls forced to drink water from the filthy-watered ditches into which the drains of their own buildings discharged. Decrepit bridges crossed these polluted waterways, sending up a malodorous reek that could keel over strangers to the vicinity. The water in the little river was often blood-red, the colour swept down from the leather-dressers upstream.

The worst of the buildings huddled around the sides of the Folly Ditch, a foetid inlet of the Thames. A wooden bridge, perilous for the pedestrian, crossed the ditch, planks missing and the handrail down on one side. To fall into the Folly Ditch was almost certain death. There were few ways to recover the unfortunates who did. Less chance of anyone wanting to be bothered even trying to mount a rescue. Decomposing corpses, human and animal, added to the deadly filth of its water and the miasma above.

This foulness of the locality, and the deadly intentions of the surviving residents, kept the casual onlooker away. Constables on their beats avoided the district. There was nobody living on Jacob's Island worthy of their protection. The police had hardly bothered to turn up and give security to the men sent to demolish the island. Time and again these improvers had been driven away. Most recently on the direct order of Randal Margam Boone.

The place would have to be abandoned soon. Boone knew that, for his connections at the county council had remarked, not appreciating his interest, that a greater force of labourers was to be sent there in the coming months; to wreak destruction to the rookery, to build warehouses where men might labour for sixteen hours a day, too exhausted from wage slavery to want to indulge in the island's more traditional criminal activities.

Boone was already considering other locations across the city. He had the power to become the king of anywhere he wanted. But for the moment, Jacob's Island would suit his purposes. He had become immune to its dirt and odours. Just being there was an adventure straight out of the writings of his heroes, Defoe and Dickens.

And now, this very day, there was the added pleasure of coming to Jacob's Island to murder someone.

Seventeen

Margam Boone, lawyer of Gray's Inn, sat in a carriage in the Strand, muttering curses against his younger brother. He hadn't minded visiting prospects in shops and night houses to demand the keys to their little empires, but this was ridiculous.

To have to sit in a carriage awaiting who knows what, like some common errand boy...

He leant his head out of the carriage window. It was well past dawn and nobody was in sight. He sniffed the morning air. So many better things he might be doing. Up on the riding step sat a burly driver and an even fiercer guard. His brother Randal had loaned them to him for protection.

Randal... damn him!

Randal was the younger brother, much younger. Not the heir to the barony, like himself. The Honourable Margam Boone. Soon to be, if his father down in Brighton continued to ail, the Right Honourable The Lord Boone. Not that there were estates to inherit. His father had lost the country house in an ill-advised bet. The grand London House in Park Lane... lost in a single wager on Derby Day.

Margam Boone hoped his father's death would be painful, though preferably short.

But what was there to inherit? The villa in Brighton where the old man was spending his declining years was merely leased. As were Margam Boone's own set of rooms near to Gray's Inn. His law work brought in a sufficient income, but he found it outrageous, as a forthcoming peer of the realm, that he was obliged to get his hands dirty with work.

Margam Boone looked out of the carriage window once more. The Strand was starting to get busier, but all the passers-by seemed indifferent to the presence of his carriage. How long...

He'd been a reluctant partner in his brother Randal's scheme. As a lawyer who'd spent time briefing counsel at the Old Bailey, he was only too aware of the consequences of the law.

At first, he'd been assured, his role was only to issue the mildest of threats. But then premises began to be wrecked, shops burned down. The first murders had come not long afterwards. By then it was too late to change his mind.

It had always been the same way with Randal. Years ago, as the much older brother, he'd beaten and bullied the younger boy, whose head seemed to be filled only with literature and dreaming. Then, one day, Randal had turned upon him, smashing him down to the ground with what Margam Boone had always considered to be puny fists.

But his brother hadn't stopped there, raining down blows even when he knew his battle was won. As though inflicting pain and humiliation had become an end in itself. Their relationship had changed from that day onwards. Now he did what Randal desired, though often considering the possibility that, once the campaign was concluded, and the family estates back in funds, he might pay someone to have his brother quietly murdered.

And his partner in crime as well.

Then he would be free, free to profit from all of this... this unpleasantness. This...

There was a gentle tapping on the carriage door.

From the height of the seat he couldn't see anyone at first. But as he leant through the window, he became aware of a man standing there. An older man with long hair, a cripple leaning on his crutch.

'Yes?'

Jasper Feedle held up a packet in his right hand, a small object wrapped up in brown paper and tied with string.

'Got something for yer,' he said.

Margam Boone sniffed, reaching out and grabbing the package.

'Right, now go away,' he said.

'I was to make sure yer knows what it is,' Jasper said.

'I know perfectly well what it is!' snarled Margam Boone, starting to undo the string.

'I'm not lettin' yer go until yer tells me where me friend is...'

'I know the agreement. He'll be released, though you've left damned little time. I've been here since dawn and it's gone eight thirty.'

He unfolded the brown paper. Inside the packet was a small black notebook, a piece of black cord fastening it shut. The cord

185

was tied in a tight knot and it took Margam Boone a few moments to ease it clear of the covers of the notebook. He opened its pages and looked inside. He grunted with astonishment, and then flicked through the little volume.

Every page was blank.

'What the devil is this?' he said.

He looked up and found himself staring into the barrel of a small percussion-cap pistol.

'Highway robbery,' said Jasper Feedle. 'An' I'll trouble yer not ter move or cry out, or I'll put a hole in yer head.'

Margam Boone rapidly pulled the curtain across the carriage window and threw himself on to the opposite seat. He began to yank out the blade from his sword-stick. Then he felt a round piece of metal pressing against the back of his head.

'Leave the blade where it is, my friend,' someone whispered into his ear. 'I want you alive, but you're putting my ambition in serious peril. Now turn around... very slowly.'

Margam Boone eased his head round, aware all the time of the proximity of the gun barrel. The man holding the weapon looked more amused by his predicament than anything else.

'That's better,' said Wren Angier. 'I won't kill you if you do exactly what I say. Blowing your head off would spoil the interior of this lovely carriage.'

There came a great shout from outside. A figure fell from the carriage's riding seat and flew past the window on the side facing the street. Margam Boone recognised it as the guard. There was a yelp of pain from somewhere above his head. Then the horrible sound of a fist hitting the bone of someone's head. A second later the driver rolled down the side of the coach, falling on top of the guard.

The door with the closed curtain swung open and the cripple tumbled inside.

'Righty-o mate!' Feedle yelled out, thumping the foot of his crutch against the carriage's roof. 'Time ter depart!'

The speed with which the coach took off almost deposited the three of them on the floor. They could hear the cries of pedestrians as it tore through the morning crowds. A police constable's rattle sounded somewhere far behind.

Jasper shouted up at Sticks through the window.

'As a coach driver, yer a terrific prize-fighter!'

~

'I'm so sorry it's had to end like this,' said Angeline Wissilcraft. 'Half past eight and no sign of the notebook. Such a waste! Together, my dear William, we could have been magnificent.'

Quest stretched his hands as far as his bonds would allow.

'There's little point in killing me, Miss Wissilcraft. It won't get you what you want. If my associates won't deliver the notebook on the prospect of saving my life, they'll scarcely do it in exchange for my corpse. And killing me will mean that you'll be looking over your shoulder for the rest of your life. Which will, in consequence of the act, be very short.'

'I adore threats...'

'You've lost, Angeline. Why not acknowledge the fact?'

She drew the sharp edge of the knife very softly across his throat. She drew the weapon away and carefully licked the tip of the blade. She gave a sudden burst of laughter.

'Because I haven't lost, William. We considered the possibility that you would be... uncooperative. So we've arranged to bring in one of your pawns to keep the game going a little longer. And the next time my blade touches your throat, I'll cut a trifle deeper.'

She gleamed on spying his sudden look of concern.

'What pawn?' he demanded.

'They're on their way to snatch her now, William...'

A feeling of heaviness came over him.

She put her mouth against his ear.

'Miss Stanton,' she whispered. 'The dreadful actress might have played her last part. Rosa, William. My associates will have Rosa by the time you bleed to death. I'm sure you can imagine what I'll do to her when I get there. Your passing will be painless by comparison to hers. I've always been rather jealous of Miss Stanton, William. Knowing that she has you and I don't. I shall enjoy...'

'It won't get you the notebook!'

'Oh, I do believe it will. Your friends are probably very sensitive to the idea of a woman in pain. And they probably don't cherish the notebook quite as much as you do...'

Quest heaved himself up, causing the bed to move several inches across the floor. He pulled hard against the hempen ropes until the flesh on his wrists burned. After the moment's struggle he fell back on the bed, exhaustion and the after-effects of the philtre overwhelming him.

'So you see, William, it would be for the best if you agreed to aid me in my ambitions.'

'I've never killed a woman, Angeline...'

She shook her head.

'You won't kill me. These are the last moments of your life, William. How close pleasure is to pain...'

~

They turned the coach into a quiet mews just north of Oxford Street. In times gone by the gentlemen who lived nearby had kept their horses and carriages here, their coachmen living in the rooms above.

But now the mews was gated, the whole of the properties around belonging to the Critzman brothers. The horses and carriages that still found a home here served only the operatives of Monkshood.

'Get out,' said Angier, waving the pistol from Margam Boone towards the door of the coach.

Margam Boone looked pale and his hands were trembling.

'What are you going to do to me?' he couldn't keep the fear out of his voice.

'I'll blow your head off if you don't get out of the coach right now.'

'Save you the trouble,' said Sticks, reaching into the coach and grabbing Margam Boone by the collar, dragging him head first down on to the cobbles of the courtyard.

The lawyer looked up to see several men staring down at him, no mercy in any of their eyes.

'Take a good look round,' said the old cripple. 'This might be where yer goin' ter die.'

Margam Boone swallowed hard as he looked along the row of faces. He held a hand up towards Angier.

'I can see that you at least are a gentleman...' he began.

'What of it?' said Angier.

'I look upon you to give me protection from these... scum.'

'I was very much like you once,' Angier replied. 'No! Nowhere near as bad! A man at fault, perhaps? But I learned my lesson. Now I try to do good. But I won't spare your life.'

Margam Boone cried out.

'What do you want from me?'

'You know of William Quest?'

For a moment Margam Boone looked as though he was going to deny any knowledge. Then Jasper Feedle crashed his crutch down on the ground within an inch of his head.

'I know of him,' Margam Boone said.

'Some friends of yours have him,' said Angier. 'And we want him back.'

'I can't tell you that...'

'Then say hello ter yer maker,' said Feedle, raising his crutch into the air.

'No... no... can't you see I'm as good as dead if I utter a word?'

'Yer dead if yer don't.'

'There's no escape for you, Boone,' said Angier.

'You know who I am?' Margam Boone looked astonished.

'We knows everything about you,' said Sticks. 'From your birth upwards. Right to now. The day you're goin' to die.'

'And we know about your brother too,' said Angier. 'There's one king's reign that's coming to an end.'

'You don't know what he's like!' said Margam Boone. 'He won't spare me. He's threatened to kill me time and again. He's the younger son. He covets our father's title. Randal wants the barony. If I betray him I'm a dead man.'

'You will be anyway if you don't,' said Sticks. 'We knows all about you. You were there when Ikey Balfrey was murdered.'

'I didn't kill him.'

'Yer were outside,' said Feedle.

'I was! I was! They made me go in first. But it was the two of them that killed him. Randal and his whore...'

189

'His whore?' asked Angier.

'It was all her idea. She drives him forward. Puts the merriment in his devilry. It was her idea. To get money. To seize power. They want every criminal in London working for them. They've killed again and again. Anyone who's stood in their way. It's not Randal who has Quest. It's her! And better for him that it was my brother. She worships pain. She lives for torture.'

'Who is she?'

Margam Boone couldn't see this new interrogator. The man was kneeling behind his head, hands gripping his shoulders.

'The spymaster's sister, Angeline Wissilcraft. She's a devil... a devil... They killed Balfrey together. The two of them with pistols. But it was her idea. She started him off killing with such abandon. There've been others...'

'The whoremaster, Bluff Todd,' the voice asked. 'Who killed him?'

'Her! Just her! She wanted to do one on the streets. On her own. Randal watched, but from a distance. She's mad. Quite mad. She wants the notebook so she can control society. It was her idea to get Bendig's night house. She knows the men who go there. Wants to threaten them with their indiscretions, and...'

'Blow all this,' said Sticks. 'Where's she got our friend. Tell me right now and we won't kill you.'

'Your word on that?' yelled Margam Boone.

'Our word,' said Angier.

Margam Boon told them of the address in Frith Street.

'But you're too late!' he cried out. 'It must be near nine now.'

'Let's go!' shouted Feedle.

'We'll take the coach,' said Angier. 'Though I fear we may not be in time.'

His face against the cold stone of the cobbles, Margam Boone watched the men jump on to the carriage. Saw them speed the horses into action. Watched as the coach rattled across the stones out of the courtyard of the old mews.

For a moment he thought he'd been left alone. A sweeping of hope surged from his chest and into his brain. He reached down and used a hand to lever himself to his feet.

But then both his hands were grabbed and forced behind his back. He felt the click as a pair of darbies were forced on to his wrists.

'Thought we'd all gone?' said the voice.

Margam Boone turned.

A white-haired man in a much worn frock-coat stood there, the key of the darbies in his hand. A pair of police constables stood nearby, looking bemused at the recent performance.

'I'm arresting you in the name of the Queen,' said Inspector Abraham Anders. 'I'm sure as a lawyer you're aware of your position...'

Margam Boone opened his mouth, but no words came forth.

'I'll charge you more formally when we reach the police-court,' Anders went on. 'But at the moment shall we rest on the murder of Ikey Balfrey, and conspiracy in the slaying of Bluff Todd. There'll be a great many other attainders to follow.'

'But I didn't!' Margam Boone was almost in tears. 'Not one of them! Not one!'

'You were there or had knowledge. You threatened people across London. You'll swing, my friend. Though, if you turn Queen's Evidence against your brother and Angeline Wissilcraft, you might just be spared the gallows.'

~

The coach tore into Oxford Street, sending pedestrians flying for cover and bringing a cabriolet to a shuddering halt. A police constable yelled and ran after them, demanding that they stop at once.

'My God, Feedle! Has your man ever driven a coach before?' demanded Sergeant Berry, as he was flung on to the floor for a second time.

'Not Mr Sticks' greatest talent,' Jasper replied, wedging himself into the seat by forcing his crutch against the door. 'Never did get on well with horses...'

'Not fast enough!' cried Angier, looking at his hunter watch. 'It's damn near nine, now.'

As if in confirmation, the church clocks began to chime. The coach was barely into Soho. The look of terror on Jasper Feedle's face spoke louder than words.

~

'I want to see a look on your face, dear William. A look of horror as you die. Not for yourself. I know you won't give me that satisfaction. But nevertheless I want to see it there. You've granted me so little pleasure. But this look of horror... I demand that.'

'Demand what the hell you like!' said Quest.

'Yet it will be there, William. As you die you can anticipate the death of Miss Stanton.' She laughed. 'You're too late to save her. My men are taking her about now. We've been trailing her for such a long time. We know all her silly little routines...'

'If you hurt her...'

She put her face close to his.

'Hurt her? I'm going to kill her, William. Before the day's out. For my pleasure. I did consider just maiming her. Making it so that she could never act again. Turning her face into a work of art that would make anyone who saw her shudder. Then letting her wander away to what was left of her existence. But, no. She has to die, William. Though I'll have my fun first. Before this day is out.'

'Touch her and you'll be dead. My men will show you no mercy.'

She yawned.

'You're beginning to bore me, William.' She held a hand up near her ear. 'You hear that? The clocks are chiming. It's time for you to die, Mr Quest.'

'Come away from him, Angeline.'

She spun round. In their preoccupation neither of them had hear the quiet opening of the door. The bulky figure of Benjamin Wissilcraft stood there, his head to one side and his hands in his pockets.

Angeline Wissilcraft eased her knife away from Quest's throat and stood, very slowly.

'Brother Benjamin! However, did you find me? Ah, but then you are Queen Victoria's spymaster, I suppose.'

'Do you think me an idiot, Angeline? You've worked alongside me for so long. I know all your tricks. I've used you to do such as this to others. There are actions we've taken that I bitterly regret. But they were all done to further the safety of this land. But I'm not going to let you kill this man.'

'He won't give me the notebook,' she said.

'Of course he won't,' said Wissilcraft. 'Did you ever believe he would? And you're not doing this for the safety of the realm, Angeline. Only for power and for profit. I've had you followed so many times these past months. At first I couldn't believe what my men reported back to me.'

'I've always had ambition, Benjamin...'

'You've always had a madness. Like our mother who ended her days in a lunatic asylum. Our mother cut the parson in our town, Quest. And tried to slash several others. They trundled her away in a padded wagon.'

'Don't tell *him* about our mother!'

'You have to acknowledge that you've gone beyond the pale, Angeline. Until you do, nobody can help you. She's tried to kill you before, Quest. Fired a pistol at you from a closed carriage. I was watching you that day, Angeline.'

'You might have warned me,' said Quest.

'How could I? She's my sister, and I do love her. I knew she wanted the notebook. It didn't take me long to find out about her other activities. About Randal Margam Boone and Jacob's Island.'

'Dear sweet Randal,' she whispered. 'Such a lovely boy. You should meet him, brother. He could work for you too. The three of us all together. And I didn't try to kill William with my pistol. I just wanted to drive him into an alley.' She looked down at Quest. 'I really did want us to work together, William.'

'I'm sure you did, Angeline,' said Wissilcraft, very gently. 'She seemed taken with you, Quest. I had hopes that her affection for you might...'

'*Affection!*' she spat the word.

'But it's over now, Angeline,' said Wissilcraft. 'Please give me that knife. I've a carriage outside and I intend to take you somewhere safe. A place where you can be properly looked after. A little private establishment near Barnes. They'll be very kind to you, Angeline. I shall visit and I'm sure we can make you well again.'

Wissilcraft held out his left hand for the knife.

'I think not!' she said, raising the knife above her head and turning back to Quest.

'You really have to, Angeline,' said Wissilcraft.

She glanced in his direction. His right hand had come from his pocket. His pistol was levelled at her. Wissilcraft's hand was shaking and his mouth trembling.

'Oh, Benjamin,' she said in a reproaching voice, 'you know you can't use that pistol, so what's the point of threatening me with it? At the end of the day you'll always do what I command.'

She stepped towards her brother, a hand held out like a governess determined to confiscate a dangerous item from a child. One pace in front of him she stopped. She leaned forward and kissed Wissilcraft on the cheek. Her knife fell to the floor as her empty hand grasped the barrel of the pistol.

'Give it to me, Benjamin,' she spoke very quietly.

Then louder: 'At once, Benjamin!'

'It's over, Angeline,' said Wissilcraft.

'No, it's not!'

She reached out with the other hand, seizing her brother's wrist and pulling his arm upwards. For a moment they tussled, the pistol pointing first towards the far wall and then back at the window. Quest heard her cry out an order, but was never clear just what the words were.

Then came the shot.

Wissilcraft gave a deep cry as his face and shoulders were covered with a fountain of blood. Then he fell backwards on to the floor, dragging his sister with him. Quest watched. Benjamin and Angeline Wissilcraft lay very still, embraced in each other's arms. He heard the spymaster give out a long drawn sigh.

Quest struggled against his bonds, but the ropes refused to yield. The door was thrown back on its hinges.

The small boy, Cain, stood there, looking at the two bodies on the floor, an expression of horror on his face.

'She's dead,' he mumbled. 'She's dead.'

'Undo these ropes, Cain,' said Quest. 'We need to get help...'

Cain looked down once more. Then he stumbled across the floor towards Quest, sweeping down to pick up the knife cast aside by Angeline Wissilcraft.

'She's dead!' he said again, as he came close to the bed.

'They may not be, either of them,' said Quest. 'But we must get help. Cut these ropes. Quickly, boy!'

'She's dead and you caused it,' said Cain. 'She told me all about you. You killed her...'

'It was an accident. Miss Wissilcraft and her brother were struggling. The gun went off. Come, boy. Cut me free. They may be just wounded...'

'No, she's dead,' said Cain. 'Her eyes are staring so, but she can't see no more...'

He held the dagger in both hands, raising it to the ceiling.

'I'm going to kill you, Mr William bloody Quest. You killed her and I'll kill you.'

'But why?'

Quest felt exhausted.

'She was my mother!'

There were tears running down the boy's cheeks and a look of pure hate in his eyes.

He raised the knife higher.

'She was my mother!'

~

As the clocks struck nine, Rosa Stanton set out towards Oxford Street. It had been a bad night, with not much sleep during the hours of darkness.

There had been restless yearnings as she turned over in bed. Thoughts of her appointment at the Lyceum Theatre that morning edged out of her mind by her anger at William Quest.

He was so damned bloody unreasonable!

And yet she had seen the indications of surrender in his eyes, even as they'd argued. She knew the signs very well. Their whole relationship had been punctuated by rows, though she usually took the leading part.

Mostly, he would refuse to argue back during their spats, which was particularly annoying, given his occasionally violent nature

195

towards his enemies. Worst of all, she saw the reasonableness of his position regarding her public exposure on the stage. But she still maintained that his concerns were over-blown and unnecessary.

Quest had no idea what it was like to act on the stage, unlike his own performances on the streets of London. The chances of being recognised by old foes was one in thousands. People looked different in theatrical costumes. Make-up and the flare of the footlights banished the person who might be seen in society, transforming them into those devotees of Thespis who seemed to live in a magical world of their own.

Now that the white heat of their argument was over, she knew that it would be possible to come to an accommodation with Quest. His bad moods seldom lasted long, and she was a past-mistress at bringing him around to her way of thinking. At least on domestic matters.

As she pounded the pavements of Oxford Street, Rosa regretted not visiting Quest within the first few hours after her argument. She could have ended this nonsense there and then, getting her wish to walk the stage again granted and not having a row with Will. In truth, she missed him. But she missed the life of the stage as well.

The last time she'd walked this way she had felt like singing. Now she could barely think of anything but getting the day done and out of the way. She tried to concentrate on her forthcoming discussion with Madame Vestris. That would be a most important appointment, for they were to further discuss the schedule for rehearsals in the new production of *The Beggar's Opera.*

Concentrate on that, Rosa told herself. There's really nothing you can do about the wretched Quest until later. Put all your thoughts on pleasing Madame Vestris. That was the urgent business of the day.

Rosa wandered down through Bow Street, hardly noticing the villains being dragged into the police court. A place she had often visited in a variety of disguises. A seat of justice where she'd often thought she might be dragged if any of the activities of Monkshood had gone badly wrong.

She was in Wellington Street, in sight of the theatre, when the coach pulled in alongside her and the window slammed down.

Rosa looked up at the noise, scarcely even hearing the words spoken by the person inside.

'Pardon?'

She stepped closer.

'We're strangers in town,' the man said. 'I'd be grateful if you'd point the way to Whitehall?'

A burly man with a considerable moustache. He opened the door and put out his head, attentively.

'You need to turn right when you reach the Strand,' Rosa said, smiling at the ridiculous waxed hair above the man's lips. 'And then...'

Rosa was shoved from behind, quite violently over the carriage step. The man with the moustache grabbed her by the shoulders, as though arresting her fall.

For a moment, she thought some other pedestrian must have collided with her, creating the tumble. She half-turned, starting to protest, but before she could utter a word, a small sack was pulled down over her head.

As she was forced down on to the floor of the coach, she heard a crack of the whip and the driver cried out an encouragement to the horses. The coach rumbled away at great speed.

~

'I didn't fire the gun, Cain,' Quest said, very calmly. 'They were struggling. The pistol went off. It was nobody's fault.'

He saw the knife trembling in the boy's hand. Cain lowered the blade a trifle.

'If you hadn't been here, she'd still be alive.'

'She was going to kill me, Cain.'

The boy's eyes gleamed.

'Now, I'm going to kill you, Mr Quest. My mother was going to cut your throat. I think that's too bloody quick. You'd soon be dead...'

Cain brought the knife down until it was level with the bed.

'I shall cut your wrist,' he said. 'Give you time to watch yourself bleed to death. I like blood. I like to see a lot of blood. I want to see a lot of your blood, Mr Quest.'

The boy was crying as he took in a deep breath, before bringing the blade near to Quest's right wrist. Quest looked up at him, but saw no mercy on the young face. He braced himself for the feel of the cut, his eyes half-closed.

But even as he watched, the boy seemed to fly sideways through the air, the knife flung clear from his hand and crashing into the far wall. Quest blinked in surprise and twisted his head sideways. Cain lay on the carpet, his arms sprawled above him.

'A near run thing there, Mr Quest.'

His rescuer was so small that Quest had to force his head upwards to see him at all. A tiny man in a huge hat, a lead-weighted life-preserver in his hand. It was Jenkins, the man who had kept watch on Quest's house all those days ago.

'Shame on me for hitting a child like that,' said Jenkins. 'But it seemed the thing to do.'

The little man reached inside his coat pocket and brought out a pocket knife. He opened a small blade and began to saw through the ropes which bound Quest to the bed, which took quite a time.

'I do apologise for the state of my blade,' said Jenkins. 'My pocket knife was only ever designed for peeling fruit.'

He looked at the blade thrown from Horace's hand.

'I simply couldn't use that one,' he explained. 'One doesn't know where it's been...'

'Never mind,' said Quest, 'I'm sure you're doing the best you can, Mr Jenkins.'

At last he was free, though he felt giddy as he sat on the edge of the bed, rubbing his wrists and ankles. He breathed deeply for several seconds and then stood.

Mr Jenkins was regarding the bodies on the floor.

'I really do abhor violence,' he said.

'So do I,' Quest muttered, more to himself than the little man.

He crossed the room to where Wissilcraft and his sister were lying. Angeline lay on her side, as though she was asleep in her brother's arms, her dead eyes reflecting the morning sun that had found its way through the narrow window.

'Is my master dead?' asked Jenkins, trying not to look himself.

Quest bent over the bodies, reaching out to feel for the pulse in Wissilcraft's wrist.

'He's not dead, anyway,' he said.

The bullet from the pistol had clearly penetrated Angeline Wissilcraft's heart. But Quest could see no trace of a wound on the spymaster's body, though he was covered in his sister's blood.

'I believe he must have hit his head on the floorboards as he fell,' Quest said. 'His pulse is strong... hopefully, it will have done him little harm. We must get him to a doctor, Mr Jenkins.'

'I've a carriage outside,' said Jenkins. 'Mr Wissilcraft and I arrived together. We'd been following his sister for some days now. We debated whether to enter these premises earlier, but Mr Wissilcraft was eager to see who came in and out.'

'A pity you didn't,' said Quest. 'He might have been spared the death of his sister.'

'There was something else...' Jenkins began.

'What?'

'He was terrified of her, Mr Quest. He really was... Not that he didn't use her in his work. He often did. Miss Wissilcraft had special talents. But it was as much a question of keeping her... occupied... and then...'

There came a great noise from the corridor. A moment later Sergeant Berry entered the room, with Angier, Sticks and Jasper Feedle not far behind.

The detective looked at the three bodies on the floor.

'Are they all dead?' he asked.

'Only the woman,' said Quest. 'Wissilcraft and the child are unconscious. We need a doctor...'

'You all right, Will?' asked Sticks.

Quest gave a wan smile.

'Not really, he said. 'They threatened to take Rosa. They might have her already. Let's get out of here...'

Eighteen

They were gathered where several of the rooms had been knocked through into one long hall of grimy black walls and bare boards. The foetid smell of the Thames was hardly kept at bay, but the remaining residents of Jacob's Island were used to it.

But it didn't go without notice that the King found it unpleasant. There had been mutterings about the difficulties he seemed to have with the unpleasantness of his environment. Some of the more rebellious had questioned the rumour that he was a thief from the other side of the city.

Occasionally, the rough accent would slip, or some mannerism would give him away. A few of the river rats had walked, though some had paid a terrible price for their treachery. Others kept quiet – for now – though there were discussions in hidden corners about the veracity of the King's claims to be a leading figure in the underworld, in the world beyond the river.

At the very least, many suspected he was a flash villain and not the roughneck he pretended to be. Some alleged that it was worse than that, distrusting, even as they profited from his deeds.

They all knew they would have to leave the island, aye, and sooner rather than later, for the place was to be razed to the ground.

The very poor but honest residents had already gone, slaughtered by cholera or starvation or the hundred other diseases that preyed on the destitute Only the desperate and the truly murderous, who had nowhere else to flee, remained.

And for all their doubts, the King was putting money into their pockets.

The King had made an entrance, surrounded by his most trusted entourage, the better-paid bruisers who watched his back. The rogues who went out to give protection to the King, when he went out on to the streets of London to administer his own perverted sense of justice to those who betrayed him or resisted his will.

And all of the denizens of the place admired the King for his willingness to dirty his hands with blood. He seemed to enjoy the violence for its own sake. It was the fear of that vicious side of his nature that kept his troop of murderers and thieves in line – for now.

A naked man was tied to the long table in the middle of the room, fastened by ropes that were bound so tightly that the blood had ceased to flow in the hands and lower limbs. The face and chest were red from struggling against the bonds, but the arms and legs had turned pale and then blue even as the assembly watched.

The table was the place of execution for anyone deemed to have either betrayed or thwarted the purposes of the King. "Tower Hill", some of the residents called it, in tribute to that older place of execution just across the river.

The table had seen several men and women brutally done to death since the King had come into his own. And there would always be an audience. For the King's policy was not only that traitors should suffer, but that they should be seen to suffer.

Very occasionally he was merciful and the murder was quick. More often, the victim would scream, begging for death for a long while as the King hacked away at their bodies like a Smithfield butcher.

The King used no executioner to do his work for him. The pleasure and reward of all work is completing the task yourself, he'd been heard to whisper to his whore, the strange fair woman who sometimes came to watch and clap her hands at some particularly refined torture.

Sometimes the woman had demanded that she be allowed to participate. The woman eclipsed even the King's imaginative methods of drawn-out murder.

But today, the King seemed to be in a hurry, as though some more important appointment was occupying his thoughts. The watchers had seen him in these moods before.

This would be a speedy death.

Randal Margam Boone stood above the man on the table, the razor-sharp dagger held before him. He indulged himself for just a moment, enjoying the terror in the eyes of his victim.

'This man is a traitor!' he declaimed.

'No, sir, no, sir, I'm not, I'm not!' The victim screamed his protestations of innocence.

'A traitor,' Boone went on. 'He deserted my guard at the old blacking 'factory at Hungerford Steps. Escaped by diving into the river when my property was under attack.'

He looked around the crowd.

'Well, that's his version of events,' he said. 'That's bad enough in itself. But who's to say whether or not that's a truthful account?'

His audience murmured amongst themselves.

'Who's to say there's a word of truth in it?' said Boone. 'For all we know, he was allowed to escape. Aye, by betraying each and every one of us? His tale of swimming the river, a yarn we're expected to believe. This man stood by and watched while his brave comrades perished. Now, as a warning to all, he must pay the price...'

Boone held the dagger in front of his victim's face. Then with one deft movement sliced the blade into the man's carotid artery. A great spurt of blood shot across the room, adding to older, darkened red stains on the table and the floorboards.

Some of the men gathered around cheered. Others regarded the scene as if they were in a nightmare.

'So die all traitors!' Boone declared.

He turned away and summoned a member of his personal guard.

'King?' the man said.

'Did they get the woman, Stover?' he asked.

The rough nodded.

'She's locked in the cell downstairs,' Stover said. 'Foul-tempered bitch! She bit my hand...'

Boone grinned.

'Then I'll let you participate in her destruction, Stover. I might even let you have her before she dies. Has the message been sent to her... friends?'

'Yes, put through the door as she ordered.'

'Has there been any word from Frith Street?'

'The host's here. He says the man Quest was taken. *She* has him. That's the last we heard. But the lawyer ain't arrived with any package. He should've been here by now....'

'I want you to go out on to the street, Stover. Find out what you can. Tell the host to come up and report to me in person...'

'Yes, King...'

Boone wandered back to the table and smiled down at the bleeding corpse. He really had killed him far too quickly. No pleasure in being rushed. No pleasure at all...

'Margam Boone's singing like a skylark,' said Anders, as he entered Quest's study. 'Prepared to turn Queen's Evidence to save his rotten hide. He's put the noose round his brother's neck and a good many more. The boy Cain's more of a problem. Out for blood. We've had to restrain him. He might end up in the Bethlem Hospital...'

They looked up at him. He could see the misery in their faces.

'What is it?' he asked.

Sergeant Berry held out a filthy and crumpled scrap of paper.

'They've taken Miss Stanton,' he said. 'She's as good as dead unless Quest hands over the notebook.'

Anders looked across to where William Quest was staring out of the window.

'Well, that's it, then,' he said. 'Are you going to hand over the notebook?'

'He says not,' Berry remarked.

'Then he'll kill her...' said Anders.

'We have to face facts, gents, he may've killed Rosa already,' said Sticks.

Quest turned to face them. Anders had never seen such a look of despair on the face of his old adversary.

'Whether he's killed her or not, Boone's a dead man,' said Quest. 'I'm going down to Jacob's Island to bring this to an end, once and for all. I'll show this little bastard what vengeance means.'

Anders was reminded of a lonely beach in Norfolk, the previous winter. Of a duel between Quest and another enemy, an old foe, a man who deserved to die.

If he'd done the right thing, he would have arrested Quest there and then, brought him before a judge and jury. But the Establishment had been wary of Quest's possession of the notebook and thwarted such judicious endeavours.

Not again, by God, not again ..

'Absolutely not,' said Anders. 'This is a matter for the police, not an armed civilian. You kill Boone, Quest, and I won't spare you the due process of the law.'

'Do you think I care?' asked Quest. 'If she's dead, what would be the point of living?'

'Yer don't know she's even in the wretched place,' said Jasper Feedle. 'He might be holdin' her in any one of an 'undred lurks across London.'

Quest sat back on to the window seat.

'No,' he said. 'He'll be there. I can feel it all has to end there. It's where most of his followers are. The place he'll feel safest. I shall go to Jacob's Island...'

'But not alone,' said Wren Angier, 'I'm going with you...'

'Nobody's going anywhere,' said Anders. 'For once in your life, trust me, Quest. I'll flood that place with constables. I'll lead them personally. If Miss Stanton's there, well, I'll find her...'

'She'd be dead before you crossed the Folly Ditch,' said Quest. 'You'd never get past his guards. Not until it was too late. Rosa will be dead and Boone far away. That'd be the consequences of such action...'

'It's the only way it can be sanctioned,' said Anders.

'With respect, sir, I think what Quest said is right,' said Sergeant Berry. 'I know that locality very well. At the first sign of trouble we'll end up with another murder and the loss of the murderer.'

Anders turned on him.

'Surely you don't agree with Quest?' he asked. 'We're officers of the law.'

'Yes, sir, we are,' Berry replied. 'And as officers of the law we should do everything in our power to ensure the safety of Miss Stanton. I believe that the only way to do that is for Quest to go in alone.'

'To murder a man?' thundered Anders.

'Not murder,' said Berry. 'How would it be murder if Quest killed Boone, while he was defending himself? There isn't a jury at the Old Bailey would convict a solitary man who lashed out while defending himself against such overwhelming odds.'

'And that's another point to my refusal,' said Anders. 'If Quest goes in there alone, we'll end up with both him and Miss Stanton dead. What would be Quest's chances? Next to nothing. There could be hundreds of villains alongside their King on Jacob's Island.'

Jasper Feedle held up a hand.

'With respect, Inspector, there wouldn't be nothin' like hundreds. Not since the cholera cleared the place. Couple o' dozen mebbe? And most of 'em too ill-nourished to put up much of a fight. I knows the place, and a dozen like it in London. When push comes ter shove, it'd be the King and a few roughs.'

'Enough to do damage, to maim and to kill,' Anders replied. 'My Commissioner fears a bloodbath. We can't let that happen, not under any circumstances.'

He glanced at Berry.

'We're too long in the tooth to be pounding a beat, sergeant, but I fear we will be. You really believe I should let Quest do this?'

'I do, sir.'

'Then God help us all.'

Nineteen

In the winter months, the workers who loaded and unloaded the ships on the great reaches of the Thames, began work long before it was light and carried on for many hours into the evening darkness.

But in the summer, they at least had the opportunity to get home while there were still a few moments of daylight, the chance to spend a little time in the light with their families.

The less fortunate of the dockers and stevedores laboured on the night shift, slaving away through all the hours of darkness, lit only by the gaslight coming from the dockside walls, or the flames of the warming braziers on the stone quays. Shouting and whistling and singing as they yearned for the relief of dawn.

Being the summer, the dayshift were finishing their work as William Quest made his way along the riverside to Jacob's Island. Night-workers were all around him, sour looks on their faces, as they reluctantly headed towards their various stations and the curses of a hundred dock foremen.

Dressed in poor clothes of rough fustian, a canvas cap on his head, he wasn't noticed amongst the toiling hordes. He looked as miserable as any one of them, with his dirty face and dark stubble.

Some of the workers who did glance in his direction presumed he must have been injured at work, for he needed to use a rough and heavy stick as he walked. Not an unusual sight. Cripples and the sick were expected to work on at their trades. At least as long as they kept breathing. It was the way of the world for the working class.

Quest had faced death so many times before, in so many ways. He might have been marked by those experiences, both physically and in his mind, but he'd always survived.

'We lived to fight another day,' Jasper Feedle often said, thinking back to his time with Wellington's army, 'wounded or not.' And so he had, until he lost his leg at Waterloo.

But after that victory, his country had cast him aside, leaving him jobless, without a roof over his head. Unheeded by those he'd fought for. Jasper had found his way into crime and then screeving and ballad-writing. Those occupations had been the only way to survive, at least until the time he'd saved Josiah Quest from a gang of street murderers and been recruited into Monkshood.

But for that encounter, Jasper would probably be dead by now. A man only had so much luck. William Quest often thought of how Jasper's life had been altered for the better. He hoped Jasper and Sticks and the others would live into a peaceful old age and better times.

Quest had, deep down, never expected to grow old. He'd always been amazed that he'd walked away from so many close shaves. Ever since the first escape, when he was quite a small child. He didn't fear death, though he would miss the happier moments of living.

He paused as he approached St Saviour's Dock, situated around the foul waters of the river Neckinger. A deeply unpleasant place. There were no ships here waiting to be unloaded, just a rotting Thames barge and a couple of half-sunk skiffs. The dock was awaiting renovation, the waters too shallow for modern vessels. The stench of the river too much for even the hardiest worker.

On the far side of the dock was Jacob's Island, or what was left of it. Some attempt had been made to pull down a few of the redundant buildings. There were great piles of rubble close to one edge of the dockside. But two lines of old houses clung on, desperately, around the Folly Ditch, though this inlet of the Thames, with its tumbling old footbridge was still out of sight.

Quest turned away from the river and out towards London-street, which bridged the Neckinger river a little higher up. A couple of men, beggars, sat on the steps of a house and watched him pass by. A plump woman, trying to sell herself for a penny to a stevedore, looked annoyed as he pushed past. The dock worker looked too bereft of energy to profit by the transaction, even supposing he had a penny.

Quest was away from the riverside now, where the buildings of Jacob's Island pushed out into the surrounding slums. The roof of the nearest house had fallen, sending tiles and rafters leaning down towards the street. One side of the shattered building had been cleared, leaving an entry into the heart of the remaining rows of houses. Apart from the alley leading to the Folly Ditch, this was the only easy way into the kingdom of Randal Margam Boone.

Which was certainly why it was guarded by two bruisers, armed with coshes. They were watching Quest as he came along the street. Quest leaned more heavily on the great stick, but it obviously wasn't alleviating their suspicion.

'Wot'yer want?' one of them growled.

'Come ter see the King,' said Quest. 'Got somethin' for 'im.'

The two bruisers looked him up and down.

'Yer ain't one of his reg'lars?' said the other guard.

'Got somethin' for 'im,' Quest persisted.

'Well, hand it over. I'll see as 'ow he gets it.'

'It's a message,' said Quest. 'A private message. I was told as how no one else was to hear it. It's from his woman...'

Quest noticed the look of concern exchanged between the two men. One nodded the other to come closer and they whispered together for a few moments.

They turned back to Quest.

'If yer knows her, yer'll know the password,' the first bruiser said. 'She wouldn't send no one here without it. So sing, me beauty, or yer might just get yer head stove in.'

Quest waved them nearer.

'Don't remember her saying anythin' but the message,' he said.

'Well ain't that a pity!'

One of the men was holding his cosh above his head.

'Yer needs a good seein' to, cully,' he said. 'Then we'll take what's left of yer to 'im.'

'His skirt won't be happy about that,' said Quest, in his own voice. 'Not happy at all...'

'What's yer game?' said the first bruiser.

'Only this...' said Quest.

The bruiser with the cosh hit the ground with a mighty thud, scattering a pile of fallen bricks on the edge of the ruin. The other guard turned to see a cripple with a heavy crook standing nearby. Even before he could yell, something caught him below the jaw, sending him flying upwards for a good foot, before his world dissolved into an experience of great pain, with flashing lights before his eyes.

'Too easy,' muttered Sticks, waving his fist in the cooling air. 'If they're all as incompetent as these two, you'll have an easy ride, me boy.'

'Get the darbies on them and haul them back to Anders and Berry,' said Quest.

'There's bound ter be other guards,' said Jasper, pointing towards the dark passageway.

Quest gave the passageway a glance and nodded.

'Come into my parlour, said the spider... well, I will, but not that way...'

'You sure about the roof?' said Sticks. 'Don't look safe to me. None of it. If I blew hard, it'd tumble down.'

'It's the only way,' Quest replied, 'and I doubt Boone's thought to guard it. Fifteen minutes then. If I don't sound the whistle by then, I'm probably dead.'

'I could come with you...' said Sticks.

'Not yet,' said Quest. 'Just be prepared to come running when I blow. And if I don't, let Anders raid the place. There'll be nothing left to lose...'

Before either of his companions could say anything else, Quest scampered up a rafter to where the edge of the tiled roof was heaving in the slight breeze. He caught at an old leaden drainpipe. It swayed away from the roof and Quest was forced to kick out at a wall to send it back where it belonged.

He rolled up on to the tiles, clinging desperately as the drainpipe swept away once more, gradually arcing towards the ground, where it smashed into the rest of the rubble. For a moment he paused, wondering if the crash of the drainpipe would alert any other watchers.

Nobody appeared. The noise of tumbling debris must be a familiar sound in the vicinity of the decaying Jacob's Island, he thought. He looked down to where Jasper and Sticks, in the company of several other members of Monkshood, were hauling away the two unconscious guards.

Then he turned, scampering along the roof of the first intact building, using the ridge to hide him from the environs of the Folly Ditch.

Progress was perilous, with a great many of the tiles loose. Some had vanished altogether, leaving great holes between the rafters, exposing the rooms below. He halted above each one, to make sure it was empty, before continuing to edge his way along the roof.

A building, taller than its neighbours, occupied the middle of the line, forcing Quest to jump up towards its eaves, grasping the edge of its roof with his fingers. This extra height brought into view the Folly Ditch, sixty feet below, its foul waters black with menace as the light of that summer evening began to die.

Quest looked down, trying to avoid being overcome by the nauseating stench of the inlet and the torrid waters of the Thames beyond.

The little footbridge still crossed the Ditch, though it seemed to be in a parlous state. Rumour had it that many bodies had been lowered into the water from there. Tales were told that some of the poor, original inhabitants of Jacob's Island had brought their miserable lives to an end by throwing themselves over its wooden rail.

Buildings on the further side of the Ditch had been demolished, much of their remnants being hauled away by labourers. A long, flat space led from the Thames, giving a view of St Saviour's Dock beyond.

A few figures huddled around a bonfire of old timbers. They didn't seem to be guarding the proximity of the King's realm, Quest thought. They were just the destitute in search of warmth. He wondered if it ever occurred to the class who ruled the land that it was their greed that created much of London's crime. Probably not, he considered. He might use the notebook to bring the Class to a rude awakening.

He could hear voices now, shouts and yells from somewhere in front of him in the long building that jutted both above the Folly Ditch and the Thames. He lay down and crawled forwards, hoping that there might be a gap in the roof or at least a missing tile. But this section of roof seemed to be in a better state of repair than the portions he'd encountered so far. These renovations suggested to Quest that he must be getting close to the King's headquarters.

From somewhere below him came a raucous cheer, then a solitary voice, though Quest couldn't hear what was being said. Just a strident tone barking orders. There was another yell of approval. And then silence. Just the noise of the river, the savage crashing of water as the tide swept up from the estuary, and the distant shouting of men on a Thames Barge, riding the waves up to London Port.

Quest looked up at the sky, noting the first hints of darkness as the sun dipped in the west. He was running out of time. In daylight he might have a chance. In the dark there might be no hope of rescuing Rosa and bringing down the King of Jacob's Island.

A gallery led along the side of the old house, a fashionable feature of what had once been a pleasant property. It overhung the mud and filthy water of the Folly Ditch. Quest knew that there were windows and doors leading from the gallery to the interior.

It would be guarded but... what the devil... he had to get in somehow...

~

Randal Margam Boone sat on the edge of the bloodied table as two of his men brought Rosa Stanton before him, her wrists secured behind her back.

'So, you're Quest's bitch?' he asked.

Rosa stood silently and glared at him.

'What, no words?' said Boone. 'I thought you were an actress? Most of the actresses I've ever met never stop spouting. You're not living up to your reputation.'

She said nothing. Boone stepped across to her and kissed her on her cheek, forcing her to turn her head away.

'This is your farewell performance, my dear,' said Boone. 'I expected you to make more of it.'

'Go to hell!' said Rosa.

Boone held out his hands to his men.

'Go to hell!' he mimicked, to a burst of laughter from his followers.

'The matter is that I expected your friends to deliver a certain notebook. It hasn't come. They've abandoned you, Miss Stanton. Such a pity. It would have been a delight to know you better.'

'Did you really think he'd send the notebook?' said Rosa.

Boone feigned a hurt look. 'I really hoped he might. I write, you know. Poetry. Everyone that happens to you today will be immortalised in my verse. *A Death in London*. I'm considering that as a title. The only question is, just what kind of a death?'

'Get on with it,' Rosa replied. 'If your poetry's as boring as your character, I doubt you have a future in literature.'

'Hurtful words, my dear Rosa. Hurtful words. A very slow death then. My man here, Stover...' he waved an arm in the direction of the nearest bruiser, 'has a desire to have you. I might just let him. Such acts encourage the others in their endeavours.'

There was a cheer.

'Quest will kill you,' said Rosa.

'I'll still have the notebook. One day, and not that far in the future. Quest has other pals. How many is he prepared to sacrifice for his silly ambition to change the world?'

'He'll never bring you the notebook,' said Rosa.

'I'm sure he will,' said Boone.

'You're quite right, poet,' said William Quest, standing in the window. He held up a small object in his hand. 'Is this what you're after?'

~

Wren Angier looked at his pocket watch.

'Fifteen minutes,' he said.

He looked across London-street to where he knew Anders was waiting with his men.

'Fifteen minutes,' he said again.

Sticks caught the look on Angier's face.

'I'm not waiting any longer, police or no police,' he said. 'The lad's not come out with Rosa. He needs us now.'

Jasper Feedle nodded, waving an arm to summon the dozen members of Monkshood who stood in a nearby alley. Some were carrying life preservers, others longer coshes and neddy sticks.

'I reckons as how we've a minute or two before the police comes wadin' in boys,' he said to them. 'Bruise 'em as much as yer likes, but try not to put your necks in a noose.'

'Let's go,' said Sticks.

~

'You've brought the notebook?' Boone seemed astonished. 'Does your mistress mean that much to you? I wouldn't have done it, Quest. You're not quite the ruthless paladin I took you for.'

212

Quest held the little book higher.

'Do you keep to our arrangement, Boone?' he demanded. 'Or do you intend to renege...'

'What I intend is none of your business, Quest,' said Boone. 'You're here alone, outnumbered. I've two dozen men here to overwhelm you. I can have the notebook and still kill you and your whore.'

'You think so?' said Quest. 'One flick of my hand and the notebook goes through the window. It'd take a bit of finding in the waters of the Folly Ditch.'

Boone looked at Rosa and then back at Quest. His men were muttering between themselves, though Boone couldn't hear any words.

'How did you get away from Angeline?' Boone asked very suddenly. 'Do you have her prisoner?'

'Angeline Wissilcraft is dead, Boone. Your brother's taken by the peelers. It's all up with your little enterprise. There's no hope in it for you.'

Boone stumbled against the table. He clutched his head in his hands.

'Angeline's dead?'

His mouth formed the words, but Quest could hardly hear them. Boone was breathing very deeply.

'You killed her, Quest?'

There was a look of pure hate on his face.

'She died by her brother's pistol, not mine,' said Quest. 'It wasn't Wissilcraft's fault.'

'She's dead...'

The men of Jacob's Island were edging closer to Boone and Quest, talking louder now. Both men heard the tone of hostility in their voices. Quest, being nearer, could hear what they were saying.

'You seem to have forgotten the part you're playing, Boone. You've let your rough accent slip. They've gathered you're a gentleman... of sorts.'

Quest turned to the mob.

'He's been playing you for fools,' he declared. 'He's a flash cove from Chelsea, related to Palmerston, the Home Secretary. He's lured you all out from your hiding places. It was all a trap to put the mark on you. The crushers are outside, even now. Waiting for you, their darbies ready...'

'Don't listen to him!' Boone screamed. 'It's not true! You've seen what we've achieved. We can rule London if we have that notebook. Get him! Kill him!'

'It's all over Boone,' said Quest. He pointed to the King and glanced at the men. 'Take him and the crushers won't spare a second for you. It's the King they want...'

Some of the men had produced weapons, daggers and coshes. Their hungry, begrimed faces showed only mistrust. But still they hesitated.

Stover stepped forward, pointing at Quest.

'Don't believe 'im, boys,' he chided. 'Trust the King. He knows what's best for yer. Hasn't he done well fer yer since he arrived? This man's a liar, lads. Yer can see it in his face. And yer all knows me. I'm one of yer...'

'He might be one of you, but the King pays him to lie. Just look outside over London-street. You'll see the police gathering,' said Quest.

As if in confirmation, there was a great noise from somewhere in the bowels of the building. A shouted challenge, cries of warning and a pistol fired.

'They're coming for you,' shouted Quest. 'Now's the time to overthrow this King. Get him before he sells you all out...'

Boone stepped nearer to Quest, even as the men took another step forwards. He reached inside his jacket and produced a pair of pistols. One he waved in the direction of the men, the other at Quest. The men of Jacob's Island, hesitated at the sight of the weapons.

'Now, don't be stupid, any of you,' he said. 'I'm the one who's telling the truth, not him. We're under attack, so fight back. We'll meet later at the lurk in the Borough. Go to it, men. Don't be fooled...'

'You'll all swing if you listen to him,' Quest countered.

'Shut your mouth!' said Boone.

But Quest could see the fear on the poet's face. The men were coming too close, murmuring their own suspicions and edging each other on.

Boone pressed a pistol hard against Rosa's throat.

'Give me that bloody notebook!' he demanded. 'Now Quest, or I'll shoot the girl.'

'Very well,' said Quest, throwing the notebook towards the furthest wall of the building, close to where there was a gap in the wall and a flight of steps led down to the Folly Ditch.

The King of Jacob's Island walked backwards to where the notebook had fallen. He put one of the pistols on the blackened floorboards and picked it up, stuffing it inside his coat. He picked up the weapon and brandished both guns in the direction of Quest.

'You and your bloody interference led to the death of Angeline, Quest. There's no poetry without her. So I'm going to kill that bitch of yours, Quest. Just so you know what it feels like.'

His glance moved swiftly from Rosa Stanton to Quest. He wanted to see some terror in the eyes of his enemy. Instead, he saw only an expression of coolness. Quest had a pair of pistols levelled at him.

Boone threw himself backwards towards the flight of steps, even as Quest's pistols barked.

One shot broke away a slice of brown London brick near to his head. The other tore into his shoulder. Boone's own pistols fired randomly towards his men, dropping one dead, a ball through the forehead. Another man yelped with pain, clutching a shattered kneecap. This attack caused the remainder to shout with fury and rush forwards towards the steps.

Quest dropped the discharged pistols to the ground, reaching inside his jacket for his third gun. He pulled back the hammer and ran across the room to the steps, waving away the charging crew of riverside villains.

Stover stepped into the gap in the wall, pulling out a pistol of his own. Quest saw the barrel lining up with his face and barely two yards away.

A shot echoed across the room. Quest saw Stover, his eyes widened with shock, grab his throat. He watched as the blood soaked the man's chest, saw his mouth trying to gasp out a word. Stover fell down on to the steps, head facing the river.

Quest glanced over his shoulder. Wren Angier was standing midway across the room, lowering a smoking duelling pistol. Sticks and other members of Monkshood, were shepherding the King's men against the interior wall of the building. Jasper Feedle was cutting Rosa's bonds with a great dagger.

The staircase down to the Folly Ditch was in a parlous state of repair. The handrail had long vanished and several of the steps were missing. Boone must have known its dangers well, for he was already stepping down to the wharf-side, which ran between the crumbling buildings and the foul-stinking ditch.

By the time Quest descended, the King was at the end of the long footbridge which crossed the water towards St Saviour's Dock. But Quest could see that the wounded man was slowing down from loss of blood. Twice Boone stumbled, using the remnants of the handrail on one side to steady himself.

Boone turned as Quest walked out on to the bridge, reaching inside his own coat and producing a fresh pistol. The movement caused the notebook to fall from his pocket. With great difficulty Boone reached down and picked it up.

He aimed the pistol at Quest.

'I've got this!' Boone yelled, a kind of triumph in his voice. 'She'd have been pleased I defeated you!'

'Look at it,' said Quest. 'Not quite your taste, I believe.'

For a moment, Boone didn't seem to grasp Quest's meaning. He waved the book again before examining the little volume. There was no lettering on the spine, but as he threw it open, he saw that the pages were printed, not hand-written.

A pocket edition of the poems of William Wordsworth.

The poet, the King of Jacob's Island, laughed hysterically, throwing the book into the mud below and lowering the pistol.

'No taste, Quest! No taste at all!'

'Come off that bridge!'

Both men looked along the wharf. Inspector Anders and three uniformed constables were walking towards them.

'Boone, you're under arrest!'

Boone laughed again.

'I don't think so,' he shouted.

He raised his pistol very quickly, aiming it at Quest.

His weapon and Quest's discharged in the same moment. Quest felt the pistol ball skim through the long locks of his hair and heard the thud as it buried itself in the tattered wall of the building behind him.

Boone's hands reached in to clutch the middle of his chest. Quest saw a river of blood pour from the poet's mouth. The stricken man tried to say something but couldn't utter any words that the watchers could hear.

As he leant against the handrail, it collapsed almost instantly, sending him falling backwards into the Folly Ditch.

Quest caught a glimpse of a pale face as the dark waters swept over the poet, plucking him backwards towards the growling torrent of the River Thames.

Quest lowered his pistol, finding Anders at his side.

'Self-defence, I believe,' Quest said.

'Self-defence,' Anders echoed, very quietly.

Twenty

'It's as though there's no end to it,' said Rosa, as she and Quest sat in his study in the house in Tavistock Place. 'I just know that one day, you'll go out and never come back. We both came close enough this time.'

'It's the price we pay for what we do,' said Quest.

'Do you ever consider that the price is too high?'

'All the time,' Quest replied.

She stood by the fireplace and adjusted the battered old fire-screen. It was a scorching day and both the open windows admitted a great deal of noise from the street outside.

'I was unfair to you, Rosa,' said Quest. 'You came to London to act on the stage. I've taken that away from you for far too long. I've been unreasonable. I want you to go and play the part and be a triumph.'

She smiled.

'I always intended to,' she said. 'I get a thrill from acting, just as you find fulfilment in fighting for a better world.'

'Then there's no difficulty between us, not if we recognise and allow for our various activities.'

She knelt down beside him.

'I'll tell you what I believe we should do...' she began.

'What?'

'I think... I really believe we should spend a few months apart...'

'No!'

'Oh, yes,' she went on. 'Just a few months. To see how we really feel about each other.'

'I know how I feel about you...'

'Do you? I wonder... I'd like those months, I really would. Acting upon the stage. Not knowing, day by day, if you're in danger. Three months, say. Is it too much to ask?'

He rested his hand on the back of her head.

'I'm not sure I could last three months without you. Listen, what if I gave up this life? Monkshood and all the rest? Settled down to a quiet life here, and in the country at Hope Down.'

She smiled, took his hand in hers and kissed it.

'Don't make promises you can't keep, Will.'

She pointed to an unopened letter on the table. It had arrived in the morning post. It bore the bold and unmistakable handwriting of Isaac Critzman.

'I've seen you glance at that letter, *Mr* Quest. All through our conversation. We both know that Isaac never writes letters unless there's trouble afoot. You're aching to know its contents. It's not two days since we left Jacob's Island and you're already yearning for some new adventure.'

He kissed her cheek.

'You know me too well, my love,' he said.

'I'm not saying I won't share adventures with you again, Will. But let me have some little time to myself. Not just to act, but to find out how much I miss you.'

She leant over and kissed his lips.

'Time to leave the stage,' she said. 'Just for now...'

She stood up, blew him a kiss, and left the room.

THE END
But William Quest will return...

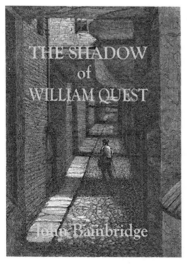

A mysterious stranger carrying a swordstick walks the gaslit alleys and night houses of Victorian London. What is he seeking? London in 1853 - a mist-shrouded city where the grand houses of the wealthy lie a stone's throw from the vilest slums and rookeries of the poor. Who is this man so determined to fight for justice against all the wrongs of Victorian society? What are the origins of the mysterious William Quest? In a pursuit from the teeming streets of London to the lonely coast of Norfolk, Inspector Anders of Scotland Yard is determined to uncover the truth. To an explosive climax where only one man can walk away...

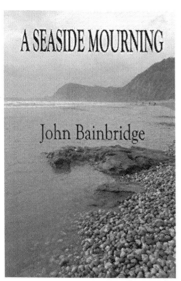

An atmospheric Victorian murder mystery. Devonshire 1873. In the sleepy seaside resort of Seaborough, a leading resident may have been poisoned, Still coming to terms with his own mourning, Inspector Abbs is sent to uncover the truth. Behind the Nottingham lace curtains, certain residents have their secrets. Under growing pressure, Abbs and Sergeant Reeve must search the past for answers as they try to unmask a killer.

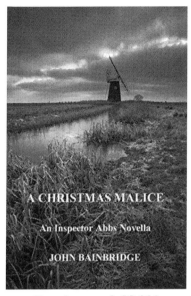

Christmas 1873. Inspector Abbs is visiting his sister in a lonely village on the edge of the Norfolk Fens. He is hoping for a quiet week while he thinks over a decision about his future. However all is not well in Aylmer. Someone has been playing malicious tricks on the inhabitants. With time on his hands and concerned for his sister, Abbs feels compelled to investigate..

This complete mystery is a novella of around 33,000 words. The events take place shortly after the first full-length Inspector Abbs novel, *A Seaside Mourning*.

Meet Eddie Chance – Edgar, if you want to annoy him. Back home in sleepy Tennysham-on-sea, the newly promoted head of C.I.D. is nobody's fool, if far from perfect. In a 1930s world of typewriters, telephone boxes and tweeds, Inspector Chance isn't expecting to investigate his first case of murder. But when a body is found on the promenade, his worst nightmare is about to begin...

How do you hunt down a faceless assassin before his ultimate kill? You get Sean Miller... Sniper. Mercenary. Adventurer. He'll stop at nothing. Do whatever it takes. As the shadow of the Nazis falls across Europe, a sinister conspiracy begins a secret war closer to home. Miller's chase leads from the dangerous alleys of London's East End to the lonely glens of the Scottish Highlands. But where do his loyalties really lie? Who will take the final shot in the Balmoral Kill?

A hooded man has come to the forest. Sherwood Forest. Come to fight for the poor and desperate. Come to fight for freedom against the overlords imposing tyranny on those who can't fight back. Embittered after a failed rebellion, armed with a longbow and a sword, Robin of Loxley faces his greatest challenge – defeating the despotic Sheriff of Nottingham, the deadly Sir Guy of Gisborne and the cruel Master of Newark Castle Sir Brian du Bois. Proclaimed wolfshead in Sherwood, Loxley becomes Robin Hood In the struggle against injustice Robin Hood fights alongside the other wolfsheads of Sherwood. Their deeds will become legendary.

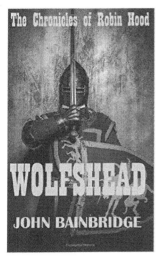

The fate of a silver arrow brings blood-soaked terror to the peasants of Sherwood Forest. England faces uncertainty as the king falls in battle. Nottingham Castle is seething with intrigue as the Sheriff's power is threatened and Sir Guy of Gisborne faces an old nightmare. Robin's fight is more desperate than ever. Friendships are tested as the outlaws confront a new depth of evil. When even the villagers have turned against him, Robin Hood discovers the true cost of being made wolfshead. A hunted man – and this time it's personal...

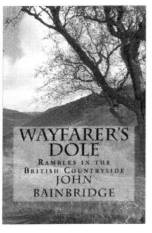

In a series of solitary journeys on foot the writer and novelist John Bainbridge explores the ethos of rambling and hiking in rural England and Scotland. On his journey he seeks out the remaining wild places and ancient trackways, meeting vagabonds and outdoors folk along the way and follows in the footsteps of writers, poets and early travellers. This is a book for everyone who loves the British countryside and walking its long-established footpaths and bridleways.

GASLIGHT CRIME

If you've enjoyed this book please consider leaving a review on the Amazon site. It really helps all independent authors. Thank you.

Please visit our blogs:

www.gaslightcrime.wordpress.com

www.johnbainbridgewriter.wordpress.com

If you'd like to be on our mailing list join our contact list by emailing us at gaslightcrime@yahoo.co.uk

We only send news about publishing and giveaways. We never share data.

You can now follow John Bainbridge on Goodreads.

Made in the USA
Coppell, TX
30 April 2020

19365967R00132